Tin

Devils Reapers MC
Book Four

By *Ruby Carter*

~ Tinhead ~

** Warning **

***

Cover designer: Les from germancreative on Fiverr
Editor/Proofreader: Lauren Whale on Fiverr
Proofreader: Hannah Hughes

~ Links ~

Come and join me on Facebook, Instagram and Twitter to keep updated with my work!

Just click on the links below!

linktr.ee/rubycarter

https://www.facebook.com/rubycarterauthor/

https://www.instagram.com/rubycarterauthor/

https://twitter.com/rubycarterauth1

The Devils men have an Instagram account!
@devilsreapersmc

~ Dedication ~

Thank you to my haters!

You make me want to be a better writer. It takes a lot to pour your heart, soul, and personal experiences into a piece of work and then bare that part of yourself for the whole world to see.

Just because you may not see the talent shining through doesn't mean it's not there; you've made me realize that a lot of others see the flawless 24-carat diamond in my work.

So thank you, seriously.

I'm still going to do me, and you do you.

Go ahead and do what you do best...

~ Acknowledgements ~

Lauren Whale— Yet again you have pulled out the big guns again and helped me so much with my 4th book!! You're always there to throw ideas or snippets at. Thank you millions xxx

Bee Bird—TINHEAD is finally here! You've been bugging me for his story ever since the first edition of *Axe* and now he's here! I hope you love him! xx

Aleisha Maree, AKA my Kiwi Bird— Know that you are stronger than you give yourself credit and are one tough cookie!! Roll on some sprint sessions too. Love ya xxx

Hannah Hughes, AKA my Lil' Magpie—Thank you for being there for me to throw ideas at, sprinting sessions with me and especially let me share parts of *Dagger* with you… You don't have to wait too long for him. Thank you for your continued support and cheerleading. You rock love ya xxx

Claire Shaw and **Shakkia Courtney**—Thank you both for being amazing girls and the sprinting sessions. Love ya xx

To my girls, who are my biggest support system, thank you for being my cheerleaders and your continued help with my craziness! Love you all loads xx

In no particular order, I'd like to thank Aleisha Maree, Bethany Worrall, Hannah Hughes (my crazy-ass magpie) Shakkia Courtney, Nicola Dooley and once again Naadira at BookedMercy for your awesome teasers.- You never fail to bring it, and you really upped the ante with Tin's!
You are all honorary Devils Reapers members. Xx

To my BETA Gang— You girlies rock!! Sorry for making you cry. xx

To my Jam Jar Lovers (Jammers) AKA my Street Team— Hannah, Shakkia, Naadira, Aleisha, Nicola, Erin, Alley, Vicki, Leslie, Bethany, Nicole, April, Leslee, Peggy and April.
Thank you for all the support and sharing of my posts.
xx
To my Readers Group—Thank you all for your continued support, love and sharing my post. xx

To my readers—I am forever grateful for the amazing reviews, support, and love you continue to give me and my Devils Reapers men.
I hope you all have a firm grip of your panties, girls, as Tinhead's about to rip them off!! ;o)

~ Contents ~

~ About the Book ~

To his club, Tinhead is the joker of the pack. One of the Devils Reapers MC's most desired men, he has no shortage of admirers or bedmates, but eyes for just one woman; the elusive Jade Smith, whose connection to him runs deeper than he thinks...

All too aware of their shared past, Jade is determined to refuse Tinhead's advances at every turn, sure she has no interest in the MC's confident clown. When she is faced with the opportunity to get even, she is shocked to find that revenge isn't as sweet as she thought it would be and all is not as it seems.

As Jade learns that this clown is more than his cover, she finds herself drawn ever closer to Tinhead, and it becomes clear that his head is a minefield that only she can navigate. As Tinhead's past threatens to overwhelm him and he stares down the barrel of impending doom, both love and life are put on the line.

When faced with an ultimatum, will the Devils Reapers' newest member find the strength to follow his heart and fight for his future, or will the weight of his former life prove too much to bear?

~ Translations ~

Ritirate gli uomini! Stupidi coglioni! - Stand down! Stupid cunts!
Buon pomeriggio - Good afternoon
Buona sera - Good evening
Scusi - Excuse me / Sorry
Prego – Please / You're welcome

~ - ~

"Now if there's a smile on my face
It's only there trying to fool the public
But when it comes down to fooling you
Now, honey, that's quite a different subject…
…It's only to camouflage my sadness."

Tears of a Clown - Hank Cosby, Smokey Robinson, and Stevie Wonder.

~ - ~

~ Chapter 1 Jade ~

9 years earlier...

Dylan Anderson; that's the name of the tall, lean athlete in the 11th grade who I can't keep my eyes off of. His sandy blonde hair flops over his hazel eyes as he casually leans against his locker. Libby Carson, one of the lead cheerleaders, is fawning over him as she twizzles a lock of her white-blonde hair around her finger.

As I watch them both, I think of how different my big sister Jenna and I are to your typical high school girls. Jenna is in the 12th grade, where they're all about status, popularity, and who's sucking face with who, but Jenna? No matter what day it is, you'll find her in one of the home-ec kitchens on her breaks, whipping up yet another one of her concoctions for me and Momma to try. I love my sister to death, but where she has her head in the oven, I have mine in fashion design books and all the latest magazines for inspiration, seeing what new thing I can sketch a design for to join the collection in our shared bedroom.

I'm too busy dawdling and trying not to drool over the sight that is Dylan Anderson that when I eventually make my way to my own locker, I don't notice one of the girls from my Art and Design classes coming toward me. She barrels into me, knocking my thick brown rimmed glasses clean off my pimple-ridden face. They clatter onto the floor, practically bouncing over to Dylan and his locker.

Oh my God! Kill me now! *I internally scream.*

I don't dare look up, but I hear the squeak of shoes against the polished linoleum of the hall, getting closer and closer. Through blurry eyes, I see a pair of dirty white Nike sneakers eventually come into view, but my eyes stay fixed to the floor.

"I think these are yours."

The deep, smooth tone of Dylan's voice hits my ears, stopping me in my tracks. I freeze, not knowing where to look at first, then slowly straighten up and lift my head to see the boy himself standing in front of me. He absently flicks his head to move his hair out of his eyes, but it doesn't work and his fringe flops back over his face, I can't help but gawp.

After a few seconds, I realize I have been standing there staring at him like a crazy bitch, and nervously lick my lips as I squeak, "Oh, thanks."

Grabbing my glasses out of his hand, I make a quick exit before someone sees us together, although I doubt anyone would assume the school heartthrob was dating the quiet nerd with bad skin, glasses, and a vintage clothes habit.

As I stride off in the opposite direction and reach the end of the hall, I hear him holler out. "Yo, wait up! I didn't catch your name."

Hell no, there's no way he's talking to me...is he?

I glance both ways down the hall to see no one else except the hall monitor at the far end. Shocked and confused about why he wants to know, I do the only thing someone like me does. "It doesn't matter, thanks again!"

I scamper away, heading straight to my English Lit class, where Jane Austen is calling to me. I'm convinced Mrs. Mortimer is determined for us all to fall helplessly in love, making us study all these classic romances. Well, I won't, that's for damn sure. I'm concentrating on my studies, and then I'll be busy setting up my business as a designer or dressmaker, whatever I can get my teeth into. I don't have time for boys.

I eventually make it to Mrs. Mortimer's classroom, and glance over my shoulder to see Dylan Anderson still standing where I left him, a confused look covering his beautiful face. He could be a cover model; he's definitely what my Momma would call a heart-breaker.

***

Night of the Halloween School Dance...

"Sweetie, just hold still and I'll attach the tail."

"Momma, be careful! It took me hours to make this."

"Jade, quit ya bellyaching will ya? I know exactly how long it took you—me and your sister helped you cut the scales out," she tells me, the exhaustion clear in her voice as she pins the tail to my bodice.

The soft, warm glow from the big light in the living room hits every scale; greens, purples, blues and golds shimmering in the light as it catches the glitter covering each one. I readjust my equally glittery turquoise top and shift the heavy plait my thick strawberry-blonde hair has been styled into to keep within the theme I was going for.

"There ya go, sweet, all done. Stand up, let's see what it looks like."

As I stand up and shimmy over to the floor length mirror, all those late nights and weekends of work become worth it. I stare back at what just might be the best mermaid costume ever, if I do say so myself.

"Ahh! JJ, you look amazing!" Jenna comes barreling through the door, her hair and cheeks dusted with flour from the major bake-off she's just competed in.

I grab my glasses off my nightstand and shove them on my face, as I've already applied my mascara and light blush with some lip gloss to finish. I swivel around and show my little family what I've created with their help. It's been just us girls ever since our 'sperm donor' ran out on us—alcohol and loose women won out over his family. I don't blame him really; after all, alcoholism is an addiction, and we are so much better off without him anyway. 'What doesn't kill ya only makes ya stronger' is definitely a true saying for us Smith girls. We stick together through thick and thin and have grown stronger than I thought possible.

"Are you ready to go, sweetheart? You sure you just want me to drop you off at the door? I can help you walk in— "

"Momma, no! Just dropping me off at the door is fine, thanks."

Sheesh, I can't have Momma taking me in! everyone will see…and by everyone, I mean Dylan.

***

We pull up to the high school and Momma jumps out of the car to help me out—the mermaid tail is difficult to stand up in at first as the tail doesn't leave much room for your feet, but once I'm moving and get a momentum going, there's no stopping me. I crack open my door and shuffle on my butt to the edge of the seat.

"Here hon, put your arm through mine and try to stand, and I'll hoist you up at the same time. On 3?"

"Okay."

"1, 2, 3," Momma counts, pulling me up, and I stand up in one smooth motion.

"Careful of the sequins, Mom!" I squeak out in a panic. I've worked so hard on this outfit; all the sequins have been hand-stitched into the tail, and I don't want to ruin it.

"All right, there ya go, darling. See you around 10, okay? Don't be late, missy, or I'll come in and find you."

I seriously don't know why she says stuff like that, it's not exactly like me and Jenna are the popular kids. They say we're 'quirky' because we don't stare at ourselves in the mirror or hang around the lockers twirling our hair and drooling over all the jocks, but really we're just artistic in our own ways.

"Mom. I'll be here early. You know it, I know it, and the freaking cheerleaders know it too."

"You never know, sweetheart; you may be slow dancing with a boy."

"Mom. No. That's never gonna happen, and that's the way I want it. I'll see ya here at 10."

I scuttle off to the ramped part of the entrance to get into the school, then take my time lazily roaming the halls, going past the school's trophy cabinet. Even though it's past school hours, it's still lit up like a beacon, the silver and gold shimmering in the light. As I get up close to it, I take in all the awards. This is the first time I have really gotten this close before—all the 'it' kids hang around it, and you always get gawked at if you get anywhere close to it, let alone walk past it. I take my time to inspect it. It has to be 10 feet long at least. One side of the cabinet is mainly awards from basketball and football teams of all ages, some of them dating back 30 years. The other is swamped with trophies for track and field, and the top shelf is tightly packed with medals and cups that only date back over the last four years, almost all of them bearing the name of a certain athlete…

I'm suddenly aware of the baby hairs on the back of my neck standing on end, and I shoot daggers at the glass of the cabinet to see if I can spot anyone behind me. My gaze flicks to the left, and the reflection of a lopsided smirk greets me.

"Looking for anything in particular?" his smooth drawl asks me. Without turning around, I answer the face in the cabinet.

"No, actually. I'm appreciating everyone's talents, and I'm taking my time; I'm not normally allowed close during school hours." I can't help jutting my chin out in defiance, but I don't know why I'm giving him shit—sometimes I can't help running my smart mouth; Jenna and Momma are always telling me it's gonna get me into trouble.

Cool fingers wrap around the top of my arm, swiveling me around. I'm met with carefully gelled back hair, a white dress shirt, and a black cloak that skims the floor, reaching past his matching black trousers and polished shoes. His face is powdered white, and fake blood drips down from his pouty rosebud lips. My eyes finally meet his sparkling hazel ones, then he looks me over. Oh God, I bet he thinks I look a real doofus! Well, at least I'm not a walking Halloween cliché—even if he does pull it off well. Really well actually…

"What's that meant to mean?"

I instantly straighten my spine, lifting my chin in the air. "I mean that us 'normals' aren't allowed to even walk down this hall without you 'popular kids' glaring daggers at us, so this is the first time I have actually been able to look at the trophy cabinet. Don't worry, I won't stay long; I need to go in and help with the finishing touches to the gym." It wasn't my intention to get snarky with him, but I have no filter. I shuffle back to the other end of the trophy case—the end that isn't covered with the words, 'Dylan Anderson, 1st Place'.

"'Normals?' What's that meant to mean, that I ain't normal or some shit?" he asks with a confused look on his face, the frown forming the cutest little crinkle in his forehead.

I can't help myself, and pivot on the ball of my feet, blurting out, "God, you just can't see it, can you? Either that or you don't want to. Just forget it, that's the way it has been for years, and will continue to be for the rest of time. See ya around, vamp."

I storm off, my heels click-clacking on the polished floor as I head to the gym to make sure Izzy White hasn't popped all the balloons. The freaking girl is obsessed with the smell of them; I'm always catching her stealing the ones we use for experiments in Science class, then sniffing them and sneaking them in her pants pocket.

"Look, you little brat, you don't know shit! Jesus, why are ya busting my balls about a freaking trophy case?" Dylan yells after me.

I stop where I am and glare over my shoulder at him, shooting daggers so hard I squint.

"Forget it! Your small brain would never get it anyway. Have a good night... jock jerkwad!" With that, I rush off, leaving the stupid jerk behind before he can say another word.

The spot where he lay his hand on my arm continues to burn as I enter the hall and make a bee-line for Izzy. As I reach her, I can't help risking a glance over my shoulder, and sure enough, Jerkface is still in the hall, giving me a smug, lopsided grin and raising an eyebrow. I can't help thinking that if he were the real Dracula, he would have taken his fill and sucked me dry already.

I don't even know why he's here, who let him in?

The smile drops, and he gives me an icy glare, his eyes glittering in the lights on the stage. His face is stoic for a moment, then he stalks off, and I let out a heavy breath I didn't know I was holding in.

***

I stand by the refreshment table watching people from my grade and the grade above dancing, drinking and having fun. The glitter balls we hung from the ceiling earlier are hitting all the strobe lights and spotlights in the room, casting sparkles like fairy dust that are gone as quickly as they appear it looks so magical.

"Gurrrl! D'ya wanna dance?" my best friend Kelly asks me, shimmying toward me. We've been inseparable since middle school—thick as thieves, my Momma says. Kel's half-Mexican, and her gorgeous skin tone is stunning, even though she never wears makeup other than mascara—not that she needs it, her freaking eyelashes are outta this world. Tonight, though, she's made up as a gorgeous purple glittery sugar skull, a black bodysuit making sure all your attention is on her face, which is painted in a white base with different shades of purple around her eyes and the tip of her nose, and matching eggplant-purple lips with little black lines stretching across them vertically. Stick-on jewels are dotted over her forehead, and she looks every inch the perfect advertisement for 'Day of the Dead' or rather 'Día de los Muertos' even though she's a little early for the celebrations. She doesn't get to go to Mexico much anymore and she was born here in Tennessee, but she tries to keep her traditions and heritage alive in some way.

I gaze up at her. I hate to dance, and she freaking knows it. I'm usually the girl who loves watching others dancing and enjoying themselves and prefers to sit back herself, but I can feel the deathly stare of a certain jock jerk coming from the far corner of the gym, where his cronies and all the popular girls hang onto his every word. I lift my chin up and grab ahold of Kel's hand.

"Oh, why the hell not?"

At that exact moment, 'Moves Like Jagger' comes blaring through the speakers as us, and a couple of other girls around us scream and run to the dance floor. I turn back around to look at Kelly and beam with excitement, and she gives me an equally enthusiastic grin back. She tugs at my hand, pulling me onto the dance floor with everyone else. We eventually find a spot and start throwing our hands up in the air and waving them. My hips flick back and forth as much as I can make them wearing my mermaid outfit, and I shuffle around as Kelly tries to twirl me on the spot. Kel's mouth's moving, but the music's so loud I can't hear her.

"What?" I try and shout in her ear,

She moves closer and screams in my ear, "I said, the sequins and glitter on your outfit are making this whole dancefloor look magical!" Her breath tickles my inner ear, and I can't help the laugh that bubbles out of me.

We carry on dancing—or 'shaking what your Momma gave ya' as Kelly puts it—losing ourselves in the music. Feeling like I can finally relax, I close my eyes and just let the music run through. It touches every part of me; I love the way it tickles up the backs of my arms and neck. I'm completely in the zone, feeling the bass pound so heavily I swear to God its making my organs jump aro—

"ARRGGGH! HOLY FREAKIN' SHIT!!"

My eyes spring open, bulging out of my sockets as I spin around on my heel like a drowned rat, locking eyes with the dick. Behind me, Dylan Anderson's stupid face is filled with the dirtiest, smuggest smirk I've ever seen. I can feel the ice cubes and freezing cold punch dripping down the back of my neck, running painfully slowly down my spine.

My gaze flickers to the empty bowl that's in his tight grip. "Wha—"

Before I can even finish a word, Dylan cuts in, not giving me a chance to give him shit. "Look, you're definitely not 'normal' now! Swim along, you little freak!" he snarls as everyone surrounding us erupts out into fits of laughter, cackling like a coven of witches.

I know they're all pointing and staring at me, but I can't seem to tear my gaze away from the smug grin covering this jerk's face! I eventually look away, my head bowing so low that my shoulders are practically curling over my chest, then I stare down at my handmade outfit. The sequins and fabric are absolutely soaked, the scales I drew over my arms in make-up washed away like they were never there. All the hard work I put into this outfit I was so proud of has been completely ruined in the blink of an eye. The fabric I made the mermaid tail from ironically isn't waterproof, and I can already see it starting to shrink.

I want to argue back, but I think I'm stunned into silence; I would never let anyone treat my sister or friends this way. I pivot, but the puddle around me sends me slipping and sliding all over the floor. The pack of animals behind me bursts into more fits of laughter, but I gain my composure and hold my head up high in my best attempt at blocking them out. Their laughter echoes in my ears as I storm off, and Kelly runs after me as I head out of the gym towards the main entrance of the school, tears burning my eyes as they spill down my red hot face, leaving a scorching trail down my cheeks.

"Jade…Jade, stop. Please…let's go get you clean—" Kelly breathlessly tries to implore me.

I spin around and cut her off. "No, Kel'. I'm not going back in there! I have never felt so humiliated in all my life. Who the hell does he think he is?! I'm going home."

"Hon, let me go grab our jackets and I'll call my Dad to come and pick us up. 'Kay?"

As I listen to Kelly call her Dad and explain what's happened a few feet away, I'm glad she stopped me. We both know my Momma would be down here like a shot if she knew, giving Dylan what for and probably whooping his ass.

One thing's for certain; I hate Dylan Anderson. I hate him with every fiber of my being.

If I ever see him again it will be too soon…

~ Chapter 2 Tinhead ~

Present day...

"Fuck. Yeah! Just like that...Don't...stop...Tinhead! Don't. Fucking. Stop!"

I keep pounding into her cunt, fuckin' her with everything I have. I'm off my game tonight; it's probably the drink. The whole clubs been partying since this afternoon, and I've been gettin' smashed with all my brothers. The party is still going even though it's 3am, but I'm fucking the shit out of one of the club girls. I don't know which one, all I know is that she's face down on my bed and I've got a tight grip on her hips. The girls know what they signed up for, and they're always up for it. They offer free pussy—when you need to unwind, it's there, and I fuckin' need this.

I gain more momentum, working out my frustration with a sharp tug of her hair as I slam back into her right to the hilt. Jerking with urgency, I feel a wave of pleasure zing up my spine as she clenches down on my dick, her walls starting to flutter. Sweat has started to collect on my forehead as I'm chasing the pleasure I find in all the girls I sleep with—or fuck, whatever ya wanna call it. Some call me a 'playboy', others call me a 'man slut' but I call it sharing the 'T Dawg' around. They didn't call me Big Dick D at school for nothing, and even the women I met in the Army loved fucking my dick.

"Fuuuck!" I roar as I come furiously inside her, making the girl—Jewel, I recognize her now—twist around to look at me, her deep violet eyes suddenly becoming a familiar pair of cat-like ones as her whole face seems to shift, making my hand go limp in her hair as I come again with a jerk. I pull out and collapse to the side of her, rolling on my back as I do.

That was fucking freaky, like a ghost coming back to haunt me.

I'm still staring at the ceiling trying to work out what it could mean when a snort of laughter interrupts my thoughts. I flick my gaze over to Jewel, who's still laying on her belly in my bed, propping herself up with one arm.

"Tin! I wasn't that bad, was I?" She shoots me that stunning smile of hers, shaking her head and making her purple-streaked dark bob bounce. Shit, she is definitely something else. She's got the juiciest, perkiest ass you ever seen, but perfect small tits that don't even need a bra. All the club girls are sexy, minus maybe Brandy. She's too stone-like if ya ask me, and a total nympho—she's had me and Dags spit roasting her before—but it's made her so loose she needs to lay off all the dick.

"Nah babe. I think I've had too much to drink, I saw a different face when I was fuckin ya."

"Aw, Tin, does that mean I'm going to have competition? Ya know you're my favorite," she purrs at me as she reaches out and runs her forefinger down the middle of my six pack towards my now-flaccid cock. She takes it in her small fist, squeezing it gently as if hoping for a second round.

"Ha! Not likely Jewel, ya know you're the only girl I need. We got an understanding." I close my hand around her fist, tightening her grip, but suddenly feel the rush of those six—or was it seven?—whiskey chasers fill my head thick and fast, hitting me like a sledgehammer. Reluctantly, I peel her hand off me. "Doll, I think I'm gonna crash for the night. I'll catch ya in the morning, okay?"

I watch her scoot her ass off my bed and pull up her denim skirt, then tug her strappy red top over her head and pull on her sandals. She turns to look at me as she pats her hair down smooth. "All right, catch ya tomorrow, I need to crash myself. See ya later, stud."

***

After a quick shower, I jump back into bed and can still smell the sweet aroma of sex.

Shit!

My head swims suddenly and the room spins, spots and swirls covering the back of my door.

I don't think I can keep my eyes open…any…longer…

***

BEEP! BEEP! BEEP!

"Fuckin' shit, balls, ass! What the hell is that?" I peel open my eyes—which are gritty in the corners and dry as sandals in the Sahara Desert—then squint at the shafts of sunlight blazing through my blinds.

Grunting with the effort, I roll over, stretching out the cricks in my back as I shove my hand in my pants pocket and grab exactly what I'm looking for. I pull it closer to my face, trying not to slam it into my nose as the screen lights up, nearly blinding me before coming into focus. There's a text from Axe:

Prez: - *Church at 10am. No excuses.*

I look up at the time in the corner of my screen and groan.
Shit! I only have five minutes to get ready.
I jump out of bed, swaying around as I try to shove my long legs into my jeans and boots, then I grab the first shirt that I find out of a drawer in my dresser, folded exactly how the Army taught me. I'm still the same as when I served even now; these habits are ingrained in you from the moment you join, and besides, I like the order. I need it like I need to breathe, just like fuckin'. I love losin' myself in pussy; doesn't matter where, doesn't matter who, I need it to escape…

"Shit!" Remembering the time, I snap out of my thoughts and glance at the clock. I've only got a few minutes to get my ass to church, otherwise Axe is gonna have my ass. I shove my arms into my cut, gliding my palm over my '*Prospect*' patch. I'm still fuckin' proud I get to wear this.

I swing the door open and stride out toward the main room with my spine as straight as an arrow, nodding towards where Sue, Dani and Zar' are chilling and chatting on the couch as I make my way towards the Prez's office. Dags walks through the door just ahead of me, and I catch it with my fist before it swings shut behind him, entering. I mentally count the figures around the table, realizing that everyone else is here and I'm the last one in.

"Tin, you're gonna have to stand where you are; Dani's got one of the chairs out in the main room." Axe slams his gavel down on the worn, aged table, right in the spot where the wood is slightly warped from it. "All right men, as you know, we're trying to keep off of the pigs' radars in regard to gun dealing. Well, after a discussion with Rebel in the Missouri chapter, I agreed he could talk to us all about a proposition he has for us, and then we'll all have a vote. You all know the rules. Tin, Wrench, you get your first proper vote on this. We have to be in a majority to decide on anything, if we're not at least 6 in favor of whatever we come up with I won't pass it. Okay?"

A bunch of 'Aye's go around the room, and with a sharp nod of his head Axe signals Flex, the V.P., to call Rebel, the President of the Missouri chapter. The dial tone echoes around the room.

"Speak!" Rebel's deep growl booms through the speaker,

"Yo, Reb'! It's Axe, my brother. You doin' okay? I got the whole Tennessee chapter on loudspeaker here. So, what ya got for me?"

"Axe, my main man! Everyone cool? It's not my story to tell, so I'll hand you over to Red."

"Yeah, sure thing bro, hit us," Axe says. He shoots us a confused scowl, then we hear Red move closer to their phone.

"Y'all ok? All right, well, as you know, each chapter tends to look after each other in regard to our finances—or at least the majority of us do. So, I put a deal to you; to join forces, using all our shared contacts and clientele to make deals and split the profits down the middle, 50/50. Would you be interested?"

Red's words have all our ears pricking up. Flex and Dags raise their eyebrows and nod in agreement, but Doc leans forward.

"Red, it's Doc. The offer sounds good, son, but why's this any different than any other deal?"

"Doc, that's a great question. Well, while I was visiting family in Florida recently, me and a few of my family members went into a well-known place called Indigo—a real nice joint, kinda a bar-come-gentlemen's-club. I didn't wear my cut in that part of town on account of the fact there's a lot of rival clubs and I didn't want to bring any shit to my family's door.

"We were all sitting in a private booth my brother Kai arranged, and by 11pm, we were wrecked. Around that time, these fuckin' big dudes stride up to the end of our booth, all decked out in black. Brother, they were bigger than Bear and Flex put together! Well, y'all know me; I don't care who you are, I ain't intimated by you. These two meat-heads stared me down and told me the owner of the club wants a meetin' with me. I told them to fuck off, because it was my down time and I needed to regroup, but these fuckers didn't take no for an answer. I got hauled up by my arms and dragged off to their back room."

My eyes go wide. I can't help wondering what the fuck they wanted from Red; he's the most chilled out of the Chapter VPs unless you mess with his club or Trixie, his little girl who's cute as a goddamn button. Even Dags knows he's a hard fucker to crack, but you should see the sparkle in his eye when Trixie comes up to him with a treat or hands him a daisy just because.

"Shit, man, were you okay? They didn't try fucking you up or anything?" Flex asks, a deep crease forming between his brows.

"HA! No, brother! Nothing like that. I got my ass dragged up 2 flights of stairs through some heavy-as-fuck metal doors—the kind you get in banks, ya know? On the other side, they throw me onto the floor like a sack of fuckin' shit. As I hit the deck, I see black dress shoes come into my line of sight. I look up, and standing over me is this dude dressed in an expensive-looking black suit with a white dress shirt. He proceeds to tell me that he knows who I am, and starts spouting shit about my life, the club, and Trixie. I punched him clean in the fuckin' face at that, nearly breaking his nose, which seemed to amuse the fucker but not his goons. He told me that he hasn't gotten dirty in a while, and while he would love to go toe-to-toe with me, that's not why he sent for me."

"Hell, what's this gotta do with us? Cut to the chase, Red." Axe interrupts, leaning his crossed legs against the leg of his chair.

Just then, Rebel comes back on the phone. "We should meet. I don't wanna be talking about this shit over the phone. You ok to meet us halfway, at ours and Pops' old meeting place?"

"All right, is next Tuesday okay? Same time?" Axe asks.

"See y'all there," Rebel replies, hanging up without another word.

"What ya thinkin', boss? Ya know Rebel would never steer you wrong with anything he suggested, he's gotta be one of our oldest friends. Ya Pops never had a bad word against him." Flex says with a questioning look.

Axe doesn't say anything at first, but stalks the length of the room, circling the table as if prowling for the answers as he rubs his palm over his stubble. We all know to leave him to his own thoughts until he comes out with his decision, and once he has, no one— Well, except maybe Dani, his Ol' Lady—can change it.

He suddenly halts, and all of our eyes flick over to him to wait for his decision. "All right, I say we go and listen to this deal Red has for us all. I've known Red as long as I've known Flex; I know he would never deceive me and I trust him as much as I trust all of you," he declares as he leans back into his chair at the head of the table. "Any aye votes?"

The whole table erupts with unanimous 'aye's— no one will say no; The club's faith and trust in Axe is utterly unwavering. It's exactly like in the Army; if you don't trust your boss, then what's the fuckin' point.

"Then it's agreed by unanimous ayes!" Axe slams the gavel back down and continues, "All right, onto other matters. We have the next rally coming up on May 20th, and Dags came up to me the other day with a great idea. Dags, you're up."

Dagger is a quiet man. When I first came into the club, he didn't say a word to me for weeks. Eventually, I helped him on lookout for Axe and he finally spoke to me. He told me he had been watching me, sizing me up, and that I would do good here. He's very much a 'sit back and observe' kind of man. We all are in our own way, but Dagger? Shit, he takes it to the next level until he's ready to speak. He'd be a pretty damn good FBI agent or spy.

Dags finally clears his throat and rubs nervously at his copper-colored beard. His raspy voice vibrates through the room as he starts to speak. "Well, I had the idea that instead of doing our usual rally and partying like we normally do, what about we do a sponsored bike ride between three of the chapters and all the proceeds go to the charity that helped Bear and Jenna?"

Silence falls over the room. It's not that we don't agree, but that just might be the longest we have heard Dagger speak since I joined, and he's thought of something pretty kick-ass to boot.

Bear sits right next to our Sergeant-At-Arms, practically gawping in awe at his brother; it's no secret they have a close bond. "Fuuck! Dags, man! Are you trying to make me cry? I fuckin' love the idea, and I'm honored that you would choose our charity; it's no secret they're struggling with just paying their bills now." He slings his arm around Dags' back and pulls the man into one of his well-known 'Bear' hugs.

Before I know what I'm doing, I push my chair away and stand up, slamming my hand on the table as I shout "AYE!"

Bear and Dags follow suit, and within seconds, we are all doing it. I feel the vibrations of my brothers through my palm and in the atmosphere—including Axe, who slams the gavel down in agreement.

"So that's decided! We set up the rally as a joint sponsored bike ride with three other chapters, and all proceeds are to go to charity! All in favor?!" Axe shouts.

"AYE!" we all bellow out in unison. The sound is deafening, but it's definitely worth it to see the look on Bear's face. As brothers, we're bound through the club, but that bound tighter and entwined that runs deeper than blood for each other. The love and respect we have for each other makes us more of a real family than sharing DNA would.

~ Chapter 3 Jade ~

"*Boom, badoom, boom, boom, badoom, boom, bass!*" I sing at the top of my voice. I'm in the kitchen in the bakery whisking eggs and getting ready to pour them in the frying pan when my older sister Jenna comes strolling through the door with another order. Her head tilts to one side, and she stares at me with pursed lips as I carry on singing in her face, doing my best impression of Nicki Minaj.

She can't help but giggle at that, and eventually she joins in with my singalong. "*Boom, badoom, boom, boom, badoom, boom, bass*! *Yeah that's that super bass.*" We dance wildly, then come to a halt in a breathless mess in the middle of the kitchen.

"Jade, you are nuts! You do realize that, don't ya?" Jenna says breathlessly.

"Um, hello? Sis, this is me you're talkin' to! Of course, I freaking know it! It's the best way to be obviously; you're the exact same. Bear is obviously a sucker for the cray-cray too." I nod to the swing doors leading into the kitchen, where my sister's partner Bear stands wearing a bemused grin with one eyebrow arched in amusement. He looks scary, but underneath the thick dark beard and burly exterior he's a big teddy bear who adores the bones of my sister.

"Cupcake…You look gorgeous dancing, it's like you're free as a bird," he tells her huskily from the doorframe, staring at her hungrily.

My sister hurries over into his arms, standing up on her tippy toes to wrap her arms around his thick tattooed neck, and whispers something against his lips. I don't hear what it is, but it doesn't take a genius to see how much they love each other. They've stuck together even after all they have been through, and their bond is completely undeniable. I'm in complete awe of them both, not just because of how fiercely they love, but their sheer strength.

"Oh, Sis, I came in to give you an order! Table 2 wants a stack of the 'Bear pancake special'." Jenna turns and grins at me, then pulls Bear back through into the busy bakery-come-café with a tug of his big hand. Business never seems to slow down, which is great for us, but even with Jenna, Maggie and myself working around the clock we are still stretched. I know Jenna wants to bake more, but with Maggie struggling with the big crowds out front at the moment, neither of us want to leave her side, even though she's improving all the time.

***

I start putting the finishing touches to the 'Bear pancake special'— a stack of 8 pancakes dusted with powdered sugar and a handful of chocolate chips nestled in the middle of the stack so they melt and ooze out. Once I'm done, I decorate the plate with a strawberry syrup outline of a cupcake. It's the largest dish we serve, but Jenna's man has quite an appetite— I don't know where he puts it all. They're just for him, no one else is allowed to have them. When other customers see them and request them, Jenna always gives the customer a proud beaming smile and apologizes, but explains they're only for her man. It shocked me the first time I saw it happen; Jenna would normally accommodate anything her customers wanted, but not with Bear's pancakes.

I finish up and stride through the kitchen doors hearing them softly flap closed behind me, then round the counter—where Maggie is doing well to keep up with the morning demand, bless her heart.

I grin as I approach Table 2. "Here ya go, Bear, your special! Enjoy, you big lug!"

I jokingly nudge his elbow, and he gives me one of those grins that still makes my sister swoon like she's freaking in Casablanca. Once Bear has his food, I spin on my heel to go and help collect customers' empty plates and cups.

Just then, in walks the self-confessed 'God's gift to women'. As if! He came into the bakery last year asking for some of my 'goodies', and I told him where to go. Ever since then, he keeps pushing my buttons, thinking he has a chance with me if he keeps coming here like Bear did with Jenna. That shit ain't happening; he's a man whore! He fucks everything he sees, and I've heard him spouting shit out about all the lays he's had. He needs to grow up, if you ask me. You would think someone who's been in the Army would be more mature, but not this douche.

He stands there with an impassive expression, running his fingers through his dark blond hair. It's cropped, but not so short that he looks like he's still in the Army—it has some longer lengths in it. The stupid goofy smile he plasters across his face a moment later is fake. I can clearly see it's all bravado, so it's not for my benefit, that's for damn sure.

I don't want it to be either; hell-to-the-no! It must be for my sister and Bear.

Before I can take another step, he stalks closer to me, brushing past me as I stand there dumbfounded, then sits opposite Bear and gives me a wink. I go to carry on collecting the plates and cutlery when the douche grabs ahold of my elbow so abruptly I nearly drop some of the plates I have collected from Table 3.

"Sheesh, doll face, you okay?" he asks lightly. I know he's baiting me, trying me to get me to say exactly what's on my mind. "D'ya mind getting me what Bear's havin' and a cup of coffee? Thanks babe."

BABE?! Seriously? I feel like I'm gonna throw up in my mouth.

I don't let *anyone* call me babe except my sister, but especially not that walking advert for STDs. I tilt my head to the side and look him straight in the eye, trying not to grit my teeth as I practically spit, "Sorry, that's for Bear only, Jenna's orders. But sure, I'll get you a coffee; be back in a sec."

I stifle the smirk that's burning to spread across my face as I walk away, turning my back on him to carry on collecting plates and cups.

Jade 1, Tinhead 0. How do you like them apples, Double Douche?

I collect every single piece of dinnerware from the vacant table and slowly make my way back into the kitchen, having to go back past Bear's table but completely ignoring Tinhead. Yeah, maybe I did it on purpose, and maybe it was childish, but I don't care about my customer service when it comes to him.

"Maggie, can you grab Bear's friend a coffee? Thanks, sweetheart."

I've just rounded the corner to go through to the kitchen when I overhear Bear ask, "Yo, Tin, what the fuck have you done to Jade?"

I stifle a giggle as Tinhead sighs.

"I don't fuckin' know, Bear, she's had a beehive up her fuckin' ass since I asked her for some 'goodies'. I did want to hit that, man. I still do.

The dickhead has no shame whatsoever. How dare he say that to the man who might as well be my brother-in-law!

I don't hear the rest of the conversation as I stroll into the kitchen. Jenna is hot on my heels, and comes through carrying more plates.

"Sis, what the hell is up with you? Ever since Tinhead came in, you look like you swallowed a rotten egg or something. What has he done? I'm sure he didn't mean it, he's really lovely."

"Nothing, it doesn't matter. We all can't get along; one person may get along with someone when another may not. Don't worry, okay? Anyway, when is your next meeting with the counselor? Is it today or tomorrow again?"

I know for damn sure it's tomorrow, but I want her off my case—she doesn't need to be worrying about me and my issues with one of Bear's 'brothers'. She and Bear just need this time to heal.

"Oh, its tomorrow, babe. You want me to ask Maggie if she can come in early tomorrow?" she asks slightly anxiously. She's always worrying too much about the bakery and never enough about herself.

"I asked already, don't worry. I was thinking about what we talked about the other week. You know, about looking at getting an extra pair of hands to help around here? I found a good catering agency whose staff specialize in serving, cleaning, and managing the register. What d'ya think?" I ask. We may share managerial responsibilities, but Jenna will always have the final say as she's the one who owns the place.

"I think you're right. I know Maggie's struggling out front on her own when we aren't with her, and I would hate to drive her away with the pressure; she's such a good little worker. Has she said any more about her Daddy?" Jenna enquires.

We both know she's not safe there, but she feels obligated to look after her Daddy. It's almost like she's the parent—if her child was a drunk bum.

"No, has she said anything to you?" I reply, knowing her answer already.

"No. I might mention it to Bear and see if he will look out for her for me."

"Sounds a good idea, Sis. All right, you go help Mags while I stack the dishwasher. We'll chat about the agency and getting an extra pair of hands to help us around the place later."

***

"JJ...?"

As if I wasn't suspicious enough about the use of our joint nickname for each other, the pleading lilt to her voice as she walks out of the bathroom with a humungous duck-egg blue bath sheet wrapped around her tells me she wants something. I look up from the book I'm reading on my phone and raise a brow.

"Ye-es? How can I assist you, sister dearest?" I ask sarcastically.

Jenna just rolls her eyes at me and shakes her head at me; she's used to my sarcasm.

"Well, I was wondering…would you come to a baking competition with me? I was scrolling Facebook and I saw an ad pop up for one. I don't think I would be able to win or anything, but it would help me get back in the game. My counsellor did mention that I needed to start doing things I enjoy again, she says it's therapy in its own way. Sorry, I'm ramblin'. Ya don't have to, it's a stupid idea…" she says, her face falling.

"Sis, I think that's a great idea. When is it? I could help ya with ads and promos to take with us; it would be a great way to get your name out there."

"You sure? Oh my gosh, that would awesome! It's a good 5 months away, but I wanted to run the idea past you before I registered. Bear thinks it's a good idea but doesn't want me to feel like I *have* to do it. Oh my god, that reminds me! I forgot to tell ya that the club are having a rally in a couple of months—I think Bear said late February—but instead of having the usual party at the club, they're planning a sponsored ride with two other chapters and all the money is going to go to the charity that are helping me and Bear with counselling. Isn't that amazing?! I couldn't believe it when Bear told me earlier, especially not when I found out that *Dagger* came up with the idea! I swear to God, he's quiet as they come, but that was one of the sweetest and best ideas I've ever heard."

"Aww, what a freakin' boss! He did not?! I'd noticed he'd got kind of an angry vibe—more so than Flex had before Zara—but he's very thoughtful and quiet too."

"Another thing...the club are having a little party on Saturday at 8pm, d'ya wanna come with me and Bear?" She's asks with a pleading look. There's a tiny spark in her eyes—when the light is starting to come back, how can I refuse her?

"Do I have to, Sis? I know Bear's your man and all, but I don't wanna feel uncomfortable being there."

"Jade Smith, I will not let anyone make you feel uncomfortable there! Zara and Dani will be there too, but do ya need more back up? Want me to let ya bring your sidekick, Kel'?" she jokes. We were best friends in school, but after we graduated, Kelly's parents kept moving around and we lost touch. About a year or so ago, she came waltzing into the bakery pretending to be surprised to see me, even though she knew full well whose it was when she saw the artwork I designed on the front window—cartoon versions of me and my sister standing back to back.

"I don't need back up, I'm big enough to protect myself if anyone tries anything. Can I still bring Kel', though? She's desperate to try a biker of her own!" I chuckle—trying and probably failing miserably to hide the fact that I need my girl with me.

I fight the urge to sigh in relief as my sister's jaw practically drops onto the fluffy rug in the living area.

"S-she what? She does? Why am I not surprised? After all, she did tell me she would have climbed Bear like a tree!"

We both burst into giggles at the memory, Yup that's my best friend; she's just as bad as me. Well, maybe she's 50% worse.

"Well, to be fair, it does seem like everyone else is getting swept off their feet by these bikers, I'll message her now." I tell my sister.

I pull out my phone and bring up the message thread between me and my 'Gurl' as she calls us, typing out a quick text:

Me: - *Hey beaut! What are you doing on Saturday around 8pm? P.S, how was your date with Dr. Vet? xx*

"I've messaged her. Fingers crossed she can come, but if not, don't worry, I'll still come," I tell Jenna as she leaves the room, secretly praying that Kelly is free and game.

Please don't let me down, Kel'! I think to myself.

To my relief, my cell phone buzzes a few moments later:

Kel: - *Hey Gurl! :) Oh my freakin' God, I'm still on it atm. His body is HAWT, but he's defo a shrimp! He's just gone to the bathroom…Nothing as yet, why? Xx*

I can't help the snort of laughter that escapes me as I read my best friend's message.

Shrimp? What the hell is she talking about?

I quickly message her back.

Me: - *Girl! What the hell are you talking about? What's a shrimp?!*

Kel: - *He's got a nice juicy body, but there's nothing going on upstairs! :P He's coming bk, msg me later xx*

"What did she say, Sis?"

I look up at Jenna as she walks back into the living room with her PJs on and shake my head, giggling like a little girl. "There's never a dull moment with Kelly. She called her date a 'shrimp' because—and I quote—he's got a 'hawt' body, but there's not much going on upstairs!'"

Jenna's face breaks into a grin and she plops down on the couch next to me, giggling with me. "Yup, that girl is something else! She's certifiably nuts, that's for damn sure!"

***

2 weeks later…

"Bear, will you put me down? You don't need to carry me into the clubhouse! I said I was coming, now quit messing around!" Jenna squeals as Bear carries her in his big burly arms, heading straight towards the door of the clubhouse.

I can't help the big smile that spreads across my face as I watch my usually unflappable sister become completely flustered and embarrassed by the whole scene playing out. To be honest, it's her fault for joking she'd take Bear's 'loving' away and stay home tonight. Jenna told me a few weeks ago that they still haven't had sex again yet, but Bear's been patient and understanding—unlike many men would be—and told her he'll wait until she's ready. They've been doing other stuff to get by, and if this reaction is anything to go by, Bear wants that just as much. He puts Jenna back on her feet, slowly sliding her down his front, then growls, "Here ya go, Cupcake. inside ya go! You ain't leaving, at least not until I get you on your knees taking me—"

"Bear! For fuck's sake! That's my sister, and I am right here, ya know! Sweet baby Jesus!" I interrupt abruptly. I think the big lug must think everyone else disappears when he says shit like that to my sister.

"Sorry, Jade! When I'm talkin' to your sister, everything else blurs. When ya find the right man, they'll be like that with you," he apologizes as he leans down and captures Jenna's lips.

"Hmm. That's doubtful, Bear. One, I don't want a man, and two, you, Flex and Axe are a dying breed. JJ, I'm going to go take this into kitchen for you," I say, nodding toward the lemon and lime cheesecake Jenna made this morning. It's freaking huge, and my as I can practically taste the sweet and sour tang of the topping and creaminess of the cheese. My mouth fills with saliva; I can't wait to have a big piece later.

"Okay Sis, see you in the main room," she replies distractedly, giggling as Bear kisses her neck.

***

After I've put the cheesecake in the fridge to keep cool and firm up, I go off in search of an empty bathroom—I really have to pee. I head down the opposite hall to the kitchen where the bedrooms are, all of which are completely vacant as everyone is either out in the main room or outside smoking, drinking, and eating—Doc's barbecuing again. I round the corner and see the sign on the bathroom door, letting out a giggle. The spout of a gas pump represents the men's room, while the ladies' sign is the opening to a gas tank.

"Fuck! No! No! Don't fuckin' leave us!"

The roar makes the laughter die on my lips, and my heart stops.

"Shit, please!"

Guttural screaming pierces the air a moment later. Whoever it is sounds like a wounded animal. The hoarseness in their voice stabs my heart and ears like a rusty blade, It's a sound of complete pain.

Should I go see…?

"No! Don't kill him!!"

What the actual fuck? Is that Dagger?

The voice seems to be getting hoarser with every word, then falls silent. I move from where I've been standing frozen in limbo in the doorway of the women's bathroom, looking over to the room up ahead where I think the sound may have come from.

I decide my best option is to pee, ignore what I heard, and get back to Jenna and see the others, but as I shuffle to a toilet and plonk my ass on the seat to pee, I can't help the words running through my head.

"No don't kill him!"

Shit, I hope that wasn't Flex! I know he had his dark days, but Zara said he's gotten better with each passing week…

I need to stop being such a 'nosey parker' as my Momma would say, but it's my downfall—I'm too thirsty for knowledge not to be.

I flush the toilet, clean up, and check myself in the cute heart-shaped mirror hanging on the wall over the sink. The walls are painted a pale lilac with silver touches here and there, and perfumes sit on the corner of the shelf mounted next to it along with a pack of makeup wipes. Yup, you can tell Dani has most definitely fixed this place up since she's been here, God only knows how it looked before she came around. I double·check my outfit in the mirror once more—cute white cut-offs that show my tanned legs off and a cute red tank top paired with my comfy leopard-print high-tops—I decided if I have to be here, I was going to dress for comfort. My hair hangs loose in waves down my back that reach to just above my bra, and the look is set off with red lipstick to make it pop. Yup, I look the mother fuckin' bomb!

I swing the door open and stride through it, slamming right into Tinhead. We both mutter our apologies and head our separate ways. As I get into the main room and see Dani and Zar', realization dawns. Tinhead wasn't going towards the rooms, he was coming from them…was that him screaming in his sleep?

***

"Gurrrl! I'm here!"

I swivel on my bar stool—vodka and cranberry still held up to my lips—to see my oldest friend stride through the club's main room towards me. We are nearly wearing the same outfit—sometimes we scare each other with how similar our outfits can be.

She's looking stunning in a tiny black tube top that hardly covers her boobs, revealing her flat, olive-skinned stomach. The shirt is teamed with a pair of deep purple cut-offs that I altered for her and her black Chuck Taylor Converse sneakers. She still stands out even though she's five feet nothing—her booty is out of this world, and the girl knows how to work it too. I grab her by her forearm, staring at her.

"Oh my! There is some serious eye-candy around!" Kelly grins. "Dayum, it's like a sausage party up in here! Me likey! I want a sugar daddy, but who am I kidding? I'd take anything after Mr Shrimp, jeez," she says, waving her arms around.

This girl kills me; she hasn't changed a bit in all the years I've known her. Actually, no, that's a lie—she's gotten worse!

"Sooo, who's free game? Oooh, who are all those girls crowding over? Maybe I could get in on the action."

"Uh, babe, that's Dagger. He's super quiet and kinda scary. What about Wrench? He's pretty hot."

"Bitch, just because he's Hispanic? Really that's just fucking racist! Just because me and my *amigo* over there are Hispanic, we all gotta stick together or something?" There's a moment of panic where I think she's misunderstood me, then I see the glint of mischievousness in her deep caramel eyes.

"Oh my God! Shut the fuck up, you, silly cow face! I can't believe you!" I screech out, lightly nudging her shoulder.

Kelly bursts out laughing, near enough doubling over. Even though I'm still annoyed, I can't help following suit—she has such a dirty laugh.

"*Chica*, what you saying? You want a drink?" Wrench says as he walks over. He must have heard us talking about him.

Oh no, this will not end well…

I know Wrench doesn't have a chance; Kelly has always preferred white men. I catch a devilish look in her eye, and she glances around the room again.

"Sure, why not, *chico*?" She shrugs with one shoulder and giggles up at Wrench, who's towering over her just like all the other men in the room—normally we would both wear heels if we go out for exactly this reason, but it's easier and probably safer to navigate the gravel surrounding the compound in flats.

"Yo, Tin! You gonna come serve me or what?" Axe slams his hand down on the bar next to me, making me jump out of my skin—I didn't hear him coming.

He gives me an apologetic smile. "Sorry. You okay, Jade?"

"Yeah thanks Axe. Good party you got going, but is it okay if we change up the music in here?" I ask the big bad President. Well he used to be; he's mostly a pussy cat since Dani, but he's still pretty scary when he goes alpha over his Ol' Lady Dani.

"Ha! The last time one of you girls changed the music in here, there was nearly a fight. Why, you want to show off your moves to lure a guy in? You ain't soft over anyone here, are ya?" he asks with a raised eyebrow and a devilish grin.

"Oh hell no! I'm just getting sick of listening to Guns over and over," I counter, my head cocked to one side and a hand on my hip.

He just laughs and shakes his head. He's not gonna budge, so I do something that's probably gonna cost me our friendship.

"Dani! How are ya liking the music, girl?" I bellow across the room to where Dani, Zar' and Jenna are standing near the far door to the backyard chatting to Sue.

"We need to change it up if ya ask me!" she hollers back with a gorgeous smile, throwing Axe a wink as he turns to look at her.

"See Prez? Your Ol' Lady has spoken," I inform him with a smirk.

"Fine, put what ya want on, but none of that girly flowery shit." He picks up both his own drink and Dani's from the bar and goes to walk back over to her when there's a shout behind him.

"Yo, Boss!"

My heart freezes as that voice drips down my back like ice, the cocky tone rubbing me the wrong way.

"Yeah? What's up, Tin?" Axe stops midway over to Dani and turns to face him

"I wouldn't let her get what she wants. Guns are the bomb."

"Tin, I hear ya, brother, but there's one thing ya need to learn, and quick." Axe's expression is serious as he holds Tinhead's gaze.

"What's that, Boss?" I can hear the curiosity in Tinhead's voice, and Axe's face breaks into a grin at the sound of it

"Whether me, Doc, Flex or Bear care to admit it or not, our women own our fuckin' balls. I can only speak for myself, but I'm fuckin proud she does. What she says goes." With that, he strides right over to Dani, and without hesitation, he swoops in and passionately claims her lips, stealing her breath as she peers back up at him looking every inch the Pixie he calls her.

"What a fuckin' brat," I hear the douche behind me mumble under his breath.

I swivel on the ball of my foot and stomp my way up to the bar, slapping my palm on the dark wooden surface to make Tinhead look over his shoulder at me in the middle of cleaning a glass.

"If I'm a fuckin brat what does that make you?!"

"Why the fuck is she here?" I growl to Wrench between slurps of ice-cold beer. We're leaning back against one end of the L-shaped couch while Dagger and Brains have the club girls draped all over them at the other.

"What's that *amigo*? Ya mean one of the hot *chicas*? Want to share them?" he asks, nodding toward the club girls and giving me a suggestive wiggle of his eyebrows.

"Nah, fuck that! I was talking about that little brat Jade fuckin' Smith. I don't know what her fucking problem is, but every time she's around she goes out of her way to piss me off! "

"Brother, why the hell you gettin' all riled up over a pretty *coño*?"

"I don't know, but I'm not getting any of that pretty pussy, that's for damn sure. All I can think is that she don't like me, but I don't know why she ain't giving me a chance; all she does is calls me out on shit and brand me a 'man whore'."

"Listen, *amigo*, instead of fighting back and getting her all mad at ya, why don't you try talking to her? If she keeps calling you a man whore, prove her wrong…then fuck her and dump her ass!" he chuckles, wiping beer off his lips with the back of his hand.

"Shit, Wrench! I don't even think it's worth it. I get on with everyone else except her."

My eyes scan the room on the lookout for trouble. I'm always on the lookout; Axe even brought me into the club because he saw how observant I was.

I was at Ol' Jack's the day he found me, drowning my sorrows in drink—and not for the first time that week—when I saw drug dealers trying to deal behind Jack's back. I had not long come back from service, fresh off of the discharge, and I was angry...

I push the memory of my past life away, and my eyes land on the woman in question as I peer over the top of my bottle of Bud. I watch her chatting to everyone in the club, thinking she's all that. My eyes roam her body, travelling from her leopard print kicks up those long, bare legs to appreciate her thick thighs and ass. You'd expect her to be pale from her hair color, but her legs are golden-hued even in the low light of the main room.

Just then, I feel eyes on me and flick my gaze up thinking I'll be seeing Jade scowling at me, but instead I see Kelly smirking at me. She gives me a cheesy smile with a little wave, trying to catch the attention of her best friend at the same time. When Jade eventually peers over her slender shoulders, I raise my eyebrows, my lips turning up at the corners in newfound admiration for the bratty fireball glaring daggers at me.

Hmm...maybe Wrench was right. It's time I tried a different tactic...

***

"All right, men, I want you all ready to ride out for the meet up with Rebel and Red by Perkins Creek in Paducah. It should take around 3 hours give or take, so

I need you ready by 7:45 sharp, " the Prez orders, stopping his pacing around the church table to plant his fists on his hips. It's 6:45 now, which is later than church would usually run, but we're all intrigued about this deal that Red's offered.

"We all don't need to go. Wrench, Brains, Doc, and Bear, I need you stay here with the women. Bear, bring Jenna over here to keep everyone together. The rest of you are coming with me. That's it." As Axe slams the gavel down on the table we all pile out of the room, most of us going to our rooms to get ourselves ready. I round the corner to my room and see Jewel waiting for me at the door, propping her body up against the wall. She's wearing a skirt so short it should be a belt, thigh-high fishnet stockings with knee-high boots and a black scoop-neck vest top.

"Hey Tinhead, d'ya fancy a quickie before you gotta ride out?" she asks as she rubs her delicate palm against my chest.

"Nah, Jewel. I gotta get packed up, doll, we're leaving in an hour. I'll catch ya after we get back, you can come and keep my cock warm then," I chuckle.

She responds with a fake pout, her bottom lip sticking out at me. "Ohh…what about a blow job instead?" she asks as she squeezes her boobs together, trying to entice me.

"Sheesh, you're getting as bad as Brandy! Naw, I'm all right, but like I said I'll catch ya later. After sitting on my bike for six-plus hours, I'll need some TLC," I grin, deciding to throw her a bone for her effort.

"Sure thang, Tin," Jewel responds in a defeated voice, striding back into the main room as I go about packing my saddle bag up just in case we have to stay overnight for any reason, then throwing in extra ammo. I take my favorite lady from the closet—I owned this handgun before my deployment, and it's been with me since I got home—then tuck a hunting knife into the strap on my ankle. After a moment, I decide to pack light and leave my sleeping bag behind; even if we do crash there, I don't mind where I sleep. Being in the Army, you learn to sleep wherever you can, no matter the terrain. I've slept in dusty trenches with nothing but a backpack; out on the road will be a cake walk.

***

We finally leave the club a little over an hour later after everyone takes their last piss. The buzz of my khaki V-Rod Muscle vibrating under my ass never gets fucking old. I got it cheap off a guy who seemed determined to sell it quickly; I later found out he was selling it to pay for his daughter's medical bills, so I posted an extra $1000 in his mail box—no note, no explanation. I got more than enough to survive on and then some when I left the Army anyway.

Some may wonder why I hang with the club if not for the payouts or the roof over my head, but I joined because it gave me a purpose again. These men are my family; there isn't a thing I wouldn't do for them or their women. I even got sucker punched by Flex just because I was trying to encourage him to pull his head out of his ass and approach Zara, for crying out loud. Don't get me wrong, I get my fair share of the cash we make after bills and necessities, but that ain't why I stay.

I love the feel of fresh air whipping against my cheeks and through my hair—it's no wonder most of my brothers have a beard. I'm riding behind Dagger on his gunmetal gray Street Bob, his copper hair plaited to the top of his back and whipping every which way the wind takes it. Flex is up front ahead of Dags, then the Prez is at the front. We're blazing down the road to get there on time, but I don't think I've ever felt so free.

**

After a quick piss stop about two hours in, we're back on the open road and it doesn't take us too long to eventually come into Paducah.

Axe pulls left, then right, then left again so many times that even I can't keep count. That's probably why they chose this place—the pigs would really struggle to follow our route because it starts with so many turns and bends. To my surprise, the road to Perkins Creek the road is straight as a ruler. There are hardly any streetlamps here and we're miles from the closest city, so the black inky night cloaks us. A little while later, Axe starts to slow down, and we all follow suit. He heads down to an overgrown clearing, and we all start to slow to a stop and park alongside Axe. We made good time, so once we've swept the area for pigs lying in wait so we sit and wait for Rebel, Red, and their chapter to arrive.

Dags swings around on his bike to chat to me. "Tin, you down for a three-way when we get back to the club? Jewel's busting my balls about me doing her and wanting you in there too. The way that girl's going, she's gonna turn into a fuckin' nympho like Brandy," he says. His voice is gravelly, with a deepness only a select few men I know have—one being my old Sergeant Major who had a habit of smoking cigars and screaming our names over and over. I think Dags must have always had it naturally; I can't imagine him without it truth be told; I bet the man had it when he was four.

I smile to myself at the thought, then I answer him.

"Fuckin' hell, you too? We spit roastin' her again?"

Fuck, what else have I got to look forward to when I get back to my bed?

There's a flash of strawberry-blonde hair in my mind's eye, but it's gone just as quick. Nah, that ain't *ever* happening... at least not until I can get her alone and see if I can figure out what the hell's wrong with her. Either way, I can't say I ain't tempted to bend her over my bed and fuck her, tugging on those thick locks as she screams my name...

Shit! This ain't the time to get a chubby out of nowhere, especially over some fantasy pussy.

Dags just smirks at me, a glint in his mint green eyes. We've both done a few threesomes before, including with Brandy. I've gotta hand it to him, he's 40 soon and he's still pretty buff. He might be able to drink me under the table but there's no beer gut in sight; he works out as much as Flex and Axe.

My observations are interrupted by the distant hum of bikes approaching. I flick my gaze to the Prez, who just nods in acknowledgement as the bikes start to rumble down the main road until they turn down into the clearing.

Rebel is up front on his mint-condition 1989 matte midnight blue Softail with Red not far behind on his red custom-painted 2008 model, his long black plait carried by the wind behind him. Next is Kreed, their Enforcer he's a big fucker, he's got be at least 6'6" and is built like a brick house. He's followed by Screw, their newly patched-in member. I've not met him yet, but I've heard good things from Dags.

We all get off our bikes, striding across the grassy ground to greet them, Axe and Flex embracing their counterparts.

"It's good to see you, brother. Are the Ol' Lady and the little guy keeping well?" Rebel tosses his greying black shoulder length hair over his shoulder as he speaks.

"Yeah she's all good, so is my boy," Axe beams proudly.

Red pulls out his pack of smokes, pushing one out of the pack and putting it up to his lips to light.

"Was the ride up ok? Y'all didn't get followed our anything?" he mumbles around it before inhaling deeply. I watch the cigarette burn bright orangey-red in the darkness of the night.

"Nah brother, we were careful. Ya know me, always vigilant. We got straight through with no problems, and no pigs either. Come on, I'm curious about all the cloak-and-dagger shit behind this deal," Axe says curiously as he leans cross-legged against his bike staring up at Red and Rebel.

Rebel nods to Red. "It's your story, you tell them."

His gaze turns to Axe. "Let him get every fucking detail out first, Axe; I know what you're like," Rebel smirks as he pulls out a smoke for himself and Kreed before silently offering one to me and Dags. We both shake our heads, wanting to know what this is all about.

Taking the last drag from his smoke, Red flicks the butt on the floor in front of him before stepping on it. "All right, so you know what happened while I was visiting family? The man who brought me to meet him wanted to know if my chapter wanted to go into a deal with him—apparently he's been keeping an eye on the club and likes how professionally we operate without being sloppy about how we do business or being greedy. Well The deal he put to me was that if the chapter put in 50 grand for some *products*, he could distribute them for us. Well as you'll be aware, we ain't got that kinda cash to give away willy-nilly, so I asked could we go in the deal with another chapter and split the deposit and returns. He agreed, but he wants me to be the front man of the op as he hardly knows about the Tennessee chapter. I'm sure he already has spies on the lookout for y'all."

Red flicks his eyes to Rebel, and an unsure look flits across his face as Rebel gives a slight raise of his left eyebrow that a quick glance around tells me no one else saw. There's not a lot I don't miss; I notice everything, even down to how many dogs we rode past in the nearest neighborhood—12, to be exact—so a fuckin' eye twitch in the dead of night is child's play. My eyes were trained to see even under the cloak of darkness, and they've never failed me.

Axe finally breaks the silence a moment later, not able to help himself. "So, who's this deal with, Red? I need to know all the facts before I put my club into this," he asks firmly, his tone unwavering.

"Shh!" Red warns in a whisper.

Who the fuck is gonna hear us except a couple of bullfrogs in the rushes? I think. A moment later, it becomes clear why he's cautious.

"Have ya heard of Matteo Giordano? He's Italian Mafia."

"Shit! Fucking hell, how did you get on the radar of the fucking mob?! What have ya been doing?" Flex blurts out. Suddenly unable to stand still, he stalks the length of the row of bikes with his hands on his hips.

"That's the thing, brother, we haven't done a damn thing to catch the attention of this guy! All our deals are small compared to the Mafia, but like I said, he's seen how the Missouri chapter operate and came to *me*, not the other way around. That's why I approached you first, Axe—we operate very similarly. He said that if we put in $25,000 each, we will triple—possibly quadruple—that in return," Red replies, leaving the last part hanging in the cool night air. He crosses his long arms across his chest.

Axe hasn't said a fuckin' word, but I know he's thinking of how this could benefit Dani and Ryker as well as the club. I glance over to Flex and Dags, wondering what they're both thinking. Neither of them seems overly worried. Time seems to pass in slow motion, but we all know Axe is thinking every single detail over, and none of us want to disturb him. Even the bull frogs stop their chorus until he finally breaks the silence of the night.

"Tell him I want to meet him to finalize details, but yes, the Tennessee chapter are in."

~ Chapter 5 Jade ~

"Who the flyin' fuck does he think he is?!" I shout down the phone to Kelly the morning after the incident at the club.

He thinks he's God's gift, that's who. Well, not to me, that's for sure. I like my men with no dicks on their heads for starters! He really thinks he can charm his way into any woman's bed? Um, not mine!

"I know, Jadey. Look, you need to tell—"

I cut her off before she can say another word. "Nope, not fuckin' happening! I am not giving him the ammunition. He just needs to stay well away from me, otherwise I won't be held accountable for my actions. Anyway, how's things? You got much planned today?", I ask, trying to change the subject as I don't want to talk about the dirtbag at the club. I made it clear how angry I was after—even Bear tried to ask me what was up—but didn't even get so much as an attempt at an apology.

"I have a girl coming into the shop with her bridal party soon for a makeup trial for her wedding, then later on I have some free time, so I'm going to try and update my site with some makeover pictures. D'ya wanna be my model again?" Kelly's got her own little store across town. It's attached to the hair salon there—she needed the extra space rather than just the pokey room she used to work out of when she started out. Some of her looks are incredible. If I ever need my makeup doing for a special occasion or a costume party, she's my girl; she just shines in those areas. I'm so freaking proud of her; she's worked her way up from a tiny corner room to her own shop. She manages it singlehandedly, from taking bookings to filing taxes, making sure she gets all the money for herself.

"What's the theme this time, babe?" I ask cautiously, wondering what she's conjured up in that head of hers.

"I'm not sure, I just want to try out some new makeup colors. Please? You know you want to really," she pleads. She never needs to, she knows how much I enjoy seeing her masterpieces. Her website's gallery is filled with pictures of me wearing almost everything this girl has done, including makeup, prosthetics—you name it. Just last week I was made up to look like the White Rabbit out of *Alice in Wonderland*, complete with whiskers, fur, and contact lenses. I didn't want her to take it off at the end of the shoot—it looked beautiful.

"Okay, I'll be there. What time?" I ask, already looking forward to gossiping about her latest conquest or date fiasco.

"I'm not sure how long this booking is gonna be… How about we say six to be safe?"

"All right, babes. I gotta go, I need to help Jenna in the bakery and then I was looking at making something with this gorgeous fabric I brought off the Internet. D'ya fancy being my mannequin if I'm gonna help ya out, babe? Please!" I implore in a sugar-sweet voice. The fabric is the most gorgeous shade of turquoise; I really think it will look stunning with her coloring.

"Hells yes, free clothes! You're not my best bitch for any other reason!" she jokes.

"Girl! Why d'ya think I stuck around so long? You give free makeovers anytime I want!" I bite back with a hint of sass.

"Shut up! You love me, bitch!"

"Yeah, yeah, whatever. Go suck some cock!" I giggle. I freaking love Kelly. We are crazy together, but I adore her as much as Jenna.

"I best get going myself, I'll call ya later. Love ya gurl!"

And just like that, the whirlwind disappears off the line. I carry on getting ready, opting for my slim-fit dark green leggings with a charcoal oversized distressed-effect Rolling Stones shirt and shoving my feet into my worn black Chucks.

Now to tackle my mane…

I look at myself in the mirror, deciding on a firm favorite for my look today. I flick my hair upside-down, running my fingers through the thick, wavy strawberry-blonde locks I love. I gather it up at the top of my head, scrunching the ponytail and twisting it into a bun before tying it off with a band once, twice, then thrice to keep it secure and pulling a few strands of hair loose from the front so it doesn't look so severe. Once that's done, I grab the finishing touch—my favorite black bandana—and wrap it around my head, tying it off at the front in a cute bow.

**

"Oh my freaking GAWD! Zara, you did not?!" Jenna bursts out laughing. After we shut the bakery, Zara and Dani came over and we've been having a good catch-up on today's events.

"I said 'Dude! I don't mind giving you your first tatt, but I don't want your pacemaker going off and you dying on my table.' That's not even the best part; his wife came in, and she was around 80-ish…and covered everywhere except her neck and face! How shocked were we, Dan'?" Zara says wiping the corners of her eyes.

"We both couldn't believe what we were seeing! They looked totally cute for each other, though. Actually Jenna, they were like you and Bear in the future, but role reversed! She had purple dye in her hair, and she rocked it."

"Dani Cooper! I'm not quite there yet ya know, but thanks," Jenna tells her, rolling her eyes.

KNOCK KNOCK!

I stand up on my tippy toes to peer outside, and I see Flex and Bear on the other side of the locked door.

"Yo Sugar, you in there?" Flex asks, the glass making him sound slightly muffled.

Zara smiles. "Ha! Right on cue. Catch ya later, girls! Jade, take loads of pictures of what Kel' does with your make up, won't ya?"

"Sure thang! Don't worry Dani, I'll chat to her about doin' your postnatal pamper session too."

"Aww, thank you babe. I best get going, otherwise my Ol' Man will come for me!" She slides out of the booth, giggling. She's so strong; sometimes I stop and think about all the things she's gone through and I'm even more blown away by her.

Jenna's at the door letting Bear in and he steps inside, elbowing Flex out of the way.

"Cupcake, what treats you got for me?" Bear growls before capturing Jenna's mouth.

"Bear Jameson, you can wait until after dinner to get your dessert. I'll see you lovelies tomorrow, yeah?" Jenna tells the girls as Zara's slim body molds against the lean, muscular figure of Flex. His long beard looks like it's a had a fresh cut, and he's smiling at her—he's definitely seemed a helluva lot lighter since being with Zara.

Dani stands at his other side, eager to get back home to Axe—and Ryker, her beautiful baby boy. He's absolutely adorable.

"Yeah, see ya tomorrow babes," Zara and Dani say in unison. The door slams closed behind them, then I hear the truck rumbling to life and pulling away into the night. I look to my left and see Bear pressed flush against the back of my sister, no doubt whispering dirty things in her ear.

"All right you lovebirds, I'm gonna go to Kelly's." I tell them.

"Lock up on your way out, JJ! See ya in the morning, love ya!" I hear Jenna shout from the stairs to our apartment. Shaking my head, I grab my big powder-blue overnight bag and head over to my best friend's.

***

"Kelly! Oh my freaking God, are you serious? You never said to that you wanted to turn me into a goblin! I thought you were going to give me a glam look?" I stare completely bewildered at my best friend from where I sit in her makeup chair in front of her huge ornate shabby-chic mirror.

"I know, but it's great practice for me! Please babe? I promise I'll make you look beautiful! *Please?* Then we can go out for a drink and I'll find ya some cock!"

I choke on my diet soda, spluttering my mouthful everywhere. This girl never ceases to amaze me.

"I don't need any cock, thanks for your concern!" I argue, stabbing a bony finger in her butt cheek.

"Gurl, you so do! When was the last time? I've not heard a mention of any action for months! It's like a bike; once you get back on, you'll remember how to ride. Besides, isn't getting a little dusty down there?"

"Oh my fucking god, you did not just say that! Cheeky witch! For your information, it has *not* been months and months."

I think...has it really been that long?

"That face you're pulling right now means you don't know when the last time was either. Come on, please just come out for a drink? If ya don't get any, we'll come back to mine and watch chick flicks and have drinks." She cocks a hip to one side planting a hand on the other one with a teasing smirk. She's tied her thick black hair up in a messy bun with a few strands framing her face like mine.

"Oh, go on, do what you need for your site."

I give in too easy, but I love seeing Kel' in her element. Last week, she turned my face into an elf from the *Harry Potter* movies, which was absolutely amazing, but it took her four-and-a-half hours! The week before that, I was a Minion, and my face had hints of yellow for days afterward—I looked like there was something wrong with my liver! Grinning to myself, I watch my best friend beam with excitement as she removes my makeup and sets about prepping the base.

3 hours later...

"Are you ready? 3...2...1..." Kelly tugs the towel away from the mirror in front of me, and I can't believe my eyes.

Staring back at me...isn't *me*. A lime base covers my whole face, with dark shades creating deep frown lines over my brow and forehead. They merge underneath my cheekbones, which have been given more definition with dark green outlines. Hints of black contour my nose and the column of my neck, with lighter accents making my collarbones and hairline pop even more. Finally, my lips are stained black to round off the look. My eyes keep scanning my face—every time I look back; I find something new. It's absolutely amazing!

"Jade? You're kind of freaking me out over here, what d'ya think?" Kel' asks uncertainly.

"Kel', its fuckin' awful...ly amazing! I can't believe you did all this! You never fail to surprise me with these transformations, and you blow me away more each time. Never question your talent!" I tell her with a stern voice.

"Oh, heck no, babe! I know I'm pretty awesome. I just need to take some pics and a 360° video of the look, then I'll start taking it off and do you some nice makeup before we head out," she tells me.

I just give her a little nod. "'Kay babe, no problem."

Kel' swivels my chair to get the best lighting for the pictures, then snaps about 100 every which way, steps back and starts filming, gradually getting closer to me then slowly turning the chair all the way one way, then back again the other way before pocketing her phone again.

"All right, babe, I can turn you back into a princess now! D'ya need or a drink or a pee first?"

"Nah, I'm all good, Kellybean," I reply, screwing up my face and nose and giving her a cheeky grin at the nickname—I haven't used it since middle school.

I close my eyes as she gets to work, enjoying the feel of her swiping all the makeup off my face.

***

"I'll have a large vodka and cranberry, please!" I shout over to the bartender in the new bar across the road from Kelly's shop. He's pretty cute to be honest; he's got the floppy-haired Jonas Brother look going on; his hair a hazelnut brown that matches his eyes.

"Biatch! That hottie is checking you out, you got to get up on that pogo stick and work it!" Kelly screams into my ear.

The music in the bar is nearly deafening, blaring through the speakers in each corner. Don't get me wrong, I love going to Ol' Jack's, but if we want a good cocktail this is definitely the place to go. I peer to the side to stare wide-eyed at my best friend before giving her a death glare. She just gives me her cheesiest smile and shrugs at me. I follow her eye gaze and watch the barman make our drinks, and I can't help admiring his ass as he turns to reach for his shaker.

Hmm, nice…

"I'm just goin' to the bathroom, babe, be back in a few. Can you order me a Bud? I want something different," Kelly announces, surprising me.

"Yeah, sure babe…since when d'ya drink beer?" I ask, but she's already hopped off her bar stool.

She looks over her shoulder, gives me a small smile, shrugs, and strides over where the bathrooms are. The bar isn't exactly high-energy, but at least they got some solid tunes playing. I bop to Calvin Harris as the hot server comes back with our drinks.

"Here ya are, miss."

"Thanks. Can I have a bottle of Bud too please?" I ask him to try not to make it too obvious I was checking him out even if he is hella cute.

"*Chica,* where's your girl at?"

I turn my head and find myself face-to-face with Wrench, who wears a cheeky panty-dropping smile. He leans to one side to grab his beer, and I see Sir Jerk-Off staring back at me with his signature smirk. He winks at me, and I flick my head away from him in disgust.

Where the hell are ya Kel'?!

I turn to Wrench, avoiding Tinhead's stare from over his shoulder.

"I don't know, I think she must have flushed herself down the toilet," I say with a smile.

"Let me go and see if she's okay…the place is gettin' busy now," he responds rapidly.

I look around and see that he's right. The bar is getting packed, and before long, the girl next to me is rubbing elbows with me. I turn back in time to see Wrench walk towards the restrooms.

Freaking great, now there's an empty space between me and Captain Doucheface!

As soon as my gaze falls back on the bar, he's in the space Wrench just vacated, getting far too comfortable for my liking,

"Look, I don't know why you hate me so much. Will ya at least let me get you a drink?" As his smooth baritone voice reaches my ears, I try not to cringe.

"Got one," I blurt out abruptly.

"I can see that, but I'm trying to be nice here. C'mon, at least tell me what I've done wrong, I'm sorry for callin' ya a brat," he implores, gazing at me with the full force of those baby blues of his.

"Nothing. Please just leave me alone. I don't know where the hell Kelly's got to—"

I'm interrupted by my phone vibrating in my purse. As I take it out and open the message waiting for me, I swear to whoever is up there that my best friend is dead when I see her.

"It looks like we have been set up!" I grind out from between clenched teeth, looking up at the blond ex-army womanizer.

I flick my phone around and show him the message:

Kel: - *Sorry, don't hate me. He's cute, and you two need to get to know each other…even if it is just to clear the cobwebs away in your pussssay! Love ya bitch xx*

Jade flashes me her phone, which has a text from her friend on the screen. I don't see it all as she whips it away from me as if thinking better of it, but I saw all I need to see…

Kel: - *Sorry, don't hate me. He's cute, and you two need to get to know each other…even if it is just to clear the cobwebs away—*

"Got cobwebs down there, doll face? *Shiiit*, how long has it been?" I can't help asking.

She gives me that stony glare of hers in answer, but her neck starts to get blotchy and she flicks her head abruptly towards her drink and starts taking huge gulps, apparently determined to get drunk as quickly as possible.

A laugh bubbles out of my mouth as I watch her trying to practically inhale her drink, which makes her stop and choke, sending her spluttering and coughing and bringing water to her eyes.

I decide to put her out of her misery—even if she is a complete and utter dick to me, I can't let her choke to death or Bear would have my balls. I do the decent thing and slap her firmly on her back, making a thudding noise.

"D'ya…have to…hit me…so freakin' hard…you douche?!" she says, spluttering between each word.

Even now, she looks goddamn smokin' hot. Her eyes sparkle in the bar's lights as she quickly flicks them downwards to see my hand covering hers on the bar countertop—even I didn't realize. After a second, she tugs it free, pulling it away like I have a fuckin' disease or some shit.

"Easy, tiger. Look, why don't we make the most of it? It's obvious you just need a good fuckin', and that text just confirms it," I tell her with a dirty-ass grin.

"Hell no, I ain't sleeping with you! I wouldn't even if you were the last man on this planet, I don't know where you've been or what STD's you got. You're never gonna get anywhere near me, or my cobwebs!"

"Sheesh, you definitely do need a good *hard* fuckin', you little brat."

"Will you shut the fuck up talking about me like a piece of meat! You think you're God's gift to women? Well, let me tell y—"

I slam my mouth on hers before she can finish, wrapping my hands around her small waist. Her lips slam shut like a vise, not budging an inch until I run my little finger across the gap where her black top has ridden up, tickling the soft bare skin and making her gasp. She giggles and ties to fight me, and I don't get to pursue the kiss before she chomps down on my bottom lip so hard I swear to God the hellcat has taken a chunk out of it.

I whip my face away. "Shit! Do you have to bite my fuckin'—"

"Who the hell do you think you are, forcing yourself on me?"

"Well if I didn't, you'd still be bitchin' about how fuckin' awesome I am and how you want me to clear out those cobwebs of yours. Hush your mouth. You can kiss me, fuck me, whatever, but shut the fuck up!" I growl.

Her face flushes with anger. "Like that's ever—"

I abruptly interrupt her by placing my forefinger on her plump lips smeared with lip gloss to shush her.

Her eyes widen and her jaw juts out in protest.

I bend my head to whisper in her ear. "Quit kidding yourself, I know you fuckin' want me. Whatever issue you got with me doesn't stop the fact I can practically hear how fuckin' wet you are for me and our eyes are as wide as fuckin' saucers. Instead of denying yourself, how about you let me take you on a date to get to know me for real?"

As I pull back, removing my finger from her lips, her eyes look wild with rage. I raise my eyebrow in challenge, silently daring her to take it further. Within a half a minute, see her eyes flash with a menace I haven't seen in a very long time.

Shit, this girl does have it royally in for me.

"Fine, you can take me out. One time, that's it, and it's *not* a date." She tries to keep her tone sweet, but I can hear her try to hide her distaste as she looks skeptically at me.

"Good girl, don't act like a spoilt brat now. I'll be in touch to arrange something," I say in a low tone, leaning close to her face.

I watch her breath hitch, and the scent of her sweet apple perfume wraps around me.

I push away the urge to hold her close and breathe it in deeply.

Shit!

I won't become one of my brothers, I'm not gonna be falling hard and fast for no-one. Nah, this is all about finding out what makes this girl tick…and why the fuck she hates me so goddamn much.

***

"Remind me why all of us have to be here again, boss? You know I don't like to leave Jenna at the moment," Bear pipes up as we wait at the rendezvous point. He never goes against orders—none of us do—but his discomfort is clear. It's totally understandable after what happened to him and Jenna, and Axe knows it.

"I know brother, I know. Red and Rebel said every single member of the club has to be here to meet Giordano before he'll do business with us, and it's fair enough—I'd be the exact same, you know that. I don't like leaving the women and my boy without any of us either, but that's why I asked Rebel's men to go to the clubhouse and keep watch," Axe replies gruffly, a deep crease forming across his forehead as he hops off of his bike and waits for us all to follow suit. I pull off my lid, hanging it off my handlebars before I stride up to the rest of the men. I can't help but stand back in awe of the monstrous but beautiful mansion in front of us.

There's no way this big-ass place is a house; it's like a museum, complete with grand Roman-like pillars on either side of the lily-white building. In contrast, the windows and doors scream modernity that fit right into this private gated community in Arkansas. There are a dozen steps leading to the nearly 6-foot-wide porch in front of a huge door covered with vast glass panes with intricate gothic designs on them. The door itself is made of deep caramel wood.

Axe climbs the steps and is just about to knock the door when it swings open to a reveal a gigantic man with a military-style buzzcut looks nearly. He has dark olive Mediterranean coloring and grunts out a welcome, swinging the door open further to invite us in.

I catch a glimpse of his forearm tattoo as I approach. It's a black crow in flight with an inscription above the wings, *'Familia or Death'*—pretty clear as mottos go.

Just as Axe steps through into the grand entrance, he's pinned up against the far wall by a lookalike of the meathead who opened the door.

"What the fuck?" Flex and Bear yell in unison as they get manhandled and thrust up against the wall by two more men. The rest of us move to help them, but Axe holds up a hand.

"Men, stand down. Just let them do their search; we would be the same." Axe mumbles, his face smushed up against the cream walls. One by one, we are all thrust up against the wall or the back of the door, searched and patted down, and our pockets emptied.

The dude who opened the door comes over to pat me down, and as he shoves his hands into my front pockets, I can't help my smart mouth. "Easy, dude, let's at least get to know each other first," I smirk against the wall. The meathead responds by shoving me further against the wall and gruffly mumbling something incoherent in Italian. Once the goons are satisfied h that there is nothing to be found on any of us, they let us go.

"Follow me," the big dude says in a thick Italian accent, striding down the hall.

It's lined with pieces of art here and there, but nothing personal, I notice as we follow. He eventually brings us to an archway with a set of thick dark wood double doors set into it, opening both doors wide like he's revealing lost treasure.

The room the doors open out into is vast and grand; there is a ten-foot-long mahogany table placed smack in the middle of the room surrounded by matching high-backed chairs.

As we all file into the room, the big guy who tried to cop a feel leaves the room as abruptly as he entered. "Wait here."

As we all wait around, I take in more of the grand hall we stand in. The ceiling is high, and marble and expensive wood decorate the room everywhere I turn. Famous paintings I recognize from high school art class as Gaudi pieces—and one Da Vinci piece I'm pretty sure was stolen from a gallery a few years back— are mounted on the wall under dark lights.

Shit, it must've cost a fortune to decorate this room alone!

My snooping around is halted as I hear the *click-clack* of dress shoes on the highly polished floor in the distance. I look over to Axe and Flex who are hovering near a long dark-red velvet couch. It's pristine, I don't think it's ever been used.

Come to think of it, nothing in here looks like it has—it looks like a show house…

I glance up at the corners of the ceiling where the paint meets the coving, and I know for a fact there are high def cameras there—and undoubtedly there were in the hallway and entrance where we came in too. The untrained eye wouldn't have noticed them—not even

Brains—but we used the exact same ones in the Army. I'm impressed by the fortress this man's built; I suppose a man like him can't trust anyone—including his own staff.

"Be on guard, all of you," Axe mumbles under his breath, no doubt hearing the footsteps himself.

My eyes can't seem to stop honing in on a painting over the ornate fireplace; a riot of black, red, and orange with flecks of white. It reminds me of all the bloodshed and destruction I saw in Afghanistan...

Chills run down my spine and my vision starts to get blurry at the edges, so I whip my eyes away from not only the picture, but the memories—just in time for the man himself to appear at the door frame in a dark gray suit and black dress shoes to match the lightly-gelled coal-colored hair that contrasts his olive skin. He doesn't say a word, but he doesn't need to.

He exudes dominance and authority; I don't need any introduction to know that this is Matteo Giordano—the man who's on top of the FBI and Interpol 'Most Wanted' lists, the Boss, the Don, and the head of the Italian Mafia.

As the meathead who patted me down follows him in like a good little lap dog, he steps into the room, his dark eyes scanning us for any hint of deceit. Axe does the exact same thing for a few seconds, and eventually Giordano breaks the silence.

"Nico, leave us; I'll call you if I need you and Lorenzo...but I won't as long as our guests behave." Matteo shoots us all a glare, then dismisses Nico with a sharp flick of his head.

As soon as Nico leaves, Matteo stalks the length of the room, not saying a word. His gaze is fixed on the painting hanging over the fireplace—the one I was just admiring.

"You see all this you're standing in? I built this whole empire up from the ashes. My *Padre* nearly destroyed the Giordano name before I got involved, but what you see if the product of my hard work and excellent business deals. I haven't had a bad one...yet."

As he pins us all with an ominous glare in turn, I bristle before I can help myself. I don't give a fuck about his intimidation tactics; I'm not even intimidated staring down the barrel of an enemy gun.

"I won't risk all I have built from nothing lightly, Axe," he says, locking eyes with the Prez. "I don't know much about your chapter compared to Rebel's, and I don't know if that's a good or a bad thing, but I do know you covered your tracks well after what went down with your woman's ex and her kidnapping."

Matteo's eyes flick to all our faces in turn again. "I need to know I can trust you *all*—not just the president—and have the loyalty I will offer you shown back to me, otherwise this isn't going to work at all."

"Thank you for meeting us and humoring the idea of this partnership, but let's get one thing straight—if you expect me and my men to trust you and yours, I expect the same in return from you." Axe steps up only a few feet in front of the boss, both men on an equal footing. Axe hasn't got so much as a flicker of uncertainty in his eyes; I can tell he knows that if he shows so much as a hint of weakness, Matteo will be sucking at it like a fuckin' vampire.

They haven't broken eye contact at all since Axe addressed Matteo. Matteo stares right into Axe's eyes as if trying to read him to see if he can find any bullshit. He will find none; my Prez is a straight-talker.

To my surprise, Matteo then slaps Axe on the shoulder so hard I hear Axe's leather cut creaking. A fleeting look of respect crosses Matteo's face.

"One thing I admire is someone standing up to me, and you and Rebel have that in common. I don't stand any shit, and I expect my business associates to be on an equal footing. You're right, you do deserve to meet my men and have their trust too."

Matteo tilts his head to one side.

"Nico! Get in here; bring Lorenzo, Tomma and Leo!" he hollers through the thick wooden door. The next minute, Nico and three other men come storming in with their guns drawn, ready to shoot anyone at point blank range. Whether these men have served in the military or not, they still carry themselves like true soldiers.

"Everything okay, boss?" asks Nico. He scans the room, always on the lookout.

"Easy, Nico. Stand in line. I have asked Axe and his men to trust me and mine, and he wishes the same treatment in return. That's why you're all here. Axe, this is Nico, these guys are Tomma and Lorenzo, and this *grande* motherfucker is Leo, my right hand."

Tomma has a similar haircut to Nico but a similar build to me, Lorenzo is stocky but also has a buzzcut, and Leo is fuckin' huge, taller than Flex.

Fuck me, dude's gotta be at least 6"5 if not 6"6 and is scarier than Dagger, complete with a Scarface-style psychotic glare in his eyes, It's apparent that Matteo likes his henchmen to be of Italian descent—they're all olive-skinned with dark hair.

Axe introduces each member of the club, but we're met with nothing but scrutinizing looks from them all.

When he's done, the room falls silent as the corners of Matteo's lips turn upward, then he breaks the silence. "Gentlemen, *buon pomeriggio.* I look forward to doing business with you."

~ Chapter 7 Jade ~

3 days after agreeing to the non-date…

"Hey, Jade! Can you grab the tray of brownies and the lemon tartlets out of the fridge for me?" Jenna hollers from the front of the bakery. I pick up what she needs, grabbing some extra salad items as well. I still can't believe I was stupid enough to agree to go out with the one person I detest. I think he knows I've been considering bailing—he messaged me an hour ago setting a date and time, but I've not even replied yet. Sighing, I pull out my cell and look over at the message again. I can't help my lip curling on instinct at the sight of his "name".

Captain. Cockhead: - *Hey! It's the man of your dreams! Nah, I'm jokin', it's Tin. You free tonight at 7?*
Ah fuck it! It's one night, and maybe I've been too hasty…
I tap out a reply before I can change my mind:

Me: - *Yeah, yeah…whatever you say, jerk! 7 is good for me. Where are we going?*

Tinhead's response is almost instant:

Captain. Cockhead: - *Aw, dollface, so eager to reply… It's a surprise, wear something that u don't mind getting dirty ;oP…and nah, I don't mean wear me — T*

Me: - *(eye rolling emoji) Haha, you're so funny! You wish, Buttcrack! You best not take me to some dirt track!*

Captain Cockhead: - *You fuckin love it really! Stop denying yourself some of the T Dawg. Nah, I won't, wear jeans and boots. C ya later ;oP — T*

I shove my phone back in my pocket with an irritated huff.

For fuck's sake! What is it that Dani and my sister say? He's "a real sweetheart, just the joker of the pack"? Yeah well, we'll see about that, won't we? I'm not holding my breath…

***

Around 6.30pm…

"Jade! Are you serious? You can't wear that on your first date with him!" Jenna exclaims from my bedroom door.

I turn to meet her eyes, and complete shock is written all over her face. Her eyes are as big as the large cappuccino cups we keep downstairs.

"Why, what's wrong with what I'm wearing? t's not a date." I check myself over in the mirror, ignoring the alarms screeching in my head. I know exactly what I'm doing. "I look fuckin' hot! I don't see what the problem is," I shrug nonchalantly.

A red-and-white checkered shirt is tied underneath my 'ample tatas', as Kelly calls them, and I've teamed it with faded pale blue denim shorts and my dark tan cowgirl boots. I admit that maybe I went too far putting my hair into plaits, but I think I look the bomb—good enough to bring a man like Tin to his knees. I have *definitely* brought out my inner Kelly tonight.

"The problem is that you've hardly got anything on, JJ! I don't want Tinhead getting the wrong idea about what type of a girl you are…he'll pounce on you without a second thought." She mumbles the last part under her breath but it's exactly what I want; even if the sound of his name does still irritate the hell out of me. I mean, what kind of name is *Tinhead* anyway? It's bad even for a nickname!

I wrap my arm around my big sis. "I'll be okay, I promise. I'm a big girl now, and I got this handled; he ain't getting any of my goodies, don't you worry." I can't help the satisfied grin spreading across my face.

This is going to be fun…

"Okay…If you're intent on making the poor man suffer like I accidentally did with Bear, then at least do it right."

I turn from the mirror in shock at Jenna's statement and catch her smirking at me with a mischievous twinkle in her eye.

"Here, this color is gorgeous on you. Knock him on his ass, babe!" She hands me a tube of MAC lipstick aptly named *Foxy Woman,* the smirk melting into a smug smile as I glide the silky smooth lipstick across my lips a couple of times and smack them in the mirror before turning on my heel to face Jenna.

"Will this do?" I say sassily, planting a hand on my hip and threading my thumb through one of my belt loops.

"Oh yes, definitely. He's probably going to be very uncomfortable all night…Oh my God, Jade, is that your plan?" she exclaims, her eyes practically bulging out of her head.

"I can neither confirm or deny that, I'm afraid." I try and fail miserably to hide my amusement at my plan, giving my sister a huge grin.

"I hope you know what you're doing, sis. You know how these biker men get when they want something; you saw how Bear was with me," she informs me with an all-knowing look.

"I know, but don't worry, I know exactly what I'm doing."

I take a quick glance at the clock on my phone and see it's dead on 7pm.

Right on time, I hear the '*Thud thud!*' of someone thumping on the back door of the bakery.

Show time!

"Can you get that for me while I grab my purse?"

"Yeah, sure," Jenna smiles as she waltzes out of my bedroom to go let Tinhead in.

I do a quick final check of my outfit and makeup. My look is perfection; exactly what I was going for. I shimmy my arms into the aged denim jacket I can't seem to part with, even with the holes. I slide my cross-body black leather purse over to finish the look off just in time for me to hear Jenna bringing Tinhead up the stairs.

I sit on my plush bedcovers, waiting for Jenna to come and knock on my door. I'm eager to get this show on the road, but I plan on savoring the moment of walking out to see Mr. I-Think-With-My-Schlong gawp at me. Don't get me wrong, like most women, I have my insecurities, but I know for damn sure I look fuckin' hot tonight.

This is going to be sweet as fuck!

KNOCK! KNOCK!

"Jade?"

I don't move, but wait a few minutes, letting him stew. There's a hum of conversation on the other side— my sister is probably asking him all kinds of questions. That's one thing that I can count on my sister for; when Momma isn't around, she steps up. It's Tinhead she should worry about, not me. I touch my phone and see it's 7:14pm.

Deciding that he's waited long enough, I check my lips again, making sure I haven't gotten any red smears on my teeth, then I lazily saunter over to open the door—only a minuscule amount at first, just enough to see the back of his leather cut, dark denim jeans, and boots in the light streaming in from the living area.

I grin like the cat that got the cream.

Perfect.

I pull the door open wide and stride through it with such purpose that my spine straightens on instinct. As soon as my cowboy boots hit the wooden floor outside my room, Tinhead's head snaps up and he pivots on his heel. His eyes go wide as his ego, his muscles tensing across the olive-green shirt stretched over his torso. I take a few more steps toward him, neither of us saying anything to one another. He stands there gaping at me like a goddamn trout until I'm about a foot or two away from him, then finally slams his mouth shut.

A mischievous glint appears in his eyes. "Holy fuckin' hairy ballsacks! Doll…*damn*… we ain't goin' to a rodeo. *Shiiit!* I wish we were now!" Tin coughs nervously, and I catch him readjusting himself—not that I'm looking or anything.

Bingo!

"So should I change?" I flip open my denim jacket so he can see the full ensemble, looking up at him with doe eyes.

Tin's nostrils flare and he grits his teeth. I don't miss the crack in his voice as he responds, "N-no! You're knockout. F-fuck, you're making my balls ache!" The last part comes out in a mumble, so I stare him square in the eyes to let him know I heard him. He's practically drooling over me; this is definitely going to be a fun night indeed.

Forget the cat that got the cream, this *pussy* has the whole dairy farm!

***

Well, at least he decided to bring the club's pick-up truck and not his bike; the thought of being squished up against his back with my thighs rubbing against his makes my skin crawl.

The drive is pretty uneventful. We trade a few standard 'yes-no' questions, but when he pulls up to where he tells me we're having our date, I can't help but gawp. He's actually shocked me, which not many people can do—minus Kelly, of course. I'm so shocked I don't even react to the fact he called it a date.

"What are we doing here?" I ask stupidly as we pull into the parking lot. "I mean, I assumed you would just park up somewhere and try throw yourself on me, not bring me to a monster truck rally!" I say, keeping the edge to my voice despite my excitement.

Tin's head snaps back at the suggestion. "Whoa, Jade! I ain't about to throw myself on you! I wanted to bring you here to show you that there's more to me than meets the eye…If I *did* want to throw myself on you, you would know about it! And you know what else?" he asks, reflecting the challenge in my tone back at me.

"What?" I sigh, already knowing what the douche is gonna say.

"You would fuckin' *love* every second. So, how about it? You still want to go in?"

I stare back at him for a moment, then flit my eyes to the sight that greets me through the truck's windshield stare back at the floodlights as the roar of engines make the windows in the truck vibrate. I know I'm with Captain Douche, but I have wanted to come to the rally for years now. I tried to get Jenna and Kel to come before, but it's not their thing—I'm not gonna divulge that to him, though.

"Yeah, sure thing. Let's go." I try to hold back my eagerness, but I'm chomping at the bit and trying not to leap out and run all the way to the grandstand.

I step out of the cab and am surprised as hell to find Tinhead right there to help me down, wrapping his arm around my waist so I'm practically flush with his side, his cool leather cut tickling my midriff.

I shove out of his grasp and jump down on my own—his touch is too familiar, and I hate it. "I'm okay, thanks though. C'mon, we best get moving; the poster at the gates says it starts at 7:30pm," I tell him as I stride ahead to join the line for seats.

Tinhead catches up with me in moments, and we join the hustle and bustle of the crowds. I keep getting weird looks as we wait…

Shit! I forgot I'm wearing something that's definitely not normal for a monster truck rally! Fudge…

I tug nervously at my jacket, trying to cover my boobs as much as possible.

"Don't hide your body, Jade! You look hot as hell!" Tin informs me from behind, the warmth of his breath tickling the back of my ear lobes. I'm still disgusted by him, but I am surprised he brought me here—I would never have thought this would have been his thing.

"I'm not hiding my body, but thanks. D'ya know where we're sitting?" I peer over my shoulder and catch a glimpse of his eyes sparkling in the light from the stadium. They're soft and dilated.

Why the hell is he looking at me like that? Stupid dick…

"Yup. It's all taken care of, doll. What meat d'ya want?"

"What the fuck? You can't help yo—" I freeze midsentence, noticing that the shithead is grinning ear to ear at me as he tilts his head to the food truck near the doors.

"I meant, hot dog or burger? What the hell were *you* thinking, Jade Smith? Get your mind outta the gutter," he chuckles, wrapping his arm around my shoulder and tucking me under his arm.

What the actual fuck?

I try and shove out of his hold, but he holds on tighter. "Nuhuh. You agreed to go on a date with me, dollface, so that's exactly what you're going to do."

"Fine, but don't start getting too friendly, you jerk. And stop calling it a date!" I inform him as we walk through the turnstiles.

Tinhead stalks up to a staff member, showing him the tickets, and he gives him directions, I follow behind, now being tugged along as he's gripping my hand like I'm about to slip away. As much as I detest him, I have been wanting to come to a rally since forever, so, I'll endure a night with Captain Douche in exchange for a free show.

I follow him down flights of steps to seats right on the front row, where only a couple of other seats taken. I can feel the jealous gazes of other fans boring into me.

"Here we are, Your Highness!" Tinhead stops in front of two seats on the end of the row, taking the outside seat and spreading his legs wide enough that I barely have enough space for my own on the inside seat next to him.

"Hey! Close your legs, wouldya? I get that you men need enough space for your junk, but I doubt you're packing that much!" I decide to spread my own legs right up against his to emphasize my point.

"Easy, tiger! These seats aren't wide enough for my long legs, ya feel me? Also, how d'ya know what I am or ain't packing? I never had any complaints about my dick before, but do you wanna test that theory?" he shoots me the dirtiest smirk, the laughter lines creasing around his eyes.

I want to wipe that fuckin' smirk off his stupid face...

My hand clenches instinctively, but I just raise my eyebrow in response.

"Seriously?! Does that line actually work on women?" I shake my head at him, then flick my eyes back to the people surrounding us. The crowd gets rowdier, the noise filling my ears until I'm barely able to hear Tinhead, or should I say *Pinhead*.

A few moments later some of the trucks roar to life, getting ready to perform. I take a long slurp of the diet soda he handed me in the truck, waiting for his response. When it comes, he has to yell over the noise. "You bet your sweet *short ass*...the ladies love it, they eat that shit right up—by the end of the night *I* end up eating *their* ass."

I choke on my drink as the last words pass his lips and stare at him, stunned at the fact that this wannabe playboy has just shouted about his sex life when there are kids only four rows back...at the exact moment the music dips enough for everyone to hear.

"Jesus! Did you really have to say it that loud, if at all? What is wrong with you? Have you got a screw loose in that thick skull of yours?!"

He sits there with a proud, smug grin across his face.

"Yeah, pretty much. Why d'ya think they call me Tinhead? It's hollow up there. You want anything to eat? I'm gonna grab a quick bite before they start."

As he leaves, I notice that although his smile hasn't shifted, his eyes seem to have lost their spark.

Hmm, interesting. So the joker of the pack does have some flaws...

Fuck! Why the hell did she have to go and ask about where I got my name?

I mean when Zar' asked that time, I was ready and my hackles were up, but Jade? Fuck, she caught me off guard completely. It almost feels like she's trying to get to know me.

I make my way towards the food vendors, but my mind can't help running through what just happened. I know she doesn't really; I see the way she flinches when I'm near and slams her guard up, even though she may have agreed to come on a date with me. Sure, there are moments when she tries to see through the façade I have built up, but it's pointless. No one can break through, and that's just how it has to be. It's still bugging me why the fuck she's got beef with me, and the stick she's got shoved so far up her ass doesn't help.

If she's like this with me, God help other men. Sheesh!

I eventually get what I have been searching for since we got here—the best hot dog stand this side of Tennessee, 'Donny's Dongs'. I shit ya not, those are the tastiest bastards ever.

Donny greets me like an old friend as I walk over. "'Sup, Tin? I didn't know you were coming down, I would have put your special to one side for you! You with Wrench?" Donny's an alright guy; he's greasy as John Travolta and his white wife-beater barely covers his pot belly, but other than that he's pretty sound. We've been friendly since the club helped his business out a few months back.

"Nah, Donny, not this time. I got a chick out there, but she's hating on the T-Dawg so I'm trying to win her over...it's the hardest fucking shit I have ever had to do."

It isn't, not even close, but I can't help the shit I spout. Most people know about my time in the Army, but other than Zar' and my brothers, no one has ever asked for details...except Jade wanting to know about my name just now.

Damn it, I know that look in her eyes, she's tenacious as the devil and will keep pushing 'til she finds out all she wants, and if I'm going to find out what put the stick up that juicy ass, I'm going to have to give her some answers too. Little does she know, I've seen the devil—stared down the barrel of a gun at him, in fact...

"Here ya go Tin, the works, just for you. Enjoy— it's on the house. Does your date want anything?" he drawls.

I grin. "I'll tell ya what, Donny..."

***

As I make my way back to the seats with the food, I notice the rally has started. I see the 'BoneKrusher' come in to view, yellow and black stripes decorating the side of its cab. The custom Jeep M715 monster charges at 'The Zombie'. I turn around to see bleachers of loyal fans dressed as zombies and others with black and yellow striped faces. Their roars and screams are fucking deafening as I search the crowd for Jade. I eventually see her strawberry hair shining at me like a beacon, the artificial light illuminating the gold and red pigments. Making my way over in a few strides, I get to my seat and plonk my ass in it. Casting my eyes over to her, I'm left stunned and smiling by what I see. Jade looks completely awestruck at all the trucks, her eyes dancing around like she's a kid in a candy store.

Slap me on the back and call me a pussy, Jade Smith is enjoying the rally! Well, I never thought that would happen.

I don't think she's noticed that I'm back, and if she has, she's doing a good job of pretending I'm not there. I could care less about the truck rally, but this has to be the most amusing thing I've witnessed.

I clear my throat gently. "Ahem. Here, for you," I smile as I thrust the hot dog under her nose.

Her shoulders slump as soon as my voice reaches her ears—she clearly didn't know I was there after all. "I said I didn't want anything."

Her gaze flicks down to the hotdog, and I bite back a laugh as she clenches her back teeth and curls her lip. "Seriously?! Who the hell d'ya think you are? How exactly is *this* going to help your fuckin' cause, huh?!" The fireball shoots flames at me with her gaze, then stares down at her hot dog decorated with the words *'Tin's dick'* written in mustard and ketchup and squirts of mayo at the end of the sausage.

"What can I say? I thought it would break that icy exterior of yours. Besides, you looked a little peckish, and what's better to nibble on than Donny's dong?" I give her a smug grin, flashing my pearly whites.

"Donny's dong? Fucking hell, Tinhead! Well, ya know what?" She snatches it out of my grip and shoves a third of the hot dog and bun right into her mouth, taking a huge mouthful like a pro. Once that's gone, the second mouthful goes down a treat, followed quickly by the last part.

Without missing a beat, she swipes the back of her hand across her mouth, smearing all the sauces across her cheek and making herself look like a clown.

"Happy now?!" she demands, raising a neat auburn eyebrow.

Trying to get a reaction from her, I lean down, put my lips to her ear, and rasp out, "Oh, more than you know, dollface. So how was Donny's dong? Was it *juicy? Tasty? Satisfying?*"

"It was all that and much more, and ya know what? I know for a fact that was the best dong I will *ever* have!" Jade spits before whipping her head back to watch the trucks.

Yeah, she may be tenacious, but I'm stubborn as a mule. This girl *will* tell me why the hell she hates me so much, and then I'm gonna fuck her hard and watch that fiery hair fly around as she bounces on my cock. This hellcat will be begging for it...

~ Chapter 9 Jade ~

Before I know it, we're on the way home from one of the most mixed nights I've ever experienced. I fucking loved every minute of the monster truck rally…but then there was Captain Douche.

I look over at him in the corner of my eye. "So, Blockhead, who told you about monster truck rallies?"

Tin glances between me and the open road. He's using one hand to drive even in the inky black night; his left arm is stretched taut, showing his toned bicep off

"What are ya on about now?"

"Who told you about me wanting to go to a monster truck rally? Was it Jenna or Kelly? Come on, tell me so I can kick their ass for such a crappy idea." I stare at the side of his face, waiting for a reaction.

His expression is stony and unreadable for a moment, then the corner of lip curls upwards, his short golden whiskers glinting in the full moonlight beaming down on us. "No one."

"Huh? What d'ya mean, no one?"

"No one told me that you, Jade Smith, like monster truck rallies."

"What are you talking about? Quit lying, Tinhead. What kinda name is that? Bear's makes sense, but yours? Well, it's the dumbest fucking shit I ever heard." After the look I saw in his eyes earlier, I know I'm picking at one big scab he doesn't want to scratch off. I see his mind shut off and his expression go blank—I know that look well.

"Like I said earlier, you were accurate about my name...but I never got the idea from your sister or Kelly. Anyway, I saw you back there. I saw your face light up like the fourth of July—you like monster truck rallies."

I sit there for a moment, trying to come up with a retort and observing every flicker emotion that crosses his face.

"Nah, it was at the lack of company I had at that precise moment, actually. So, how long you been in the club?" I change the subject quickly, not wanting to let him know that I had the best night with the monster trucks. Tinhead doesn't reply right away, so I grab my purse from my lap check my phone to see a text from Kelly. The girl's certifiably crazy, that's for sure...

Kel: - *So, how did the date with the "enemy" go? Are ya gonna get some sausage?*

Me: - *Hell no, it wasn't a date! Girl, are you nuts? I already ate a sausage tonight anyway. Call ya later x*

Just as I'm about to tuck my phone back in my pocket, it buzzes again:

Kel: - *WHAT? You gave him head?! Fuck, girl, what are ya doing?*

Me: - ***rolls eyes at you***

Looking up from my phone, I glance back over to the giver of 'Donny's dong'. He still hasn't responded and he's completely in a world of his own, just driving back to the bakery on autopilot.

"Tinhead?"

"Yeah?" he breathes out in hardly a whisper.

"Did you hear my question?"

He shakes his head to snap out of his daze. "Yeah. Yeah, I did. I zoned out, sorry dollface. I've been prospecting in the club coming up a year in January."

Even though he's called me his current favorite endearment, his voice holds no banter or humor, devoid emotion. He pulls in behind the back of the bakery and parks up, but doesn't switch off the engine, staring blankly.

Okay...

"Well, I guess this is me. Thanks for tonight, Tinhead. it's been...eventful." I roll my eyes in an attempt to provoke a reaction, but there's no flicker of anything, he just keeps staring dead ahead at the dumpster behind the bakery. I place my hand on his forearm to wake him from la-la-land or wherever he is, but as soon as my fingertips touch the hair on his arm, he grabs my own forearm, his nails biting into the skin there.

"Get off me, you scum!" he screams in my face, his eyes as black as the crows that circle carcasses over Dead Man's Peak.

What the hell?

I have never seen him this way. His eyes aren't just black, they're dead, with no light dancing in them. My heart's racing; as much as I hate the jackass, I wasn't expecting to see him like this. After fighting to swallow a few times, I'm eventually able to squeak out, "Tinhead. Tinhead, it's Jade. Are you okay?"

As soon as the words leave my lips, his eyelids flicker, and I see the exact moment he comes back from wherever he's been. His eyes fixate on his grip on my arm, but gradually he comes back to himself and lets go like I burned him—but not before I notice his hand trembling.

"Fuck!" he growls as he swipes his hands down his face, distorting his features by rubbing at them.

"Tinhead, are you okay?" I ask, genuinely worried about him.

No, I think, catching myself, *I'm not worried, I'm curious; he's obviously got problems.*

I'm met with silence, but I'm not touching him again in case he lashes out again.

To my relief, he responds a moment later. "Yeah. I just zoned out, doll, nothing to it." I watch as he composes himself again and flicks his head in my direction. He tries to smirk, but his usually boyish grin barely touches his lips, never reaching his eyes.

"Okay, if you say so Tinh—"

"I do say so! For fuck's sake!" he snaps at me, almost giving me whiplash from his verbal hairpin. This time, I lose it.

"Who the hell d'ya think you are?! Don't snap at me like that, you fuckin' prick!" I growl at him. I grab the door of the truck, jumping down before swinging and slamming the door.

Seriously? I ain't standing around waiting for him to treat me like shit a moment longer.

I storm up to the back of the bakery, unlocking and re-bolting the door before marching up the stairs to the apartment. I notice the corner lamp in the lounge is still on—Jenna's old habit, she's been leaving a light on at night since we were kids.

I'm still reeling from what happened downstairs, slamming my purse down on the kitchen counter and toeing off my cowboy boots before kicking them haphazardly near the front door.

I make my towards Jenna's room like a woman on a mission. As I near the door, I hear noises that no sister wants to hear, but at this point I'm past giving two fucks about it and knock loudly. I step away from the door while I wait, hoping I don't see anything I don't wanna.

After a second, I overhear Bear grumbling, "Cupcake don't...come on."

"Bear, stop that!" Jenna gasps, chuckling. "Jade, are ya alright? Bear! Will you stop th—" Jenna breaks off in giggles, followed by a squeal.

"Yeah. Can I talk to you...both?" I pace up and down in front of Jenna's door, feeling conflicted.

I hear shuffling and padding on the other side of the door, then it opens. Jenna's hair is disheveled, even though she's tried to keep it under control. She has Bear's black Devils t-shirt on, which hangs past her thighs, and her eyes are wide with pure concern.

"JJ! What's up? You look like you've seen a ghost."

"I...I don't really know how to explain it. Is Bear coming out? I need to speak to him too?"

Jenna glances over her shoulder, and I hear the clank of Bear's belt buckle. "He's coming, sis. What is it? You're worrying me. Did you not have a good night with Tinhead? Did he give you some of those terrible one-liners?"

"Yes...and he went all weird on me in the truck. There's something not right about him."

"Jade, you okay?" Bear asks in his deep baritone as he comes out of Jenna's bedroom shirtless and barefoot with just his jeans on. He strides over to Jenna, picks her up around her waist, sits down on the couch and places her in his lap. I see her melt at the gesture.

"What's going on, darlin'?" he asks with a frown of concern as he absently caresses Jenna's arm.

"Promise me you won't go raging over to the clubhouse?" I ask hesitantly.

"Darlin', I don't think I can make that promise: you're family. Tell me what it is."

"Well, at least don't react until I finish! Oh, fuck, I can't even explain it really. I'm probably overreacting…but Tinhead kinda flipped out on me in the truck. He went deathly quiet, so I touched his arm to check he was okay, and he grabbed ahold of me and called me scum!"

I glance over to my sister to gage her reaction, but that may have not been the best idea—she looks murderous; her eyes wide. "He What!?! I'm gonna kill him!"

Jenna marches over to me to check me over. Seeing the slight pink marks on my arm, she grabs her Chucks from by the door to shove her feet in them.

"Where the hell d'ya think you're going Cupcake? Get your ass back here! Leave it to me and the club, okay?"

"No, Bear! This isn't just club business, this is family! I knew club business would come first a lot of the time when we got together, but this is *my baby sister*! He can't touch her like that!"

Bear moves to stand right in front of her, grabbing her hips and pulling her flush to his chest. "Cupcake, I know what he did was wrong, but I'm trying to keep calm. I don't know why he did this, or what's up with him. I know he can be easy with the ladies, but fuck, I have never heard or seen him treat a woman wrong. If nothing else, Axe would *never* allow that shit, even before Dani. Leave it to me, okay? I'll go see what's up with him. You both okay with that?"

"Bear Jameson, if you think I'm not going to the club with you, then you can—sorry Sis—suck your own fuckin' jam jar!" Jenna flushes beetroot red, then tugs on Bear's nipple ring sharply to emphasize her point.

I can see Bear is pissed and trying to reign it in. He stares down into my sister's eyes, and after a good few seconds, he huffs "Cupcake, there is no way in hell I'm suckin' my own cock, you know your lips are the only ones I want wrapped it. Stay here, your sister needs you."

Jenna nods, relenting, and I walk over to him.

"Look, Bear, I don't want to cause problems for you and the club; I just didn't know if Tinhead had some weird personality quirk I didn't know about."

"Jade, darlin', don't worry about it, okay? Leave it with me and try and get some rest."

I watch Bear stride back into Jenna's room, his back straight with purpose, then I look to Jenna, who's still standing where Bear left her. She gazes after him longingly

"JJ, Bear isn't going to do anything stupid, is he? It's probably just me overreacting."

Jenna gives me a sympathetic look. "Jade, that's one thing you don't do, babe."

I sigh. "I know, I don't think I am. As much as I dislike him, I'm worried; it was like he was on another planet."

"I trust Bear, he'll find out what's going on. I'm furious with Tinhead for treating you this way, but Bear's right—it's so out of character. Are you still shaken up?" Jenna walks over to me to wrap her arm around me and presses my head into her neck, but after a minute I can't stand it any longer.

"Jenna, get off me! Ew, you smell like sex and Bear!"

"I see tonight's events haven't disturbed your sense of humor. Okay, JJ." She chuckles, releasing me, then asks. "Do you want a cookie and some warm milk?"

"What cookies do we have? Please say you've got a new invention."

"Girl after my own heart," Bear says as he strides back out fully dressed, his cut firmly in place with the word '*Enforcer*' emblazoned over his left lapel. He grabs Jenna from behind, swooping down to give her a big kiss and tickling her neck with his thick chocolate-brown beard.

I roll my eyes; they'd be cute if they weren't always like this.

"Bear, as much as he's a mega bastard…you won't…ya know…kill him, will ya?" I don't care what happens to him, but I would hate for Bear to go to prison because of me.

"I promise…but I can't promise Axe won't. Right, I better get moving, Axe is expecting me. Don't wait up, okay Jenna? Get some sleep." He grasps her chin, tilting it so her lips are a hair away from his, then devouring her mouth as she tugs on his beard. I swear I hear him growl.

Jeez…this is exactly why I need to move out.

Bear straightens up. "Right, I'll catch ya in the morning, Jade. Try not to worry, okay? Love you Cupcake."

We both watch Bear exit the apartment, then I turn to Jenna, grasping her hand. "How about those cookies, then?"

Anything to distract myself from what's happening over at the clubhouse…

~ Chapter 10 Tinhead ~

I stride back through the clubhouse doors, not paying any mind that I'm slamming the door behind me and making a beeline straight for the bar. I need a drink, and it's gotta be large…

I replay the image of Jade's face in the truck, the sight of fear taking hold of her beautiful turquoise eyes and her horrified expression. I don't know what made her yell at me like that; it's not like she hides the fact she hates me, but that was extreme. I pull a glass down off the shelf behind the bar and pour two shots of the purest Russian vodka we have. I neck it back straight, enjoying the burn of the alcohol. It's like a balm right in my bloodstream, soothing and numbing my soul and dampening the voices in my head.

"Yo, Tin. You alright bro'?" Feeling a little off-kilter, I swivel around on my heel to see Flex walking towards the bar from the other side of the clubhouse. He's got demons like I do, but they seem to go easier on him these days.

"Hey, VP. I'm good, just needed a hard drink. Just finished my date with Jade." I chuckle, trying to shut out the doubts and questions swirling around my head.

"Ahh, I see. The little fireball still givin' you shit, or have you been able to crack that nut?" he asks as he takes his seat.

I turn my back on him to get his usual—a Bud with a JD chaser. "Ha, no chance! Whatever it is she has against me, she's still got her panties in a twist about it. What ya gonna do?"

"I hear ya brother. Don't make my mistake; if there's anything there worth exploring, do it. I nearly lost Zar' too many times…"

"You don't need to worry about that man, T-Dawg isn't the settling-down type. I like my dick how I like my fingers—in different holes," I tell him, plastering on the grin I have mastered since I joined the club.

Flex spits some of his Bud out on the clean wooden bar top, chuckling. "Fucking hell Tin, give me some warning before ya say shit like that!"

"What's that?" Dagger grumbles as he sits down next to Flex, slapping him on the back. He isn't into small talk, so always slips right into conversation.

"Prospect here was just telling me he likes his dick how he likes his fingers…in different holes!" Flex roars out, laughing at my joke.

"Fuck yeah, Prospect! A man after my own heart! You up for a—"

"YOU! What the ever-loving fuck! With me to the Prez, NOW!" Bear yells as he storms through the clubhouse door. His eyes look wild, like he's about to go on a rampage and I'm the red cloth. He freezes and stands there, not moving from his spot. I place the glass and bottle I had in my hand on the counter. I know what this is about, but I ask him anyway to keep up the pretense.

"What's up, Bear?"

"Don't start that shit with me, Prospect. Flex, is Axe still in his office?" he growls out to the VP, who looks between me and Bear, confused.

"Bear, what's this about?" I ask as I round the bar, walking past Flex and Dagger. I've always gotten along with all my brothers in the club, so seeing Bear like this does sting—he welcomed me into the club more than Dagger did.

"You want to explain anythin', Tinhead?!" he yells right in my face. I can see he's trying hard to keep his anger under restraint; the thick vein in his temple pulsates like crazy.

"I don't know what—"

Axe interrupts me before I get to finish my protest.

"What's all this fuckin' shouting about? I was just about to go home to Dani. You better have a good excuse for stopping me from getting back to my woman."

"Yeah, I do. *He* grabbed Jade and called her scum!" Bear roars, fisting the neck of my t-shirt in a fierce grip before shoving me away.

"What the ever-lovin' fuck?! No, I didn't!" I protest. My eyes don't leave his, and I don't let them betray any of the fear or confusion I feel—that's one of the many things I learnt in the Army; never shy away from the enemy. Sure, Bear isn't my enemy, he's my brother, but I can't show weakness—I'm not a fully-fledged member yet.

"Tinhead, Bear, in my office now; we're not doing this in here! You better fuckin' explain yourself, Tinhead; I will not tolerate any mishandling of a woman of any kind, you know that." I don't miss the venom in Axe's voice—he's holding his true reaction back. I know not to answer him until we are back in his office, so I follow them both down the darkened corridor as a sinking feeling of dread settles into my stomach like a cement block in the ocean—complete with waves crashing over it in the form of the vodka swirling around in there at the moment. I follow Axe and Bear into the office and shut the door behind me with, the latch barely clicking shut before Axe throws the gavel at my head.

It vibrates off my eye socket with a smack, and I instantly grab my eye. "Fuuck! Boss!"

"You have five minutes to explain to me why I shouldn't cut you out of this club right now!" he growls.

"I don't know what happened, but I never grabbed her, and I would *never* call her scum. Is that what she's saying? I'd never do that, you gotta believe me Boss." I implore, looking between Bear and Axe.

I don't understand what happened; I'd never hurt her!

"She had fingerprints over her forearm, Tinhead! How the fuck d'ya explain those?!" Bear bites back at me, staring me down with his nostrils flaring.

"I don't...I can't explain it. Fuck! I swear, Bear, I would never hurt a woman. Guys, you know me! Please, you gotta—"

"Well, how the hell do you explain the marks?! She said you weren't yourself, that you flipped out on her after she touched your arm. She noticed you were deathly quiet on the drive back to the bakery." Bear's eyes have softened slightly, and he tilts his head to the side.

Fuck I hate that look; I've seen it in my comrades before I left the army and from old friends who don't—and can't—understand, but not from Bear and the rest of my brothers in the club; they would understand more than most at least.

"Tin, is this somethin' to do with the Army and what happened over there? You know we never ask about it out of respect to you but if it is, we got you." The hard edge is gone from his voice now.

I try my best to speak, but instead I just give them both a curt nod of the head and look at Axe.

"I swear to you Prez, I would never intentionally hurt a woman; I don't remember her even speaking to me. I was finding it hard to concentrate on the road; I just wanted to drop Jade off and get back here." I don't dare remove my eyes from Axe's, hoping he can see the sincerity in my eyes.

After what feels like a lifetime, he slaps me on the arm with such force I know he was meaning for it to hurt, but I don't pull away or wince—I had to block most pain out to survive Afghanistan, and old habits die hard. I quickly shut those memories down.

"Make sure it stays that way. If you need to talk or anything like that, I may come across brash, but my door's always open. I hope you could come to me if you needed to, and if not me, at least one of your brothers."

"Yes, Prez," I quickly comply, not really letting the words sink in. I know I can't let the Prez see my weakness. I'm trying my hardest not to let on that my insomnia is gradually becoming worse as it is—that's why I was tired in the first place.

"You owe Jade an apology. I want ya at the bakery first thing in the morning; I'll be waiting for you," Bear says. I know he ain't messing around; Jenna will have his ass for if she thinks he didn't make a stand.

"Don't worry brother, I'll be there. I would never hurt her on purpose, ya gotta know that."

Bear sighs. "Yeah, I know. I did say that it wasn't like you."

"So we cool?" I ask, apprehension clear in my tone.

Bear looks to Axe, then Axe looks me over and nods. "Yeah, we're cool, brother. Go and catch some Z's—and that's a fuckin' order, Prospect, " Axe barks, reminding me that I'm still not a fully-fledged member.

"Sure, Prez."

I turn on my heel and exit the office, sweat dripping down my spine and my pounding heart threatening to rip out of my chest as I make my way back to my room. I hope that I can find some solace in sleep tonight, but I'm not counting on it.

As I get into my room, I lock my door behind me, not wanting anyone to bother me—I have too many thoughts whirling around my head to act any longer.

Stripping out of my clothes, I start folding them completely on autopilot, arranging them into tight bundles on the chair in the corner of my room and tucking my boots underneath it. I grab a bottle of water out of my mini fridge and drain it dry in a couple of gulps, then stand at the side of my bed wishing I didn't need sleep. Staying awake would be so much easier than having to go through this every night I'm alone in here. I untuck my bedsheets in readiness for what's to come.

Most people find sleep with ease, but me? Well, most nights are filled with fuckin' a girl or two and drinking until 3am to block the thoughts out, but after that I don't sleep; not really.

I slide underneath the cool, crisp sheets, sweat sticking the sheet to my back. I lay there with nothing but the dull rumble of the bass from the main room to distract me.

Thump, thump, thump, thump…

I concentrate on the repetitiveness of the beat as I lay there with closed eyes hoping for a decent 4 hours sleep—even that would be better than none at all.

Thump, thump, thump…

***

Strobes of crimson and orange light cloud my vision…

The bitter smokiness of a blazing fire infiltrates my senses…

A little Middle Eastern boy playing soccer waves at me from across a dirt road, then he's gone in an explosion…

Dirt and dust swirls in a cloud around me. Broken glass is scattered across the floor in front of me, tempting me to step on it and break it some more…

There are so many grenades—too many to count—as well as rows upon rows of guns of all sizes; AKs, rifles, and more. I don't see or feel anyone else here, it's just me. I stare at all the guns.

The zing of whizzing bullets fills the air. They narrowly miss me, clipping the top of my helmet...

Gunfire surrounds me left and right, and then it's my turn. In the dusty atmosphere, I see a lone armed figure, the Afghan blazing down on him. I can't see his face; just that he's in a uniform of some kind. It looks black, possibly the uniform of the Taliban, or maybe the insurgents…

Whispered words swirl around me from all angles, echoing like they're falling down the rabbit hole to Wonderland.

"Do it. Just kill him already..."

"He's one of them! Do it, pull the trigger!"

"Kill or be killed, soldier!"

"KILL HIM, NOW, OR I'LL KILL YOU! Carry out my order and kill, don't maim!"

"Do it now! NOW! Kill him! You've done it already, do it again!"

"Take his life!"

The voice repeats these words again and again, but the worst part is that it doesn't belong to a superior...

It's my voice.

I bolt up in bed, sweat dripping off my brow and soaking me. My heart gallops as my chest constricts, and it's a fight to breathe normally, but I know I need to calm down. Every time I close my eyes even to blink, I'm back there.

Scarlet blood like wet rubies...

I push the thought away quickly, blinking and sitting up fully in bed. I flick the light on as I do—why didn't I have it on already? It may not do anything at all, but it's a habit—I feel like a goddamn pussy admitting that I sleep with the light on like I'm trying to keep the bogeyman away, but what I see is a hell a lot worse than the bogeyman.

I glance at my phone.

Only 1:22am? Jesus...

I peel myself off of my clammy bed, swinging my legs over the side and sitting there for a few minutes trying to calm my racing heart. I realize too late that I sat up too quickly, and the room spins. I fix my gaze on the light coming from the minifridge to ground myself, willing myself not to give into the temptation of a cold beer.

It won't help me, it never does…

Finally, the dizziness subsides. I stand up and make my way to the shower in my room, stripping out of my boxers and stepping into the cubicle. I turn the temperature dial as low as it will go; a cold shower always rights me—well, as much as I can be righted.

I force myself under the icy blast of water instantly feeling the sweat dripping down my spine be washed away by the frigid water that rains over me. I bow my head, feeling the raw, intense torrent blast over me and fighting the urge to switch it over to fierce heat. I feel my racing heart starting to slow down and plateau, so I reward myself with a flash of warmth, then shut the shower off.

I grab my towel and dry myself off, rubbing my toweled hand over my dick, the thought of where it could have been tonight making it stir to life as a flash of light copper hair swishes into my mind's eye.

After quickly toweling down the rest of my body, I hang the towel over the rail, grabbing my discarded boxers as I leave the bathroom.

***

I slide back into bed, finding that the sheets have dried. My mind still races with flashes of tonight's vivid dream. It's one I have often, but never that detailed…

To distract myself, I take ahold of my now-flaccid cock and rest my head against the headboard, willing myself to relax as my AC blows cool air over me like a calming presence. I slide my palm over the length of my dick and give it a quick sharp tug, bringing it to life and loving the pinch and tingle the gesture brings to the head. I wrap my hand around my dick, fisting myself. A few pumps in, my dick grows hard. I swipe my free hand over the head, loving the sensation. I got circumcised when I left the Army and I love it—the feeling of a tight snatch fluttering around my dick it's a lot more intense than before.

My eyes grow heavy, and my heart rate picks up again—although for a completely different reason this time. I move my hand slowly back and forth, chasing the release I need to make me feel anything. Flashes of those green catlike eyes haunt me as I chase my happy ending, the gorgeous redhead batting her eyelashes at me. I pump my hand faster and harder as the image shifts to include the sexy outfit she wore on our date—I could have come right there and then when I first saw her.

Fuuuck!

The temptress in my fantasy isn't like the real Jade, who was clearly there just to push my buttons. This girl runs her fingers casually and seductively over the tops of her breasts, pushing them together. I flick my eyes back up to her gorgeous face to see she's licking her lips slowly and seductively, tempting me...

Fuck, the thought of her wanting me like this is the hottest thing ever, even if it's just a fantasy. My hand pumps faster as I grip harder, choking my dick.

"Tinhead...come and cum all over my tits. You know you want to..." The fantasy Jade starts tugging at her cut off shorts, lowering them and shimmying them

off her hips so they float down her lightly tanned thighs, revealing her bare pussy.

Fuck, it looks so tempting I could just reach out and taste it...

She dips her middle fingers deep inside her wet pussy.

That's it, baby, nice and deep...

The hand choking my dick gets tighter, urging the cum to reach the surface and coat my hand—even if I do wish that smart-mouthed, flame-haired woman would drink it down instead.

I cup and rub my balls, imagining it was her rolling them around her in her sexy mouth. The image of her taking me between her pouty lips sends that familiar sensation zinging down my spine, and my neck arches off my pillow. I grunt as my balls tighten, my fist still clasped tightly around my dick in wait for the first stream of cum to explode and make my knees fuckin' weak.

After a few final erratic yanks, the tingling moves up my shaft, and the first explosion coats my abs and fist. I keep jerking as more coats my stomach.

Ahh fuck, that's it! Right there!

As the last jet of hot cum coats my stomach, my arm flops down to my side, cramping slightly from fisting myself so hard.

I peer down to see cum pooled in my belly button and splattered across my chest, the drops shining like milky gems in the light.

Fuck...

I don't want to have another shower, so I get up on shaky legs, grab the folded t-shirt off my chair, and use it as a towel swiping at the cum down my stomach and using it to clean my cock too.

When I'm done, I throw it in the laundry hamper and fall back into bed, hoping that the dreams stay at bay. As soon as my head drops onto the pillow, I feel my whole body relax and become heavy as sleep pulls me under once again. Before I drift off, I pray that if I do dream again, it won't be haunted by a solitary swinging black noose…

"What was said last night, Bear? Come on, you haven't said a word since you got up this morning. You didn't…finish him off?" I can't help the hesitation in my voice at the last part.

"Jade, seriously what the hell have ya been watching? Is it that MC show again? I told ya before, we're not like that. Once one of us Devils claim a woman, we don't fuck around. I can't speak for the other chapters, though."

"So what if I have? Have ya seen how fuckin' hot Charlie is? Mmm, that man is Fine with a capital F! So Tin's okay? Did he tell ya what happened at all?"

"Jesus Christ, you and Zara are as bad as each other with that show, but at least Flex spanks her ass for thinking about another man! It's a good job she asks for it…Yeah he's okay, he should be coming over soon," Bear informs me as he checks the time on his phone before pouring a large mug of black coffee. He stands next to me in the kitchen, jeans hung low and black Devils T-shirt on.

"Huh? What d'ya mean he's coming over? You could have led with that ya know! I'm still in my PJs, shit! All right, I'm gonna jump in the shower, can you ask Jenna to pop one of her pastries in the oven for me?"

"I'll do it for ya, why you got me asking your sister to do it?"

"Because last time you did, you burnt my *pain au chocolat,* and it tasted worse than charcoal!" I bite back at him.

As I near my bedroom door, I hear him mumble, "Women! I can't do shit right!"

***

I've just finished drying myself off and am applying my body cream when I hear a knock on my bedroom door.

"Sis, Tinhead's here. D'ya want to see him?"

I think on it for a minute, but as much as the dick annoys me, I feel like I need to see him to make sure his face is still intact. I doubt that Bear would lie, but I need to know if the Devils really are the same as the MCs on TV or not.

"Yeah I'll be out in 5," I call out, still perched on my bed. I grab the first panties and pants I can find—which just so happen to include my bright purple yoga pants—followed by a bra, then the oversized cream t-shirt that hangs past my butt. The neck is stretched, so it slopes down on one shoulder.

Once I'm dressed, I scrunch some of my waves cream into my hair, not having time to dry it properly today. The scent of candy lingers in the air as I finish scrunching it and check myself in the mirror.

Ugh, the bags under my eyes aren't exactly kind to me...

I quickly apply some cover-up under my panda eyes and put some lip balm on, then I unlock my door and head to the living area, rounding the corner to see Tinhead standing near the kitchen with a glaring Jenna looking him up and down, Bear's arm wrapped around her waist as if to hold her back. Tinhead must have heard my feet on the wooden floor, as he looks straight up at me. I really look at him, taking in his eyes especially, and am almost relieved to see the mischievousness dancing in them once again, although I inwardly roll my eyes at him.

"Jade, I'm truly sorry if I scared or hurt you in any way last night. Are you okay? Can you forgive me?" he blurts out before I can speak. His eyes dart frantically over my body before landing on my arm.

"I'm fine, Tinhead, honest. Look, no marks on my arm, so no harm done. See?" I hold my arm out to him to prove my point, and he cautiously runs a finger over it.

The sensation is unlike anything I have felt; not tender or painful, but a tingle that seems to seep into my bones. I pull my arm away from his burning touch, but carefully mask any kind of reaction—he'd never let it go if he knew.

"I want to know everything's okay with you. You looked like you were in a world of your own on the way home last night."

"I had a hard day. I was dog tired, and just wanted to crash honestly. I'm good, doll. After a good night's sleep, I'm back to myself. I brought these for you; I wanted to apologize, and I was hoping you would give a second chance. Would you?"

I stand there staring at him, completely bewildered as he hands me the cutest little bunch of daises tied with a pink ribbon. If I didn't dislike him so much, I would think about kissing him to thank him. I want to let him down here and now, but then my maybe just maybe…

"Aww, thank you Tinhead! That's very sweet of you, but you really didn't need to. As you asked so nicely, I'll give you another shot, but only if you make sure you get a good night's sleep the night before, I see someone got a pot shot at your eye." I smirk at him as I nod my head to the to his purplish blue bruise under his eye.

I see a tiny flicker of emotion in his eyes, then they snap back to normal—I'm not sure what it was.

"Sure thang, doll. You free next Saturday? And don't worry about this I had it coming." he asks me with those puppy-dog eyes and that megawatt smile I know he must use on other girls.

I bet they drop to their knees for it…HA!

"Yeah, that sounds good; we can't go on any long drives this time though. How about I choose what we do?"

"Is that it, Jade? I'd thought you'd at least make him sweat a bit more." Jenna pipes up as she glares over at me, hand on her hip.

"It's okay, Sis, Tinhead has explained himself. The only reason I let him come over to apologize was because I wanted to check that Bear was telling the truth about the fact he didn't kill Tinhead." I nod my head at him in a silent indication he's off the hook.

"Fuckin' hell, Jade! You can't keep watching that show. Besides, you should know by now that my word is solid; if I say it, I mean it. Just look at how I treat my Cupcake." To prove his point, he pulls my sister flush against him and swoops in, capturing her lips.

I look away, my eyes landing back on Tinhead and searching his, trying to understand him. I thought this was going to be easy, but I have to admit that I am curious about what makes a womanizing Casanova like him tick.

"Message me and let me know what time you want me to pick you up, okay? Make sure ya do, I enjoyed spending time with you last night," he tells me, stepping into my personal space. I hear him inhale deeply, then he swipes the pad of his thumb softly and cautiously across my forearm, sending that sensation through my arm again, only this time it's followed by shockwaves through the rest of my body.

I try to not gasp at the touch, but he must feel me tense, as a look of pure worry covers his face the crinkles between his brows deepening as he fixates on my arm.

"My arm's fine, really. You didn't hurt me, but do it again and I will have your balls in a vice…or get Bear to have a shot at you," I warn with a giggle, which instantly makes his frown disappear. It's replaced with that cocky all-American-boy smile. I notice it isn't really touching his eyes like it does normally.

"Sure thang, Red! Catch ya later, doll. Yo Bear, I'll see ya at the club, brother. Later, Jenna."

He pivots on his heel, and he's nearly out of the door by the time I shout out, "Red?! Really, Tinhead? That's hilarious!" I retort.

"Baby, you ain't seen nothing yet! Don't forget to message me." With that, he's out the door and his biker boots are stomping down the stairs.

"Fuckin' Red? Really? Maybe I should have got you to knock him out after all, Bear."

"He knows the repercussions if it happens again," Bear informs me seriously as I make my way back to my room. My mind works overtime to mull over what he means for a few seconds before I decide to push the thoughts to one side for now.

I gotta finish getting ready for work…

***

"*Chica*! You didn't call or text me when you got home, so you better give me all the deets from last night. Don't leave anything out," Kel' demands as she stands in the bakery kitchen, one hand on her hip like a disapproving mother.

I stare at her face, trying to think of the words to explain what happened, but finding none. "It was definitely one to remember, that's for sure," I inform her as I turn back around and start dusting the countertop with flour to make pastries. I only get as far as grabbing some dough before I feel Kelly's hand on my arm.

"Uh, no ya don't, missy. You have to tell me! C'mon, don't leave me hanging! Did you finally get some?"

This kinky bitch is like a dog with a bone when she thinks she might get to hear people's sex stories!

I know she won't let up, so I turn around on the spot to face her. "Fine, but there's nothing to tell in the date department, and we didn't have sex. He was the normal douchey Tinhead while we were out, but on the way home he was so quiet I reached out and touched him to check he was okay. He kinda flipped, grabbed my arm, and called me scum, but Bear said he can't even remember driving home or me chatting to him. When he called me scum, it didn't sound like him either: it was really weird."

I look back up to meet Kelly's eyes—she looks stunned. "Well I'm not gonna say I'm not disappointed you didn't get any, but the other stuff doesn't sound like the Tinhead I know; you're right about that."

"He came over this morning to apologize for what happened, saying that he was just tired and trying to make his usual jokes, but when he smiled it wasn't genuine; it didn't reach his eyes like it would normally."

"We all have off days, and I think he was being honest; from what I've seen, I don't think Axe would let any man like that in the club, let alone be around Dani or Ryker as much as he is."

"Yeah, you're right. I know Axe, Bear and Flex are fiercely protective over their girls; if they genuinely thought one of their own would cause intentional harm to a woman, they would be out of the club right away."

"So, how did you leave it in the end?" she asks as she walks over to the frosting bowl, quickly dipping her finger in and shoving it in her mouth like a naughty child before.

I shake my head at her. "Kelly! Well, he wants to make it up to me by taking me out again, and I agreed on the condition that I'll be choosing what we do and where we go. Anyway, enough about me, what did you get up to last night?"

Kelly stops with her finger extended just before she reaches the frosting, peering through her eyelashes at me as she beams. "Oh Jade, is that slight interest you're showing towards the club's Prospect? I thought you hated him?" she smirks.

"Kel', listen now before I slap ya upside the head. I am *not interested* in Tinhead that way; I'm just intrigued by how a guy like him ticks. I won't ever be interested in that player, I'm just finding the right time to let him down easy. Now what is that smirk about? Who is it this time?"

"What? No one! This face right here is for you *chica.* Even if you don't want to admit it, Tinhead's growing on ya."

"Kelly, get your mad ass outta here, will ya! If you haven't got any juicy details for me about your dating life, then I'll catch ya tomorrow."

Kelly laughs. "You love me, and you will never get rid of me…but before I go, I didn't fuck anyone last night. I·*did* meet a hot Russian dude in a bar though! See ya!" My best friend waltzes out of the kitchen as quickly as she arrived, leaving me hanging.

I need to know what the hell's going on. A Russian?! That girl has exotic taste.

I pull out my phone:

Me: - *You lil bitch! I can't believe you did that! Don't think you're going to be getting away with that; I want all the juicy details later. Actually, I don't think I do…x*

Kel: - *HA! Well that's what ya get for trying to deny you like Tinhead. Speak later, love xx*

Me: - *Yeah, yeah. Keep telling yaself that, but it ain't coming true until hell freezes over! Xx*

***

The day goes by quickly—the bakery is even more busy than usual due to Mags calling in sick, which she never does. Her Daddy must be on one of his benders again.

"Sis, can you come out and help me with these plates?" Jenna hollers from the front.

I glance at the clock and see it's 5pm—nearly closing time. I'm looking forward to crashing; I got hardly any sleep after what happened with Tin. I wipe down the kitchen countertops one last time and make my way back through the door to see Tinhead casually leaning against one of the booths, arms across his chest to emphasize his muscles.

I roll my eyes at him. "What are ya doing here, Captain Douche? "

"Red, why are you hating on me so much? We never cleared that up last night, so will ya tell me now? Come on, help a brother out," he implores, giving me his puppy-dog eyes.

"Quit calling me Red! My name's Jade, try using it. I don't hate you, Tinhead, but I have yet to see a redeeming factor in your personality…unless you can prove me wrong on Saturday, that is."

I leave that lingering in the air as I glare at my sister, who's behind the counter and just shrugs. She'll be getting a lecture later too.

"I'll quit calling you that when you quit calling me Captain Douche and actually try to get to know me. If you still don't like me after that, I'll step back. What d'ya say?" I search his eyes for sincerity and see a twinkle in them.

After pretending to think on it, I eventually put him out of his misery. "Fine. I'll give you a chance. Is that all you wanted? Did you ride out here just to ask me why I don't like you and if I'd get to know you?"

I scrunch up my nose in confusion. *Why would he do that?*

Tinhead shoots me a pearly white grin, then he's off towards the door. My eyes follow him, admiring his nice-looking ass.

He is pretty to look at when he isn't running his mouth…

What? Where the hell did that come from?

Before I have time to dwell on it, he turns back around and confesses, "Hell yes I did, and it was totally worth it, *Red!*"

~ Chapter 12 Tinhead ~

Friday night...

"Boss, when's the transaction taking place?" Bear pipes up as we are all gathered around the table in church, listening to the update on things with Matteo the Mafioso.

"Matteo wants to meet with us again next Friday night; he's gonna send us the coordinates and details of when. He said that Red and Rebel are gonna be there with their men too. I want you all in the clubhouse and ready to go at any time on Friday—I ain't about to piss him off. Any volunteers to stay back with the women and my boy?"

I raise my hand, but Axe shakes his head. "Nah, Tin, I want you with me; I need your expertise. Wrench, you okay to stay behind with Doc?"

Wrench nods, and I fight the urge to scoff.

Expertise? That's bullshit!

He won't say it, but he doesn't want me around the women. Fuck! I want my Prez to have trust in me—I've worked hard to be a part of this club; this band of brothers I love and need. I can't lose it; I'll do anything to prove my worth.

"Sure thang, boss. I got you," I inform him.

"Are there any objections to this deal? If there are, say so now—this is a hell a lot of money to put at risk if we ain't all agreed."

Axe looks pointedly at each of us; Flex, Bear, Dags, Doc, Brains, me, and then Wrench. All of us shake our heads back and forth.

"Good. All right, anyone else have anything to bring to the table? No? Then that's it." Axe slams the gavel down on the table, and one by one we all start to disperse out of the room.

I get to my feet slowly—it's late, and I'm drained from trying to keep everything in and looking normal.

"Yo Tin, a word?" Axe hollers at me from his office door as I go to head back to my room.

I turn and see there's a determined look on his face, so I head back to the office and shut the door behind me.

"You got anything you need to say to me, Tin?"

"No, Prez."

"Are ya sure? I saw your face when I said you have to come with me to meet Matteo and not stay back at the clubhouse. Don't ya want to be in on the deal?"

"It isn't that, I just wanted to prove that you can trust me around the women."

"I do. Tin, listen to me; I need you to help Brains up the watch security for the clubhouse on Friday. You up for that? Just say if you're not."

"Yeah, of course, Boss, whatever ya need. Is there anything else?" I ask curiously, feeling there's more to this chat than Axe is letting on.

"No, that's it, you're free to go, brother. By the way, ya don't need to prove yaself to me or anyone else. We know you, and we all trust you."

"Thanks Prez, I needed to hear that. We good?"

"Yeah, brother. Go grab yaself a drink, I'll be out soon for a quick one before I head back home."

"Okay, Boss."

I stride out of the office and head back to the bar. I round the corner to the main room and see the white-blonde hair of Zara Hart as she headbangs to Motörhead on Flex's lap.

"Zar', you enjoying yaself there? Don't tell me Dags and Bear switched ya taste from Beyoncé to some rock? Girl, you've changed," I inform her with a grin and a wink.

"Hey, Tin. You know I love me some Bey, but I've always loved rock too. How are you, anyway? Got any plans?" she enquires with a knowing, mischievous grin.

"You girls really need to quit talking about what's going on with us men, ya know!" I chuckle. "Nosy busybodies! For your information, doll, I have more than just *plans* with Jade Smith. Let's put it this way; if she doesn't end up screaming and creaming around my cock, then I ain't doing my job properly. "

Zara practically chokes on her drink, spluttering as it dribbles down her chin.

"Jesus, Tin! You want a punch for mentioning ya dick to my Ol' Lady?! Brother, go get yaself laid to ease your blue balls."

Zara nods. "Yeah, I don't need to be thinking about your dick, Tinhead. It's just so…wrong."

"Sorry, Zar'. I meant no offence, VP, but that's exactly what I plan to do."

"I know ya didn't, Tin, but watch ya mouth." He grins at me, then shoves my arm. As I try and catch myself, I bump into Jewel, who's just passing me with a drink in her hand.

"Ah shit, sorry Jewel, are you okay? You free?" I ask, giving her a wink to let her know I need to let off some steam. Her cute face lights up, her short hair bobbing around her face as she nods at me. She gulps the rest of her drink, draining the glass dry, then takes my hand in her small one, pulling her cute ass towards my room. As I close the door behind us, I see she's already bent over the bed in wait.

"Fuck, Jewel, I'm dog tired; this week has drained me. You up for some other kind of fun?"

"Like you have to ask, Tin," she smiles as she whips her shirt off to expose her bare tits. Her nipples are like perky little jewels, making my mouth water. Unbuttoning my pants, I let them fall down my thighs tugging my boxers down at the same time. The cool air caressing my dick makes it harden with eagerness. Without me needing to tell her, Jewel gets down on the floor right in front of me on her knees, grasping my semi and bringing it more to life.

"Ahh fuck, just like that..."

I thread my fingers through the hair at the base of her skull, urging her to take me in her mouth now.

Fuck, I need the release; I crave it like a drunk wants his next sip of beer.

Jewel licks her lips and gazes up at me seductively.

"Jewel, you need to wrap those pouty lips around my dick now, or I'm gonna fuck that mouth of yours raw," I growl at her, needing the release bad.

She complies instantly, wrapping her long expert tongue around my shaft as she takes me all in her mouth swallowing me whole. Instinctively, my back arches, forcing her to take my dick further down her throat.

Perfection! No gag reflex, but her throat's tight as a virgin ass.

I know I ain't gonna last as I feel my eyes rolling back in my head. I tug her hair harder the way I know she loves, and she rewards me by sucking me farther down her throat and taking my balls in her hand, rolling them around.

"Fuck! Ya keep doing that I'm gonna blow my load."

"That's what I want," Jewel mumbles around my cock. She always seems to need the sex as much as I do—maybe that's why I'm drawn to her.

"Fuckin hell! Hold on tight!" I say through gritted teeth.

Before she gets to respond, I thread my other hand through her hair and fuck her mouth with rapid jerky movements hard enough to make Jewel's eyes pop out of her head. Seeing movement in the corner of my eye, I watch her stuff her fingers inside of her and start fucking herself as I fuck her mouth. I feel pleasure shoot up my balls, then….

"FUUCK!!!" I roar, cumming loudly to the sucking noise of Jewel finger fucking herself. Popping my dick out of her mouth, I fall like a lead balloon onto my bed, panting hard.

My thoughts of ecstasy are disturbed by my phone vibrating on the floor. I barely have the energy to grab it so as Jewel finishes and rights her skirt, she passes it to me with a wink and scoots her ass out of my room. I stare down at my phone seeing Red's name flash up on my screen. A big smirk spreads across my face, and I answer it with a swipe of my thumb,

"To what do I owe this *pleasure*, sweetheart?

"Jesus, dude, you just can't help yourself, can you? I'm just calling to say you'll need to come to the bakery tomorrow at 5:30pm. Make sure you've had a good

night's sleep, but I'll be driving. See you tomorrow—
don't be late, *Pinhead.*"

Once she hangs up, a huge shit-eating grin spreads
across my face, and a feeling of warmth starts to bloom
in my chest.

Me: - *Red! What did you hang up for, doll? Thought
we could talk some more...You know you wanted to :oP*

Sugar Tits: - *I hung up so you wouldn't talk me out
of giving you a second chance. Keep it up and I'll
cancel your ass.*

Me: - *You wound me! You know you can't wait to
get up and ride on the T-Dawg! Quit your hating, I know
you wouldn't give up your chance of getting better
acquainted.;oP*

Sugar Tits: - *This is exactly what I'm talking
about...See you tomorrow Blockhead!*

Fuck, this girl loves pushing my buttons, and I'd be
lying if I said I didn't enjoy doing it back at her. She
thinks I don't realize she won't call our nights out dates,
but I know full well she's keeping her distance. She
needs to know I am all about getting to know her more;
this ain't about chasing a quick fuck or getting my dick
wet. There's something I want to explore more with
Jade. She gets annoyed at my charms, but I ain't going
anywhere; I'm in it to tear her defensive wall down and
see exactly why she's so against me. Something tells
me it's gonna lead to more than I bargained for...

After I get off the phone to Captain Crunch—AKA the Casanova wannabe—my heart races, and I fight to catch my breath between worrying about tomorrow night's event. I don't think what I have planned is the same kind of "date" that he would expect me to go for. After I told Kelly of my plan, she got nervous, warning me it would backfire in my face.

I just want to see if it will work, but if not…well, then we're both fucked!

Kelly leaves after witnessing me ring Tinhead, saying she has to run out to see her Russian. She still won't say much about him, but has informed me several times that she's 'horny as a fuckin' bitch in heat!', which tells me that either she's not put out—which is strange for Kelly—or he won't.

Hmm, I'll store that away for the next time I see her…

I glance over at the clock on my nightstand and realize I'd better crash—I've got a big day tomorrow. It's too late to back out now; I will roll the dice for sure tomorrow and let the chips fall where they may.

***

The next day…

"JJ, are you sure you're sure about all this? What if he goes weird again? Will you at least take your gun with you?" Jenna asks, nervously shuffling around on my bed with the sunset casting a gorgeous golden glow around her head like a beautiful halo as she watches me pick out my outfit for tonight.

"Yes, for the umpteenth time, I'm sure, and no I'm not taking my freaking gun with me! I genuinely think Tinhead poses no risk; he admitted he was tired, and I've made sure he won't be tonight. I thought you liked him, anyway?" I ask curiously as I pull shirts, pants, and dresses from the closet and hang them over the door for her to help me choose.

"I do, it's just so out of character for him. Besides, I wouldn't have chosen him for you, I would have chosen Brains; he's nice and quiet. All I can see is you and Tinhead clashing and butting heads...but as long as you're sure, JJ."

"Nice and quiet? Surely I'm allowed a little more than nice and quiet? Anyway, who said I am picking Tinhead for anything? I'm just trying to understand him more and find out what makes him tick. We already clash and butt heads, but that's because he's stubborn as a dog with a bone."

She casts a skeptical glance my way, then flicks her eyes back to the outfits and points. "Pick that shirt and those torn jeans with those pale pink heels, and then maybe that cute sweater? Call me if you need anything, I'm gonna go jump in the shower myself—I swear I have more pastry under my fingernails and flour in my hair than the contents of all the patisseries in Paris."

"Thank you, I will do—I might need an extra pair of hands to detangle my mane."

Jenna just smiles and slips out of my bedroom.

Once she's gone, I cast my eyes back to the items she picked out, then move them around so they're all together. She's right—my black off-the-shoulder shirt, torn blue jeans, dusky pink heels and cute cream sweater give me exactly the look I'm going for. I take a seat at my vanity and apply my body lotion like a second skin, making sure to pay attention to my hands as well—they get so dry from the constant washing and drying while I'm on shift in the bakery. As I'm waiting for them to dry, I decide on my jewelry—a simple white gold necklace with a green peridot stone set in the middle of the pendant, silver hoops, and the ring with the infinity symbol Kelly got me two Christmases ago.

Shit! Christmas isn't far off, and I've normally purchased all my presents by now...Mental note, organize a girls' day out to go shopping.

"Sis, you okay for me to come in and sort your locks out?" Jenna hollers through my bedroom door. I'm surprised she's done with her shower already, I completely lost track of time.

"Yeah, come in! I'm about to put on my 'war paint,' as Momma always says!" I chuckle.

Jenna strides in to brush my hair, grinning at nostalgic quip about Momma.

"Ha! You don't need it, JJ, you have gorgeous clear skin and the signature Smith freckles. What are ya thinking for your hair? Do you want your waves, poker straight, or are we going for volume?"

"I was thinking loose waves. If you're happy to tame my mane, I'll start the base for my 'war paint. I was thinking nude eyeshadow, maybe a touch of gold around the corners of my eyes?"

"Definitely, that'll look gorgeous and make your eyes pop. Let's get this show on the road!"

"A darker shade of red…try that scarlet one; it suits you more than it did me."

I've spent over an hour gradually doing my makeup, and as I admire my final look for the first time once my lipstick is on, I see that Jenna's made my hair look like I just stepped off the cover of *Vogue* magazine.

"Jenna, my hair looks fuckin' beautiful! Thank you so much. Does my makeup look okay?"

"You're welcome, and if I do say so myself, you look smoking hot! Now go and get yourself ready; he'll be here in 20 minutes." With that, she leaves me to get dressed and get the final touches together.

As I pull on my slim-fit jeans and am about to put on my black off-the-shoulder ruffle-sleeved shirt, I'm surprised to feel a small flutter in the depths of my stomach.

What the ever-loving fuck? I'm not nervous because of Tinhead! What the hell's that about? I'm only in this to see what makes him tick, nothing more—I hate the jerk for what he did to me!

With that recemented in my mind, the butterflies dissipate in what I imagine in my mind's eye to be a puff of smoke, and my spine straightens with more determination and decisiveness than ever before. I tug my shirt over my head, fixing the shoulders in place and untucking my hair from underneath the collar, then sit back on my bed and pull my little black gem-studded shoulder bag toward me, checking my phone. I see I've got a message from him:

Captain Cockhead: - *Be there soon, doll. Can't wait to see ya…and feel your lips on mine by the end of the night.*

He's relentless, that's for sure…

Noticing that it's nearly time for him to arrive, I recheck myself in the mirror, slip on my heels, and apply a quick spritz of my favorite perfume, I take a quick pic and send it to Kelly.

Me: - *How do I look? Xx*

Kelly's reply is instant:

Kel: - *FUCKIN' HAWT! Do everything I would do ;oP. Let me know whether everything goes to plan or not. Xx*

Me: - *Of course! We also need to talk about Mr. Russian. You haven't told me anything, and for you that's strange. Xx*

I shove my phone back into purse as I hear knocking resound off of the apartment door.

Well, Tinhead gets a point for turning up slightly early—one of my biggest bugbears is being late.

I hear laughter and the smooth tone of his voice as he jokes around with Bear. Grabbing my sweater and tucking it over my arm, I exit my bedroom and walk down the hall to see him, his sandy hair ruffled like he's been shoving his fingers through it on the way up here—somehow, he can pull it off. His t-shirt color of choice is royal blue, and he wears his cut proudly, a pair of tight dark blue jeans skating over...

I quickly shut my gaze—and imagination—down at that.

As he turns his head towards me, I see the familiar sparkle of mischievousness in his eyes, tempting me to dive into them like a swimming pool on a scorching hot day.

"Hi. You okay? Get enough sleep last night?" I ask condescendingly, my lip threatening to turn up into a smirk.

His eyes flash with a flicker of something dark—pain, perhaps—and he grabs my hand, interlinking our fingers. "Jade, you gotta know I would never harm you in any way..."

"Oh God, Tinhead! I was joking, I promise! Let's just get going, we got somewhere to be." I swiftly change the subject and tug our linked hands towards the door, realizing my mistake as the contact burns my palm.

I immediately drop his hand, but as we make our way down the stairs and out to the back of the bakery, Tinhead stops me in my tracks and makes my heart jump by grabbing my hand again. "That wasn't me last weekend, doll. Whatever happened, I need you to know that I would never intentionally hurt you or any woman, okay? You know that, right?"

I feel my spine stiffen, but I stare back at him, not breaking eye contact. "Yes, I know that wasn't you, and that you wouldn't never hurt me." Try as I might, my eyes do start to waver on the last few words, so I continue, "Come on, let's get going, okay? No cheesy one-liners tonight."

"If I remember rightly, doll, you seemed to enjoy talking about Donny's dong," Tinhead grins. "So, what ya got planned anyway?" he asks me as we walk towards mine and Jenna's Beetle—it's more hers to be honest, but I use it whenever I need to.

We both slide into the car, Tinhead having to pull the passenger seat all the way back to get his legs in. I try not to giggle, but end up blurting out a bubble of laughter at the sight of his long lean legs crammed into the car—even with the seat all the way back, there still isn't enough room. "Laugh it up, Red. I can't help that I'm tall, can I?"

"Oh, you sure can't, *Drainpipe.* Ha!"

"Fuck, Jade! Drainpipe, really? I ain't a skinny kid with no muscles, ya know. In fact, I got a pretty big muscle—"

"Fuckin' hell, your cock? You're shameful! Give it up, stud, drop all the one-liners and be you," I tell him as I put the car in reverse and then into drive. Once we merge into the sparse traffic on the road, I glance over to see him sitting there with a vacant look and the faint tug of a smile on his lips.

"What is it? You okay?"

Tinhead snaps to attention at the sound of my voice "What? Oh, yeah. Yeah. I just found it weird that you said I should be me. This *is* me."

"Okay…"

"Why did you say it like that?" he replies, a hint of accusation in his tone.

"I just said okay, Tinhead. I'll believe that if you want me to, but personally, I like people to be authentic with me. Tonight, I'm taking you somewhere I like to go and showing you who I am, so I want to know who you are."

"Fair enough. I like authenticity too, you know. It's not just a one-way street, dollface."

Instead of responding with a quick quip like I normally would, I let Tinhead's words settle deep in my chest.

Shit, maybe he's guessed what and why I'm holding back...

As I see the familiar signs up ahead, I decide to break some of the tension. "We're nearly at our stop; we'll go there and find somewhere to eat after if that's okay with you?"

"Yeah, sounds good. Where are we going exactly? I don't think I've seen this part of town before."

"You'll see. We just gotta park up behind the building, then we can go in and I'll show you a bit of who I am."

I see him physically relax as I pull up behind the town's little art gallery-come-museum, although from behind it doesn't look like much. "Here we are, we just need to go around the front to get in."

After getting out of the car, we make our way through the alley between the gallery and the florist next to it. I march through it as quickly as possible—it always gives me the creeps— but barely reach the random dumpster halfway between both buildings before Tinhead wraps his hands around my forearm to stop me in my tracks.

"Jade, let me go first."

"Don't be stupid I've done it I—"

"Not an option. We're already losing the light, and I know the dark, trust me!" he barks, making me whip my head back in surprise

His features soften as he interlinks our fingers again, that burning sensation spreading like wildfire up my arm as he does. I just nod in agreement and let him pull me through, watching him scan the walls and rooftops while keeping a firm grip on my hand.

As we get through to the end and head towards the front of the museum, I free my hand to disconnect from the searing heat radiating through my body and risk a glance at Tinhead. His eyes are black at first, but as soon as he sees me, he flicks his head and his eyes focus again.

Yeah, there's no way that's just sleep deprivation. He can tell me or his brothers whatever he wants and train his face to hide his secrets, but your body's reactions never lie, and I smell bullshit...

"Come on, this way, we haven't got long." I forewarn him, deciding not to confront him for now. We climb the grand white stone steps to go into the museum, where I see Al the security guard on patrol. "Hi Al, you okay?"

"Hi Miss Jade. Yes thank ya, can't complain; the hip's behavin' today. I have to close up in a while, but I'll give ya as long as I can."

"Thanks Al. You're a diamond."

I stride across the highly polished marble floor, knowing exactly where I'm going, but turn on my heel to see Tinhead still standing at the entrance looking completely bewildered. The crinkle between his eyebrows deepens as he silently asks me what we are doing here.

"Come on, will ya?" I instruct the blockhead. When he doesn't move, Al steps up to Tinhead and says something that instantly makes Tin's eyes soften and the left corner of his lip lift in a half-smile. Tinhead clasps the elderly security guard's shoulder and shakes his hand, then walks over to where I'm standing.

I go to walk away, but he wraps his arm around my waist, tugging me flush with the side of his body. His hand doesn't roam as I thought it would, but I still stiffen.

"Show me the way, Jade."

As we continue on, something deep inside of me says that he's not just talking about what I've arranged here tonight...

***

We finally round the corner to the exhibition room, where the lights are already on.

Bless Al, I'll have to make sure those cakes I promised him are extra-large.

"What I'm about to show you is a part of me only a select few know about, but one I wanted to share with you."

With that, I push open the door and let him enter first, anxiously worrying that Kelly was right. I watch him stroll around the large oval room, but I can't see his face, so I'm unable to read his reaction. The whole room has warm lighting, but he makes a beeline for the middle stand featuring a huge 1800s-style dress with dim lights shining on it. The mannequin stands against an artificial fireplace with a stuffed dog at her feet. He turns, and his intense gaze pins me against the door.

"What's this, Jade? Did you make all these dresses?" For once, I don't see mirth glittering in his eyes, but genuine curiosity.

I swallow hard, struggling to find the words, which Jenna would find hilarious if she was here. I look down at my feet, and my heart pounds in my ears as I say, "Uh, not really. I love Jane Austen and the Georgian era, and using that combined with my degree in Fashion and dressmaking skills, I help restore pieces for the gallery. The piece you're standing in front of was originally dirty and had holes in the underskirts, and the corset had to be reboned. All in all, it took over 100 hours to restore to its full glory. When I can spare time, I come down and help the gallery out."

I cautiously look back up at Tinhead to find him staring at me with pure pride. He closes the gap between us and wraps his arm around my waist, pulling me to his chest. I feel tiny against him; even with my heels on, I still only come up to his nose.

"Jade, thank you for showing me this part of you." His thumb finds its way underneath my sweater, rubbing at the space where my shirt and jeans meet. I try not to tense up at the heat of his touch, but I can't help it. We stare into each other's eyes as he strokes his thumb up and down my spine, but I don't pull away. Eventually, Tinhead breaks the silence in the softest voice I've ever heard come out of him. "You look breathtaking tonight."

He takes ahold of a small section of my hair and twizzles it around his finger, releasing it and tipping my chin up so my line of sight contains him and him only.

Shit, this wasn't the response I was expecting…

His other thumb comes up to my bottom lip, tugging on it slightly. My breath catches in the back of my throat as I notice how dark his eyes have become, lust and need shining in them.

I hear him grumble "Fuck!", but before I can push out of his hold, his free hand is threaded in the back of my waves, and his velvety lips are on me.

They're soft…so fuckin' soft…

At first, I freeze, but my body's urges win out.

Stupid treacherous bitch body…

I instinctively lean into him as his tongue begins plundering my mouth, seeking my own and demanding more from me—much more.

As it wraps around mine, he coaxes it more into his mouth, where our tongues get better acquainted. The taste of sea and peppermint envelopes my taste buds as his fist clenches tighter in my hair and the hand wrapped around my midriff pushes me tighter into his lean body.

I'm drowning; I need to fight to stay afloat, otherwise he's going to capsize my raft and pull me further into the depths that are him. I push away from him, breaking contact. The last part to disconnect are our lips, and when they do, all that fills the silence is our rapid breathing.

I try to draw a gasp of breath, but still haven't moved my eyes from where my gaze fell on Tinhead's chest when we parted, not daring to peer up at him as I know what I'm gonna find there.

"Shit, Jade, for someone who hates me, you sure can kiss like ya want me to fuck you, baby."

For the second time tonight, I'm speechless, not knowing what to say or do.

Why didn't I pull away quicker? I would have wanted that in another time maybe, but not now...

And yet I can't deny his lips on mine felt good...

Fuck no...this is wrong!

With that thought, a zing of forbidden desire hits me square in the chest like a bolt of lightning.

"You okay there, Red? You got no comeback?" Tinhead enquires, stepping back into my space.

I instinctively take a step back as my eyes flick up at him. Amusement glitters in his eyes, which crinkle around the edges, and his lips have traces of my lipstick smudged around them in a reminder of what we've just done.

My body is burning with need...and I can't believe that the one person I know who kisses like a god is this jerk-off!

Fuck! I could feel that kiss searing right down into my very soul, searching me and wanting—no, *needing* us to get better acquainted. The girl may hate me, but the way she kissed me back, she's got me wanting to bend her over that worn-out chair in the corner of the room and yank down those tight-fitting jeans, then spank that juicy ass of hers and fuck her from behind whilst my fingers thread through her silky strawberry hair.

I imagine feeling her ass pound me as I slide in and out of her, both of us chasing that release.

Shit, I bet she's loud when she cums...I hope she is, I would do anything to hear her utter my name as she comes undone around my dick...

Just then, Jade herself breaks the silence, interrupting my fantasy. "Um...so yeah, this is what I do outside work." She's fighting to meet my eyes, her gaze flitting between me and my t-shirt every other second, so I give her no reason not to look at me and bend down to her eye level, catching her off guard.

"What's the problem, Jade?" I ask knowing her answer as sure as I know the sky is blue and the day is long and the Pope is Catholic.

"Nothing, I just wasn't expecting that...that kiss. You surprised me, that's all. You don't need to be right in my face either, you know," she snipes, straightening her back and twirling around on her heel to head over to the display on the far side of the room. She only makes it a few feet in front of me before grasp her fingertips in my hand and give them a sharp tug, making her face me.

She doesn't fight me, but instead just stands there, nibbling on her bottom lip as her gaze scans me, searching for an answer as to why I have pulled her hand, I can't tell her the real reason, so I decide to play it safe by acknowledging the fact that she's opening herself up to me more—even though I can see she's still holding something back.

"You've definitely shown me more of who you are. Will you show me more pieces you helped to restore?" I flick my head in the direction she was heading to, silently asking her to carry on.

The ghost of a small smile passes her lips as she turns on her heel again, but this time, I still have a grip on her fingers. They're searing through me, branding her inside me.

Branding me will break me, but will she dare to put me back together again?

***

For the next 15 minutes, Jade enthusiastically shows me the pieces she helped restore back to a near-original state. Her passion flows through her. but as she talks, I'm left with more questions than answers.

"So why aren't you doing this full-time, doll? I can see how much you care and how proud you are of your work." I search her face for any tell that might let me know to back off, but not finding one, I tilt my head to one side so our eyes meet naturally.

"To be blunt about it, there's no real money in it. This is just a small-town gallery, so I do what I can to help them. They pay me what they can, but I don't do it for the money anyway; I enjoy the craft behind it all and the history that I hold in my hands. I love the contrasts with our modern styles, and I try to make the majority of my own clothes for practice. Of what I'm wearing at the moment, the only things I haven't made are my jeans—although I did style them at the cuffs—and my shoes. I even altered and put steel studs on my bag."

"Whoa! That's pretty badass, Jade! When do you get the time to do that, work in the bakery, *and* help the gallery out?"

"I still help out when they really need me, but with the bakery's demand picking up more, I've not really had time to do much. I still create a lot of my own designs, though—me and Kelly incorporate them in shoots for her makeup and special effects makeup business."

"Damn girl, all work and no play makes Jade grumpy and frustrated…maybe I *should* help ya clear those cobwebs out; no wonder you haven't got any for a while if you don't make time for anyone to get an inch in at all."

I fuckin' love the look of pure horror and embarrassment that comes over her face—her eyes are as wide as the mannequin's skirt behind me.

"Let's get one thing straight, you caveman, One, I am more than satisfied with me, myself, and I to clear my own cobwebs out—not that I have any. Two, yes, I work hard. I worked damn hard for my degree in Fashion and Dressmaking, and I'm working hard to build up my collection so I can collaborate with Kelly. Speaking of, I'm sure she would love a male perspective for her website…"

"Oh, hell naw, I ain't down for all that eyeshadow and blusher stuff you put on. If she asks Wrench nicely, I'm sure he would be down for that."

"I didn't mean the normal makeup side of things, I meant the special effects side of things! Anyway, don't take my word for it; next time you see her, get her to show you some of her gallery. We best get going, Al could only let me have a half-hour to show you before he closes for the night," she informs me.

She could have knocked me down with a feather there and then; I had no idea she arranged to keep the museum open for our date. I entwine my fingers with hers and stride out of the room, leading the way to the gallery entrance.

Jade struggles to keep up as we speed down the hallway. "Slow down, Tinhead! What's got into you?"

I stop in my tracks, grabbing her by the waist until my nails pinch into her flesh and pinning her against the wall in the shadow of the dimmed spotlights. My lips hover over hers, barely a whisper between us.

"Tell me why you brought me here and did all this, Jade. For someone who "hates" me, it's a lot of effort, Red."

Her quickened breathing is like a soft summer breeze sweetly caressing over my face. "Maybe I wanted to share something of me so you would see there is more to me than my defensiveness, and you would share something with me other than your smartass remarks. I hoped that maybe—just maybe—you would shut up long enough to see you have more to offer than that…but the jury's still out on that at the moment," she rasps out, struggling to concentrate.

"Ya know what I think?" I murmur, inching my mouth closer to hers.

"What's that?" She gasps as push my semi into her stomach.

"I think you did all this because maybe—just maybe—you realize I have more to offer *you,* too." I grin, using her own words against her and bowing my head slightly for my lips to meet hers again.

This time, the kiss is hard, demanding, and raw. As I take over her mouth, she bites my lips like the fierce woman she is, but her body tells me something completely different. She rubs herself against me, letting out gasps of desire in my mouth.

I wrench my lips away from hers, heaving breathlessly against her swollen mouth until I'm able to rasp out, "Maybe you should listen to your hate, Jade. It would be a hell a lot of easier for you, but let's get one thing straight—you want me. You may not realize it, but you *do* want me." I struggle to drag myself away from her, but do, needing to get myself in check. I stride away with purpose and thank Al on the way out. As soon as the cool early October night air hits me, it freshens my face and wakes me up.

I lean my body against the front of the building, waiting for Jade to come out and willing my heart to be still as it races like it's in the Kentucky Derby. I ain't gonna apologize for either kiss; I don't know why she's fighting the clear attraction between us. I hear the front door of the gallery open, then thump closed, so I flick my gaze back to the doors to see a flushed Jade standing there, looking at me like I'm a puzzle that needs to be solved. Her eyebrows pinch together, and those plump pursed lips stick out at me, tempting to me to suck on them.

"What the hell, Tinhead? Who would it be easier for? What are you trying to hide, and who is the real Tinhead? I don't see him behind all this façade, but I don't hate you; I just don't particularly like *this* you is all."

"Fuck off, Jade! If you don't like me, why the fuck were you dry humping me in there? I can feel you want it, so why don't we do what we clearly both need to do?" I rasp out.

She stands barely a foot away from me, so without a second thought my hand whips out and tugs the front of her jeans, dragging her towards me until we're nose-to-nose.

"I say we fuck. No dates, no getting to know each other, just fucking. You may say you hate me, but you can't deny the pull you feel when we're together. Let's do what I know we both want. Let's. Fuck!" I exhale, trying to keep my restraint, but my dick is dying to get out. Just at the sound of her heavy breathing and the sight of her tits heaving in her shirt, I'm having to readjust myself.

I examine her flushed face and her dilated eyes trying to figure out my next move, but all bets are off as soon as I see her drag her pink tongue painstakingly slowly across those scarlet lips.

Fuck! I'm done.

I drag her away so fast she's practically running behind me in her heels, although I'm rational enough to go the long way around to the car as I know it's still lit and I want to avoid that alley at all costs. It takes us an extra 3 minutes, but neither of us say a word.

By this point, we have passed a handful of people, not one of them daring to meet the steely determination in my eyes.

We round the corner back to where her car's parked, and I don't waste any time pushing her up against the driver's side door, pinning her with my hips and grinding my cock against her.

"I…hate…you…you…fuckin'…prick!" she pants as I grind against her, my cock rubbing against that bundle of nerves she's desperate to stimulate.

"Shut up, Jade! The sooner we fuck each other outta our systems, the better. You can go back to hating me, and I can go back to losing myself in a selection of pussy."

As the last words pass my lips, she stomps on my toes with her stiletto heel, "Bastard! You want to fuck me? Then don't talk about fucking other women!"

"Now, now, Jade, don't pretend you care what I do with my dick; we both know you detest me. D'ya want me to fuck you here in this parking lot? Because I will."

She hesitantly pulls away from me, but after searching my eyes she declares, "Get in the car; I know the perfect spot." She gets behind the wheel and fumbles with her belt as I jump in the car. I'm barely able to shut the door before she puts the car into reverse, then drive; speeding out of the lot, through town, and in the opposite direction.

"Where we headed?" I ask as we pull up to a red light, trying to hide the eagerness in my voice.

She peers over at me, lust still brimming in her gorgeous eyes. "This spot I used to go to; I haven't been there in a while."

"Okay, cool. Fuck, I hope it's not far, babe. The sooner you're on my dick..."

"...the better. Yeah, I know. It's not far."

As the light turns green, she turns left and drives past Ol' Jack's bar, then makes a right before heading straight down a long road until we come to a clearing hidden by shitloads of trees.

Jade slows down, then pulls up and parks right underneath a grand oak tree, concealing us under its branches. As soon as she turns off the engine, I reach across to her, wrapping my hand around the back of her neck. We melt into a clash of lips and teeth, her sweet juicy tongue sliding in and out of my mouth.

Before I know it, she's fisting my t-shirt in her grasp and tugging me across the console, but my legs are too long for me to fuck her in this small-ass car.

I reluctantly pull away. "Jade...I can't take you in here."

***

"It's fine, I'll get it valeted after. Hurry," I demand from the jerk as desire builds inside me

"Nah, the cars too small for me to give you some of the T-Dog."

He jumps out of the car, but before he shuts the door, he leans and growls at me, "Get out, bend face down over the hood, and spread them fuckin' legs!"

~ Chapter 15 Jade ~

I'm reeling inside; my head is torn between the pure lust and pure hatred scorching through my veins. My body's humming, I'm so close to exploding that I know that if he dipped my hand between my legs, he would find my body betraying me.

My pussy clenches at the thought of getting a good fucking; it's been too fuckin' long.

Can I do this? Can I sleep with the enemy?

I swear I feel a tiny bit of bile rise to the back of my throat at the thought. I wince, pushing it back down before my mind runs away with itself.

As if to remind me of my predicament, my clit pulsates with the need to be touched, warring with the part of my brain that tells me he's everything I should avoid like the plague.

Fuck, he's the enemy! I hate him remember...

I glare at him through the windshield. He's casually leaning against the trunk of the old oak tree like he hasn't got a care in the world—or just asked to fuck me on the hood of my car.

My body betrays me once again as my eyeline homes in on the bulge in his jeans, and I feel my desire burn hotter as more wetness gathers between my thighs.

My limbs move of their own accord, and before I know it, I'm extracting myself from the safety of the car and walking up to him with purpose. I risk a quick glance over my shoulder and down the gravel track we've just come down, but there's nothing here except the distant sounds of owls calling each other.

My gaze falls back onto Tinhead, and I swallow hard to gain composure but quickly find myself impulsively licking my lips at the thought of getting this itch scratched.

After this, he can get the hell out of my life for good…

"Unbutton those tight pants and slowly tug them down those thighs," he orders from where he stands, unmoving except for his eyes roaming my body with every single movement I make. He's like a predator; watching, stalking, and ready to pounce on his prey at any moment.

If I'm going to play the game, I'll play it well…

I unfasten my jeans and push the zipper down with my forefinger, never taking my eyes from his as he wets his lips and clenches his jaw. I grasp the sides of my jeans and push them down my toned thighs, watching the intense heat radiate from Tinhead's gaze. My jeans fall down my calves, leaving my black lacy thong and ass on full show.

"Now tease your thong to one side; I want you to show me how wet you are."

"Fuck off! Are you gonna get your cock out and prove how hard you are?" I bite back at him with a defiant jut of my chin. "I ain't showing you shit without seeing what I'm getting in return."

"Fine by me, doll. I ain't lacking if that's what ya think."

"I'll decide on that. Do it."

He shifts and comes to stand in front of me in one stride, eyes still locked on mine. Without a moment of hesitation, he grabs the top of his jeans and unbuttons them, letting them fall around his ankles in a whisper, then reaching behind his neck to grasp his t-shirt and removing it painfully slowly, revealing more of his gorgeous golden skin and toned abs. Letting his t-shirt fall, he stands there in just his boxers—which have the defined outline of a long cock hiding under them.

He grins, showing me those pearly whites of his. "Now drop them, Red."

"Not doing it together?" I retort with a determined stare.

"That's what I was planning," he responds with a smirk, quicker than a whip.

"I meant underwear, stupid. If you're—" My words die on my lips, as in front of me, Tinhead is naked as the day he was born, his cock standing to attention.

I know I'm gawping at him like a crazy person, but if he wasn't the biggest douche on Earth, I would drop to my knees there and then.

I instinctively lick my lips, biting down on the inside of my cheek to stop myself from drooling like a damn fool. Peering back at the jerk's face, I notice the cocky grin is wider than ever.

After dropping my panties, I turn on my heel and lay face down on the front of the car, feeling he warmth of the engine. I stick my ass out in the air just as a cool breeze blows over my bare skin, feeling delicious.

"Fuck, Jade! That ass is definitely something else, that's for sure. Now spread those legs."

I comply without saying a word.

I'm so close to the edge that if he doesn't do somethi—

"Ohhhh! Fuck!"

I writhe on the hood as Tinhead shoves two fingers deep inside me, feeling the pinch and burn as they fill my pussy.

Fuck, it has been too long! Far too long...

"Well well, Jade, I feel honored. Is all this for me, babe? You're fucking drenched!" With the last word, he withdraws his fingers then pushes them back in with such force it steals my breath. Sweet fuckin' god, that feel so wrong and right at the same time.

After a few more thrusts, Tinhead starts to slow his assault on my pussy.

Sensing his apprehension, I look over my shoulder, watching him as he gathers my juices on his fingers and spreads them between my butt cheeks.

I tense automatically. "Tinhead, don't start playing games. Fuck me!"

"Demanding little thing. Your wish is my command," he responds sarcastically.

"If that was the case, we wouldn't be here right now. Look alive and get busy, you best not leave me hangin'."

Tinhead grins, retrieves a condom from his jeans, and slides it over his pretty impressive dick, squeezing himself.

God, I must be high as a fuckin' kite from being so fuckin' horny, because the sight makes my pussy clench with need.

Don't get used to it; this is just a means to an end, that's all.

Before I can get lost in my thoughts, I feel a piercing gaze and look up. Tinhead may be the douche of the century, but he has an impressive dick. I would never tell the fool, but he is *packing* in that area. As I stare at his cock, my mouth goes dry like I'm eating sand.

"Turn back around, Jade. This is gonna be fast and hard."

I comply without a second thought; if he doesn't at least put a finger back inside my soaking wet pussy, I am gonna combust.

Tinheads thighs brush the back of mine, and I nearly melt from the contact. Before I can gather myself, I feel strong, skillful fingers grabbing my hips. He pinches and digs his nails into the flesh there, tilting my hips so my ass is more in the air, then without warning, he lines his dick up and impales me utterly and completely, taking my breath away.

"Holy. Fuck. Jade. You're so fucking tight! Hold on to the hood, Red, because I'm gonna clear out those cobwebs for ya!"

Before I can reply, he withdraws his cock and slams it back into me right to the hilt, making me feel waves of pleasure again and again as he thrusts like a madman, driving his cock deeper inside of me. He grabs fistfuls of my hair, tugging it back fiercely. "Jade…fuck. Push against me!"

I do as he asks, knowing that I just need to get to end of this and all the BS will be over with.

Jesus, he feels so fucking good…

Swiveling my hips, I grind my pussy back on him, demanding more friction.

"Fuck me, Tinhead! Just give it to me!" I scream out as he shoves himself deeper Inside me, making me burn. He leans down and bites my shoulder as he hammers into me, and I don't recognize the feral noise that escapes my mouth as he does, but it makes my orgasm come racing to the surface. I lose myself in an explosion of ecstasy as I reach sweet release, convulsing under Tinhead as I ride the high.

I feel him shuddering above me, then he bellows out my name, his nails biting into my hips hard enough to bruise. "Jaaaade! Fuuuuck!"

I look at his reflection in the windshield to see his head rearing back as he conquers my body. Everything seems to slow down, and in that moment, the joker is gone, replaced by the twisted features of a tortured man frantically seeking release.

The relief that cascades over his face as he does is distinct, like a junkie getting their fix...

~ Chapter 16 Tinhead ~

I watch her fiery wild hair swoosh around in the breeze, and as she flings her head back, I can't help clamping my teeth on the silky soft skin of her slender shoulder. Coconut blooms on my tongue, reminding me of summer nights, sunshine, and beach trips.

Mmmm...

I fight to keep control as I watch her cum underneath me, but when I get the familiar feeling of the blood pumping through my veins rushing to the surface and that zinging down my spine, cumming isn't even close to how I would describe it; it's pure euphoria.

"Jaaaade! Fuuuuck!" the guttural roar rips through my throat, my whole body spasming and causing my head to rear back as my cum spurts out of me.

The pleasure ripples through me like waves lapping sunkissed sand, and it's absolute bliss—better than any other orgasm I've ever experienced.

As I gingerly withdraw my dick from Jade's beautiful pussy, I see it's glistening from her own orgasm; just looking at that stunning sight makes me semi hard again.

"You all right there, Red? I think we cleared out those cobwebs real good," I rasp out at her between ragged breaths, a smirk touching my lips.

She doesn't say a word, but wiggles that delicious ass in the air, trying to shimmy down off the hood and grabbing her clothes off the floor before pulling on her thong and jeans and straightening herself up.

"Jade, are we gonna talk about what just happened? Neither of us have been drinking, so we can't blame it on drunken fun."

"What's there to say? We fucked? We got this over with? It was 'okay'? Tell me, Tinhead!" she snaps defensively.

"Shit, I don't know. It was more than just 'okay', Red, don't even go there with that bullshit!"

"Look, it was good, but it was a one-time deal that's it. I still can't believe we did it, but you helped a girl out of a dry spell, so thanks." Swiveling around her on her heel, Jade moves toward the car without looking at me.

"Jade, don't even think about leaving without me! You know I'll get in the car butt naked, I don't care, " I tell her, quickly pushing my legs into my jeans, then picking up my t-shirt and boxers, not bothering putting them on just in case the little witch has plans to leave me stranded. Before I zip up my fly, I tug the condom off of my semi hard-on, knotting it up.

"Don't dispose of that here! People might find our DNA."

"DNA? Who the fuck is gonna take a knotted-up bag of jizz to the Feds to get a DNA test on us? Shit, girl, you sure I didn't clear out some brain cells instead a cobwebs?"

"Ha, ha, very funny!" Jade spits sarcastically. Shut up, Captain Crunch. I need to get some food since we missed the second part of the meet up I had planned. Tacos or a burger?"

"Are those the only choices? Jesus, you really know how to show a man a good time; it's no wonder you've not had a good fuck for a while." I inform her as I slide back into the passenger seat.

I can still feel her clamping her delicious cunt around me, choking the life out of me.

I readjust my dick as I settle in the seat, and she just glares daggers at me.

"I'll have you know I can get anyone I want, thank you very much. We all can't be sluts like you. Why don't you use what little brain cells you have to decide what food we're getting," she snaps, pulling out of the spot we parked in.

"Noel's BBQ off Mall Boulevard, you know it?"

"Do I *know* it? Noel and Mary are always coming into the bakery to enjoy their traditional Sunday pie with the family."

"Well then put your foot down, Miss Daisy, and let's get going. I'm fuckin' ravenous; and I ain't just talking about the food."

"Carry on, lover boy, and I'll throw you out on the sidewalk. I told ya, it was a one-time thing."

"Isn't that what Jenna said to Bear?"

"Yeah well, I ain't my sister, and you certainly ain't Bear, so shut that thought down right now."

I can't help the grin spreading across my face— she's cute when she's mad. I decide to pull my shirt back on and tuck my now-lucky boxers in my pocket. We drive in silence until we pull up to the parking lot of the restaurant, when she turns to me with a determined look in her eyes.

"What do you want, Tinhead?"

"I'll take a helping of you with a side order of your pussy and tits and as much sex you're willing to have with me to quench the sudden thirst I have for your pussy."

She rolls her eyes. "I was talking about the BBQ. What d'ya want? The Monterrey Jack Ribs special is good."

"Yeah, that sounds good."

"But I haven't told ya—"

"Doesn't matter. I want it, I'll have it."

***

Sitting in silence next to Jade isn't a bad thing, it's actually nice to be able to sit here with a woman without wanting to hurry her away. I still can't believe I'm having post-sex dinner with Jade 'Hates My Fuckin' Guts' Smith.

The wait for the food to arrive seems to pass pretty quickly, but when I look back at the clock on the dash, I see it's been 15 minutes. We decided to take the food to go, given that Jade 'stinks of me', as she so nicely put it.

Personally, I think she smells fucking hot—her body lotion and my aftershave mixed together smells good enough to eat. In the distance, I see Mary coming out with delicious ribs, corn, fries, and smoky chicken wings.

My mouth waters instantly in readiness to tuck into that gorgeous meat. Jade cautiously hands over my box of food, then she says her pleasantries to Mary before digging into her BBQ shrimp and mango salad and a huge slice of their mud pie. Jade moans in pure bliss as she eats, and I turn to her.

"Shit! You carry on like that, doll, and Mary and Noel are gonna get an eyeful." She rolls her eyes at me and carries on eating her salad. I'm about halfway through eating my ribs, and I've already demolished the corn and half the fries, when I see her just about to tuck into her slice of that mud pie.

My hand freezes on the way to my face as she takes a huge spoonful. As she places it between those luscious plump lips, her eyes roll back into her head and she erupts in the sweetest but dirtiest moan.

"Fuck, Jade! Stop torturing me!"

"What? What are ya on about?"

"You moaning like you're still wrapped around my dick isn't helping the situation over here, ya know."

"I can't help it! Mary's Mud Pie is amazing—it's better than sex! Even Jenna's tried and failed to recreate it."

"Better than sex? Let me try this fucking pie."

"Of course you would hear that part, Tinhead. Here, tell me it isn't the real deal," she tells me with authority that turns me on as she holds a spoonful of chocolatey mud pie out to me with her gorgeous lips pursed.

Taking the mouthful, the inside of my mouth instantly floods with saliva, each chew coating my tongue, it tastes good, but it doesn't give me that intensity that sex does.

Once I've swallowed it, Jade tilts her head slightly to one side and enquires, "Well? Amazing, right?"

"It certainly was delicious, but definitely not better than sex, dollface. Especially not sex with you on my dick."

"Fuckin' hell, Tin, does everything have to be about sex? Anyone would think you're a sex addict."

"Ha, that's an addiction I wouldn't mind. You finished with your pie?"

"Uh, no. Me and my pie are going to go home, get into bed, and get better acquainted," she informs me, a cheeky glint in her eye.

***

We pull up to the back of the bakery far too quickly for my liking, and Jade cruises to a stop right next to my bike.

After a few seconds in silence, she turns to me and utters words that have me breaking out into a full grin.

"I know you want me, but the fact of the matter is I don't need or want anything but sex from you."

"Jade are you telling me that when we fucked that was average? If you are, you're deludin' yourself, darlin'.

"I'm not telling you shit. You ain't my happily ever after."

"Good, because I ain't no Prince Charming, more like the Evil King…"

I open the door, get to my feet, and lean into the door frame. "Thank you for tonight, Jade, I'll be seeing you soon."

Slamming the door, I walk up to my bike. As soon as I sit astride my baby, I know the ride back can't come quick enough, suddenly feeling desperate to let the fresh air wash over me like a relaxing balm. I kick up the stand and start revving the engine, loving the vibrations between my thighs that never get old. I don't stop to look back—I can already see perfectly that Jade Smith is staring at me through my wing mirrors as I leave the bakery. I decide to head back to the clubhouse, needing to clear my head of the images that already lurk behind my eyes. Tonight's are worse than usual; it's always a battle not to be thoroughly consumed by them, but tonight it feels like a losing one.

***

I face plant on my bed after locking up my bike and lay there unmoving for a good few minutes before I decide to drag my sorry ass out of bed, stripping out of my clothes and folding them neatly in the correct way before I put them on the chair in the corner. The cold, fresh sheets of my bed greet me, and I punch my pillows, trying to get more comfortable. I eventually close my eyes, willing myself to go to sleep and my brain to shut the hell up.

***

"For fuck's sake! Seriously!"
I roll over, grabbing my phone to see that its 3AM. Slamming my phone back on the bedside table, I try again willing myself to sleep.
I will not use those sleeping pills I have in the drawer...
I hate using them, they make my head all foggy the next morning. I need a clear head—or at least as clear as I can get it. As I try again my head fills with memories of Jade tonight; the way her eyes sparkled with mischievousness, the curve of her butt, our first kiss, her showing me a part of her life—that surprised the fuck out of me, that's for damn sure—her cheeky smile…

I can feel my eyes getting heavier by the second, so I eventually give in and think of the fiery woman herself, my head filled with visions of her red hair…

***

The blood…

There's so much of the fucking stuff, but I don't care…

Even the gunfire never seems to faze me anymore…

"Get down now! Stay down, don't move, Omar!"

"Arnie! Don't you fuckin' dare! You selfish bastard!"

A black silhouette faces in the opposite direction, unmoving.

"You there, who are you?"

As the figure turns around, flames lick at his body until they completely engulf him…

"You did this!" the figure rasps out from his crumpled position on the floor.

As the ashes from the fire blow around me and drift off in the wind, they turn back into flames, setting the very air ablaze.

How the fuck could I do this? I don't deserve to be alive when so many lives have been lost. It should have been me that died…

***

4 Days after seeing Jade...

She hasn't messaged me yet, and I've tried to hold off, but I ain't about waiting around for too long—it gives her too much time to back out on our agreement. I pull my drawer open and locate exactly what I put there the night of our date-come-hookup, pulling out my phone to take a quick a picture of the object in question and attach it to the message.

Me: - *You forgot your gift from Saturday. If you want it, make yourself available tonight. ;o)*

Sugar Tits: - *What the hell is that? A bag of milky looking water?*

Me: - *No! Damn, you're cold…Put it this way; this is all the DNA you're ever gonna need…*

Sugar Tits: - *WTF?! Are you high? Why the hell do ya still have the used condom?*

Me: - *Desperate times call for desperate measures. Now I have your attention, are you free tonight? Say around 9?*

Sugar Tits: - *You're a sick fuck, Tinhead! Anyone ever tell ya that? Fine, but make it 10, busy on a project atm. Bring the fucking condom, and don't be getting ideas about things—this IS just sex.*

Me: - *Good, see ya at our spot? ;oP*

Sugar Tits: - *Jesus, don't make me regret this.*

***

I roll up to the same spot where I fucked her for the first time, but seeing that she's not here yet, I decide to remain seated on my bike while I wait for her.

I pull out my phone to check that I haven't got any missed texts from the red-haired she-devil.

Nada, but I am a little early, so I ain't gonna worry.

Just then, I hear the engine of a car coming up the beaten track, and Jade's headlights come into view. She parks next to me and hesitantly gets out of the car, standing there in sweats. They hang off of her curvaceous body, but that doesn't deter the hunger in me as I now know what's hiding underneath them. She's dressed like this on purpose, that I am sure of.

"You're lucky, *Bone*head. I nearly didn't come, but I can't deny that you know what to do with that dick of yours."

Her smart mouth is in full throttle tonight—I'll soon put that mouth to some good use.

"Still your cheerful self, I see...do you want to clear out those cobwebs for good, Red?"

"Fuck you, Tinhead! Are you gonna shut your mouth, or would you rather not fuck?"

"Well, I was thinking you could put that mouth to some good use and suck me off?"

"You gonna lick me out first?" she challenges.

"Doll, I'll do whatever you want as long as the only noise coming out of that mouth of yours is you screaming my name."

Jade sashays her way to stand mere inches away from me, then painfully slowly tugs the zipper down on her hoodie to reveal black lacy lingerie.

Fuck!

Her creamy alabaster skin stands out against the moonlight illuminating the tiny gems on the edge of her bra so it sparkles underneath the moon's glow. She knows exactly what game she's playing; she didn't come here to get her pussy licked out, she wants to be *fucked*. Well, it's her lucky day—that I can do.

"Make me..." she rasps, sending a tingling sensation rushing through my blood straight to my dick. It begins to start to twitch, demanding to be let out.

She's fucking beautiful—no, stunning.

Her heavy-lidded eyes stay fixed on mine, but her cheeks flush; that's all the invitation I need.

I grab the back of her neck and pull her so she's flush against my body. Hearing her breathing hitch makes me harder; it's such a turn-on knowing that I'm affecting her as much she is me.

I snatch her bottom lip between my teeth, tugging and sucking, then I slip my tongue into her mouth and push her against the edge of my bike. Our tongues duel with each other as voices scream in the back of my mind that I shouldn't be doing this, shouldn't be feeling this way.

Pushing them back down, I reluctantly pull away from her lips, barely able to speak through the pure need in my voice. "Tell me you want me to fuck you, Jade."

"Ohh fuck...yes...yes, I do! But do me one thing?"

"What's that?"

"Don't talk, just fuck me—and do it hard!"

Not needing any further direction, I grab her roughly on the hips and lay her across the seat of my bike. Without uttering a word, I tug her sweats down and find that she's pantyless. I don't move for a moment, admiring her.

She looks good enough to eat…

Maybe next time, but at the moment we are too close to the edge, we need each other.

"Jesus, Jade. Spread them, doll."

She complies, staring into the darkness at the town's lights twinkling. "I said no talking! Just fuck me, Tinhead."

I give her a curt nod, running my fingers up her slit.

Shit, she's soaked already! This is definitely gonna be a quickie, but that's all good to me—I want that asshole next.

Gathering her juices, I slide them between her delicious ass cheeks, which makes her flinch and arch her back at the same time.

Hmm, interesting, she wants it in the ass too…

I make quick work of undoing my jeans and let them drop to the floor in a soft sigh. Tugging on my cock a few times, I carefully roll the condom down my aching shaft, seeing that I've already leaked pre-cum from wanting to be inside her.

The feeling of being watched has my arm hair prickling, so I glance up to catch Jade's eyes fixated on me and my cock. After a moment, they flick up to meet mine. With her lips slightly parted, she runs the tip of her tongue against her teeth.

Taking the silent cue, I ram my fingers inside of her, mesmerized at the sight of her tossing her head back. My fingers pump her hard and fast—three, then four times—and I withdraw them as quickly as they went in.

She goes to say something, but before she gets the chance, I'm balls deep inside the sweetest pussy I've ever been in watching her arch and scream out in ecstasy, her hair cascading around her as I fuck her hard with sharp, jerky movements.

"Ahhhh!"

We're both panting and moaning, chasing that orgasm and wanting to be pushed over the edge. I can feel the need inside of Jade; she needs to let all her sexual frustration out, and I'm the man to help her do it. Pumping faster and harder against her tight wet cunt, I gain more momentum, needing her to cum before I do to feel her walls close and flutter around my dick.

"Fuuck! I'm...close..."

I fist her hair so her head flicks to one side, and see her eyes burning, trying look deep into mine, but I can't return her gaze. It's too much emotion; I can't deal with what she'll see inside mine.

I clench my eyes shut and fuck her harder than ever, making her scream out in the dead of the night. My short jerky movements become more erratic as pleasure ripples through me from the base of my skull, shooting straight down my spine to my balls.

"Cuuum!" I roar at her.

As soon as I say it, the walls of her cunt clench down harder than ever. We scream and bellow in unison as I feel spurts of my cum fill the condom deep inside of this feisty vixen. I end up spasming inside her, the feeling of release washing over me again and again on repeat until the waves of sensation die down. I half collapse on top of her, using one arm to prop myself up on my bike. I give her pussy a final couple of pumps to draw the rest of my cum out.

"Fuck, Tinhead..." Jade gasps out in between shallow breaths. "I think you've bruised me."

"At least you can feel me deep inside you, doll." The smug grin plastered on my face is one of utter contentment, but I know it's not gonna last.

"Jesus H Christ. I seriously wonder."

I cautiously pull out of her wet hole, watching her juices trickle out and smear against the inside of her thighs, shimmering underneath the soft moonlight.

"Fuck, that's beautiful." I smear it more and stroke it up her ass crack, making her shiver under my touch.

Jade slides off my bike, pulling her sweats up and zipping her hoodie, then perching her butt back on my bike whilst fluffing her hair.

Arching her eyebrow, she looks pointedly at my jeans still around my ankles. I pull off the condom, knot it up and launch it at her face, making her dodge it so it goes flying over the other side of the bike.

Not giving a shit, I pull my jeans back up, tucking T-Dawg back into the cage.

"Well Red, that was something else."

"Why's that? The no speaking stump you?" she sasses me, looking hot as hell perched on my bike.

"Nah, I just wasn't expecting you to agree to a second time. Your greedy pussy felt fuckin' amazing wrapped around my dick."

Her face falls slightly—was that realization flickering in her eyes?

As she blinks, the look is gone again. She slides back off the bike and absently trails her forefinger across my chest. Even through my t-shirt, I feel her touch burn across my skin.

As she walks off back to her car, she swivels around and tells me, "Well, maybe next time I'll be on top. This has been good, but I really need to go."

"Not likely, doll. I'll always *cum* out on top," I smirk.

"Why do you do that?"

"What?"

"Always try and make a joke out of everything. You can have a normal conversation, ya know," she tells me as a frustrated crinkle forms above her eyebrows.

"Don't know what you're talking about, doll. That orgasm gone to your head babe?" I joke, trying to avert my eyes from her knowing stare.

"You're doing it again…you can't have been this immature in the Army. Anyway, I best go."

My face falls dramatically at this, and for a moment I think I was quick enough to cover it with a smile, but the searching look in Jade's eyes tells me it caught her attention.

Before I know what's happening, my vision blurs at the edges as her words echo in my ears. *"You can't have been this immature in the Army…"*

***

…Blackness.

The pure inky darkness of the night cloaks me and blots out my eyesight…

The stench of coppery blood, followed by burning flesh being ripped off the bone; tendons and ligaments hanging freely from the ivory…

Roaring blasts pierce my ears as the building explodes into the street, sending chunks of concrete and steel flying through the air like a whip, shrapnel spinning and whizzing past my ear in a blur.

A constant trickle of claret poured down a bare arm…I knew that arm.

I had seen it hundreds of time before, and would see it a million more.

Nothing changes on that arm; it's constantly the same, like a Xerox of the original picture. That picture will forever be engrained in my mind...for more than one reason.

***

"Tinhead? A-are you okay?" Jade whispers softly.

Jade? She can't be here...

"Tinhead, it's okay. You're safe...please talk to me."

I'm aware of being touched on my forearm very carefully, which surprises me. Usually, numbness takes hold deep within my bones after a flashback, but Jade's touch, I feel.

"It's okay, it's okay. You're okay, come back," she whispers.

My eyes readjust a pin-prick at a time until gradually my surroundings start coming into focus clearer and clearer. As I scan my eyes around, I realize I'm sitting down; hunched over my bent knees and clutching them for dear life. A single sweat drop rolls down my spine adding to the dampness on my back and over my brow. I swipe down my face, tugging the flesh down and distorting my features as I go, disturbing the sprinkle of sweat on my upper lip.

Jade's hand moves from my arm and I just stare at it, looking at how petite and delicate it is compared to mine. Her hand hasn't murdered people; she hasn't got blood on her hands—I have.

Lifting my gaze to see Jade's face, my eyes catch hers. There's a look of pure worry over her beautiful face, and she's crouched down next to me on the floor. She scans me all over as my heart continues to race.

"Take a big breath in…and out. Good, now keep doing it." Her soothing, soft voice flows over me, and I follow her instructions until eventually my heart rate starts to slow. I know the breathing exercises like the back of my hand, but doing them seems to please her.

The question she utters next is totally understandable, but that still doesn't stop me recoiling in shock when it passes her lips, "So, are you going to explain to me what's going on, Tinhead? And don't say nothing."

~ Chapter 17 Tinhead ~

"So, are you going to explain to me what's going on, Tinhead? And don't say nothing."

The words ring in my ears over and over on the ride back through town towards the clubhouse.

Shit! Why out of everyone is she the one who sees through me? I've worked so fuckin' hard to keep up this pretense, but she has to go and be interested and ask questions about my time in the Army...

Even the men know not to talk about it; well minus Doc, being a vet himself.

As I pull back through the clubhouse gates, Wrench nods at me in greeting from his sweep of the perimeter. I pull up next to Dagger's bike, but at first, I don't move. I just sit there on my bike replaying the conversation we just had in my head.

***

"What ya worryin' about, Jade? Nothing's wrong, I just had a weird moment, that's all. Come on doll, we best get back—"

"Bullshit, Tinhead! Don't try that crap with me. I know a panic attack when I see it; you could hardly breathe properly, and the way you dropped to the ground and clutched your legs, rocking and staring blankly into thin air is definitely not nothing."

"Jade, leave it. I'm fine.

"You are anything but fine."

"Jade, I said leave it! Quit actin' like a fuckin' dog with a bone! I'm going back to the clubhouse. Catch ya later." I jump on my bike as she springs to her feet.

"Don't you dare, Tinhead! You can't drive back after the state you were just in."

"I'm fine, Jade. Please drop it. Go get in your car and leave; I'll follow you out," I gesture with a flick of my head.

At first she just stands there, staring at me in a silent standoff, but when I don't waver, she reluctantly strides off, getting in her baby-blue Beetle. Once she's inside, she glares at me through the windshield, and I see her shake her head at me, then reverse and speed off down the off-road track.

***

"Tin, brother, everything okay?"

I look around and lock eyes with Bear, who's standing at the clubhouse doors.

"Yeah, I'm good, all good. What's things like in there?" I ask, changing the subject.

I unhook my leg from over my bike and get off, striding up to him.

As he first clasps me around my shoulder, I think it's just in greeting, but when my legs keep going and his clenched fist doesn't release me, I angle my glaze up at him, wondering if Jade called him to tell him what happened.

Relief floods me as he grins. "How's my little-sis-in-law? You both been behaving?" he chuckles.

I swipe my hand across my face and offer a weak laugh. "Ha, yeah, something like that, Bear. You good?"

His eyes flick back and forth between mine, searching.

Fuck, has Jade said something after all?

Fear grips at my heart, but it quickly subsides as Bear releases his hand from my shoulder and nods at me.

"Yeah, I'm all good. Catch ya in a bit."

I head inside and look over at the bar to see Candi working, chatting away to Brains and Doc. Deciding I don't need a drink to sleep tonight, I veer off and make my way to my bed, needing the solace of my own room—as close as I get to solace these days at least .Just as the sun and moon control the tides of the sea, I know that tonight, my nightmare will not come.

***

Friday, the night of the meet with Matteo...

"MEN! All in church now!" Axe bellows from the hall that leads back to the office in order to let us know to hurry the fuck up as it's 6.00pm. As Flex starts rounding the men up, I walk with purpose, knowing Axe must have got the call so we don't have long to get our asses out the club. I go to church as the rest of the of my brothers filter in, and Axe slams the gavel down to start the meeting, not pulling any punches. The look on his face is guarded, not giving anything away. He's got the perfect poker face; you might have been forgiven for thinking the boss was in the Army himself with a shield like that.

"I just got the call from Matteo's right-hand man; he gave me the coordinates and told me to prepare for a long ride—it's about four and a half to five hours away. Those of you who are coming need to have your bags ready to go in case we need to crash there, but I'm hoping like fuck we don't have to.

"Brains, Tin, I want you in the cage. Flex, Dags, Bear and me will be riding out of our bikes, but we will go in stages; 10 minutes between each of us, then the cage. We don't want to draw attention to ourselves. Wrench, Doc, you know the drill. I want all the women including the club girls on lockdown as soon as I leave. Bear, I need you to get Jenna over here, ask her to bring Jade too."

Hearing her name makes my lungs constrict; I've been ignoring her texts for the past couple of days.

At first, they started off as concerned, but the last message I received this morning demanding we talk— or should I say telling me to 'pull my big head out of my ass and arrange another meet up.' I know she was just trying to change tack so she can 'talk', so it ain't happening—even though I'm desperate to get back inside that sweet pussy.

"Brains, have you and Tinhead sorted the security for tonight? We hardly know anything about Giordano, but at the end of the day, he's a Mafia Boss. We need to be ready for anything."

"Yes, boss." Brains pipes up. "We got it under control complete with back-up plans as well; things that would surprise even the Mafia." He grins, baring his teeth like a devious shark. To say that I haven't really got to know Brains is an understatement, but the only time he's not in his room or office is when he's in church; he very rarely comes out of his hole.

"Perfect, Brains. Hopefully everything will play out fine, but I want to be coming home to Dani and Ryker intact. All right, let's head out in 10; he wants us there at 11.30pm sharp. Bear, you'd better call Jenna."

***

I try not to let my fears about the meeting tonight show; I usually have things like this compartmentalized in little boxes in my brain, but if one gets so much as nudged open, it's game over.

"Here are the coordinates, put them in the cage GPS; we'll be going in 5." Axe hands the written digits through the open window to Brains as I'm driving there and back I insisted I wanted to, but the truth is, I need something to concentrate on that's not Jade. I would have preferred to have ridden, but we need to take the cage for the guns.

We are exchanging everything tonight, and we all hope it runs as smoothly as possible. We all have stakes in this deal; equal parts. I have enough money to retire ten times over in truth, but I never want to touch it for myself. Yeah, that money might be tainted, but I gladly handed it over to finance my share of the guns.

***

We're about halfway there, driving in silence as Brains works on his laptop.

"It got a hidden IP?" I enquire, examining it.

"Huh? Oh, the comp? Yeah, of course…yeah. I'm just logging into the camera feeds near to the coordinates we were given now I know where we're going." Brains' head is always covered with a baseball cap—always backwards, always jet black, and always with the Devils emblem on it. It's grubby and fading, but he'd never part with it. He's from a rich family originally; like me, he may not have been born into the MC life, but it welcomed him with open arms. He left the VP position in his family company because it bored him shitless, and he craved the structure of the club, he told me once.

Tugging his cap off and running his palm over his shaved head, Brains looks puzzled. He's about my height; lean with a gage in his left earlobe and dark eyes that only add to his edge.

"Just let me know if you need anything, Brains."

Every now and then, I flick my eyes toward the rearview mirror to check no one is tailing us. Thankfully, nothing but open road follows the back of the van, and up ahead are the distant forms of Axe, Flex, Bear, and then Dags. We're all connected via a radio comms channel that's in our lids normally, but Brains fixed it to come through crystal clear in the cage too.

"When we get around this bend coming up, all pull over for a piss stop and some food if ya want it," Axe informs us. We don't reply, having previously agreed the less radio chatter tonight the better. As the bend comes up ahead, Axe starts to pull over and we all follow suit the maneuver as smooth as you like. Parking up alongside my brothers' bikes, I jump out, needing a piss myself.

"Yo boss! I'm gonna go over there," I tell Axe as I head into the bush by the side of the road, undoing my zip and letting a satisfied sigh escape, letting my eyes flick closed. As I finish off my piss, my red-haired beauty and her catlike eyes come into my mind's eye. Her image turns toward me in slow motion, her waves cascading down her shoulders as her eyes glitter at me.

Fuck, I know I need to explain myself to her properly, but I can't…

***

"How much farther Brains?" I ask. Up until now, we've been shooting the shit, discussing guns, games, girls, anything but tonight, both needing some light relief before we pull up. We've been back on the road a little over 2 hours.

"Only about 35 to 40 minutes," he tells me not looking up from his phone. I already know he's texting Candi. They've been getting real close lately, but she's club pussy, so I'm not sure how that's gonna go down with Dags and Wrench.

We've crossed over into Arkansas, but I know almost nothing about this state.

"Where are we goin' again?"

"We're heading to a place called Ozark National Forest. I'm syncing up to the cameras leading up to the place and in the parking lot."

Brains turns his screen to face me, showing me the camera feeds as we drive and listening to the pig scanner in his earpiece to ensure they aren't onto us. He hits a button, and the screen switches to one filled with flashes of black, red and yellow headlights moving in and out of each square, the camera feeds within the squares switching every 30 seconds.

Color me impressed, although after Dani and Flex, he's right to be meticulous.

I slow down on Axe's signal, tentatively creeping down the road first with him and the rest of the men are idling behind us. So far so good, but we are tense, my body thrumming with the adrenaline that's always bubbling underneath the surface of my skin; I thrive on it, and I fucking crave it, seeking it out like a long lost friend. It always greets me without fail, welcoming me with wide arms.

We pull through the gates of the National Forest with 10 minutes to spare, gingerly driving through the vast open space as before we pull up to the exact inch of the given coordinates, not taking any chances. When we're there, Brains says one single word over the radio.

"Clear."

With that, they start to filter through the gate. Axe parks next to us, facing the opposite direction, followed by the others. Once they're in position, we just sit there for a few minutes, me and Brains not uttering a word to each other as we stare at the laptop, watching the camera feeds flicker. Suddenly, I spot movement in the bottom right one, pointing it out to Brains.

With a flick of his head, he peers out of the window, nodding at Axe and the others.

After a few tense moments, two cars and a truck pull down the road towards the gate too. One of them has to be Matteo's SUV—a brand new black Maserati with all the trimmings, complete with blacked-out windows and what I'm damn sure are fake plates. He pulls into the parking lot, continuing carefully into the forest until he reaches a spot near to us that's off the beaten track.

An older the black Maserati parks opposite Axe about 15 feet away, at which point whoever is behind the wheel must notify the others to come through.

We watch on the cameras as vehicles pull along the track in their droves, kicking up dust and over their gleaming bodywork. All the cars pull up in front of us, and then the truck parks at the farthest end away from us, not quite blocking us in.

None of us make a move, waiting for Rebel, Red and his chapter to turn up. After a few moments, Brains elbows me, and that's when we see Rebel, Red, and Pincher on bikes, their cage coming into full view as they approach us.

When they reach us, their cage pulls up on the opposite side to ours, the bikes copying Axe. Once they've all killed their engines, we sit around stewing in the electric atmosphere—or maybe it's just me.

A few minutes pass, then the driver and passenger doors of one of Matteo's cars swing open in perfect sync. Nico and Tomma come out on either side, and then I see Leo come out of the back left door. Once all three are out of the car, Tomma opens the back right door, and out steps Matteo Giordano dressed all in black—most probably an Armani or Versace three-piece suit. As soon as his expensive leather shoes touch the dry, packed dirt of the forest, the button on his jacket slips open and I spot a holster with two handguns in it. He buttons it up again quickly, adjusting his black silk pocket square to detract attention. Matteo comes to stand in front of the car and casually strokes his goatee, and the rest of us take this as our cue to walk over and get this meet done with. I jump out of the cage with Brains to check the merchandise is genuine as Axe asked us earlier—there are no better people than us to examine guns, and Mafia or not, Axe won't touch a counterfeit piece. We all surround Axe and Flex, and the Missouri chapter do the same with Rebel and Red, who I notice brought along their two newest members, Pirate and Clipper.

"Gentlemen, *Buona Sera*. Shall we all get on with business?" Matteo says in his thick Italian accent, his voice deep but smooth like rich chocolate.

Axe and Rebel nod, and Matteo turns to his men. "Tomma, you and Nico open the container in preparation for the funds."

Casually, yet lithely as a panther, he approaches Axe and Rebel and greets them chatting to each of them in hushed tones.

As Matteo gives a quick flick of his wrist, a man from the last car to arrive gets out carrying two suitcases, one in either hand. I notice they're handcuffed to his wrists.

Axe glances back to Flex, giving him a flick of his head. Flex moves from his spot, goes to his bike's saddle bags, and pulls out two large bags—our cash.

Red does the exact same, and both VPs hand them to their respective Prez'. My eyes scan the surroundings, and I flick my eyes to Brains to see him watching everyone like a hawk, including the man with the suitcases.

As I watch Axe talking to Matteo, I can see the tension coming off Bear and Flex in waves like they're preempting something going wrong.

Matteo rocks on his heels, bringing his hand up to his face and stroking his beard in thought at whatever Axe has said, then beckoning Leo, who leaves his post at the truck and stomps his great weight over to his boss. Matteo's volume gets slightly louder in their mother tongue, so I'm able to hear him say something in Italian.

Leo strides back into his place, but this time hops onto the pull-down ledge at the back of the truck before pulling and tugging the locks there. Tomma obviously knows what's going on, as he flicks of a switch to reveal the biggest haul of guns even, I've seen in a fucking long time.

The lights built into the shelves inside illuminate every weapon in the vault of guns, and I idly wonder if Matteo was planning a full-scale war to own this many.

I side-eye Brains to my far right and Dags to my left, who is standing way back and observing as he does best; an impressive skill considering he's non-military. As I glance at the back of Axe's head, he turns to lock eyes with me and signals with his head for me and Brains to go check the merch—that's probably what he asked Matteo.

My spine is ramrod straight, and I don't miss a step as Brains falls in behind me. As we reach them, Tomma and Leo stand back in defensive stances; arms crossed over their chests. Leo looks almost like he's puffing his out like a pigeon, but I know he ain't: the man is built like a brick house.

Climbing the steps into the truck, I see the shelves span floor to ceiling and three rows high in the middle. The light bounces off all the guns, and each and every ever box on every row is labeled.

When I turn my head, I see the letters that I never let bother me until a certain redhead turned up—AK 47. I was numb to those letters and numbers before Jade, but now fear grips my heart.

Fuck no! Not now.

I fixate my eyes on the box just to the right of it, then breathe in, hold it to the count of seven, and breathe out.

You can do this.

"Fucking hell, where d'ya wanna start? How about I start one end, you go start at the other end, and we'll meet in the middle?" Brains asks.

Nodding, I go to the opposite side of the truck—away from the AKs, to my relief—and we start pulling down every box one by one checking they are the real deal. I can already tell it's going to take ages, but it's gotta be done.

***

After a while, Dags joins us, and as soon as I tell him what I'm looking for, he gets to work. Within 45 minutes, we are on our last box, having checked and double checked—they all look kosher to me. I jump down from the truck, landing on my feet like a cat and giving Axe a nod.

He turns to face Matteo, grabbing his hand and shaking it, much to Matteo's shock. He looks like he hasn't shaken a hand in a long time, and as Leo, Tomma and Nico reach for their guns, I realize that they don't know what to make of it either.

Matteo has to dismiss them with a wave of his hand before things heat up, as Flex, Bear and myself are right by Axe's side in a split second.

"*Ritirate gli uomini! Stupidi coglioni!*" Matteo roars at his men, pinning them all down with a glare, his eyes wild even at his right-hand man.

"*Scusi*, Axe. They are just loyal and jumpy; I can't recall the last time I shook a man's hand that didn't lead to a bloody war. In Naples, there are many, how you say…rats…and devious men around, so I would never shake the hand of a man that wasn't my own family." He throws a final glare at his men, who have now put their guns away. "Please do not be offended by this, this is my family's way."

Axe just nods in agreement; one thing all the men here can attest to is that Axe is a fair leader, but he also means every word he says.

"No offense taken, but a handshake is my way. I trust another man based on the feel, firmness and strength of his grip, and I am an extremely good judge of character because of it."

There's tension between these two, but they both have loyalty in spades and their own traditions and beliefs—which makes Matteo's nod of agreement even more surprising when it comes, his eyes dancing with amusement. He shocks me even more by clasping Axe's leather clad shoulder and giving it a gentle squeeze, holding his gaze.

"Axe, you don't bullshit me. I can see the truth in your eyes, and I admire you standing up for your ways as I hope you do me standing up for mine. I think this will be an enjoyable *associazione*. My men will help both of your chapters' men to load your vans, and I'll be in touch in a month to see how you are doing. No hard feelings."

Leaving our Prezs to close the terms of the deal, we follow our Missouri brothers to split the goods.

***

We load the last boxes in our cage before closing it and locking it tight.

Matteo nods, seemingly pleased with the transaction. "Good doing business with you, gentlemen. I'll be in touch soon. *Ciao*."

Pivoting on the ball of his foot, he stalks off back to his car, sliding in through the door Nico holds open for him. His men all pile back into their cars and truck like nothing happened, disappearing like cat burglars in the dead of night.

Once they're gone, Axe turns back to us, his stoic expression now replaced by fatigue. It looks like he's aged a couple of years tonight. "Okay, let's get the fuck out of here and get home to our women."

"Have you heard from the BDT?" Kelly asks me whilst swinging her legs over the edge of my bed in her checkered PJ shorts.

I've been in a world of my own this past week or so, so I almost don't hear her. "What was that? BDT? What the hell is that?"

"Ya know, *BDT*, big dickhead Tinhead! You heard from him?" She enquires with a tilt of her head. Curiosity shines brightly in those big deep brown eyes of hers, but she's clearly trying to hold back a snigger.

"No, no I haven't; he won't talk to me. I don't think I even give two shits anyway, Kel'. I think he needs to talk to someone about whatever's going on in his head, but he shuts down when I suggest it. I can't force him."

"HA! Yes you fucking could, Jade Smith, you even got me to tell you my deepest darkest secrets. Buuut, the only way you're gonna get through to him is if there's something in it for him,"

"Let's get one thing straight, Kel'—I never ask you to tell me your deepest darkest secrets, you offer them on a silver platter!" I sigh. "I know, that's exactly why I'm going to the club tonight with Jenna and Bear. You wanna come?"

Her eyes light up like I just gave her the best Christmas present ever.

"Hell yes! I am *there*!"

She practically skips around my room in a whirlwind, stabbing her legs into her skinny cut-off jeans, tugging of her tee, and putting her red-and-black plaid tie-around shirt on.

"Ready!" she announces, a big smile stretching across that gorgeous face of hers.

She points to my make-up chair. "Tinhead ain't gonna know what's hit him once I'm finished with you; sit down."

***

I roll up to the clubhouse in my Beetle after following Jenna, who hitched a ride on the back of Bear's bike. She looked so carefree and angelic as the wind whipped the hair that wasn't tucked under her helmet around her face, making her eyes light up. As we head through the clubhouse gates, I see Wrench's eyes widen at the sight of the car, followed by a big smirk.

Oh God, I hope no one else knows what I did with the Dickhead to end all Dickheads.

"Oh my God, I can't believe we're doing this! Well, you are, but I had to come along to watch this," my best friend beams up at me as we exit the car, walking up behind Bear and my sister.

Jenna tried to talk to me about what was going on between me and Tinhead before we left the apartment, but I haven't told anyone everything yet; I still need to try and figure most of it out myself.

Crossing over the threshold, I hear the low *thump, thump* of the music and see the man in question behind the bar, working away with his back to me.

Kelly links my arm in hers for moral support. "Yo Tin, grab mine and Jenna's usual, plus whatever Jade and Kelly want, would ya?" Bear asks. I see the split-second Tinhead's back straightens and his shoulders hunch together at the mention of my name. He tries to correct his posture, but it's there as clear as day.

"I'll grab a Vodka and Diet Coke. What ya having, Kelly?" I ask, a slight smirk on my lips.

"I'll have a Corona, please and thank you." Kelly says as we perch on the bar stools closest to Jenna and Bear.

Tinhead eventually turns around, finally meeting my eyes. At first, they light up, but after a few seconds they flicker back to blank emptiness.

"Sure thing, coming up for y'all," he declares, not letting his eyes land on anyone in particular.

He busies himself again almost instantly, shuffling and clinking glasses and bottles as Bear and Jenna are chatting to Dagger.

"Jenna, Jade, and Kelly! When did you girls arrive?" Zara Hart marches up to me, wrapping her arms around me. She's already a little tipsy; her slender arm wraps around my neck while she plants a kiss on Kelly's cheek. "I'm so happy to see you all."

"You okay Zara?" I ask trying not to giggle as I roll my eyes to Kelly.

"Me? Yeah, I'm peachy. Where are your drinks? I'll grab them." She hiccups at the end, covering her mouth and staring at me like a deer in headlights, then a bubble of laughter comes out of her.

Tinhead interrupts Zara's hysterics by placing all our drinks in front of us and sliding them towards each person, handing me my Vodka and Coke last.

"Zar', I got it. Don't worry. There ya go, enjoy."

My eyes linger on his hand, and I find myself willing him to stay and talk to me, but he walks away, and with a last swipe of the counter, the bar he flicks the worn-out cloth away, exiting the main room before slipping back down the hall.

Well, it's now or never...

I pick up my glass, draining it and feeling the vodka burn a fiery trail down my throat. Hopping down from my stool like a woman on a mission, I follow after Tinhead, going down the corridor and stopping to listen in at the kitchen

Nope, he must be in the men's room.

I stand against the wall opposite the door, waiting for him to come out. When I've been standing there for two or three minutes, I push off the wall and decide to go into the bathroom.

As I pass through the swing door, I'm hit by a district urinal smell mixed with cheap air freshener to try and mask the stink.

For a motorcycle club, the toilets are pretty clean as it goes and the bathroom itself has cream walls and black tiling—not too shabby I locate the cubicles at the end of the room to find there's only two—one of which has the wooden door wide open.

Well, that rules that one out.

As I walk inside, the *click-clack* of my heeled boots against the tiles resounds in the deathly quiet of the bathroom.

Standing in front of the wooden door, I go to knock on it, but before I can it swings wide open, revealing a disheveled Tinhead.

His hair is all over the place, sticking out here and there in any direction, and shock is written clearly on his face. I think it must be the fact that I'm standing right before him and no one else is around, just us. Tension builds in my chest; it's making my heart ache to seeing him like this.

I tentatively take a step back, side stepping so Tinhead can exit the cubicle.

He goes straight to the basin and starts taking his anger and frustration out on his hands, washing them furiously. He swivels on his heel after drying them with a paper towel grabs, completely ignoring me as he places his hand on the main door.

All my sympathy for him dissipates in a flash. *Fuck this*

"Coward!" I shout out at him as my anger bubbles to the surface.

How dare he just leave without even saying a single word!

Calling him a coward obviously was the wrong thing to say, as Tinhead whips around, his eyes black with pure rage.

Good, maybe now I've pissed him off, he'll give me answers.

"Coward?! Fuck off, Jade, you don't know the meaning of the word! Your little mind can't even compute what that word means!" he bellows from the door taking a stride to close the empty space between us. His nostrils flare and his eyes are wild with rage.

I don't understand it, but fuck, that's hot.

I can't help pushing some more.

"Yes I do, you are a coward and a big fake! You don't want to tell me what's going on in your head, fine, but don't kid yourself that there's nothing wrong with you. Trying makes you a pure coward!" I scream back at him while taking a step toward him, my chest heaving as my heart races. I wonder if I've pushed him too far, but I'm enjoying taunting the beast.

"Like hell I'm gonna admit that there's something wrong with me! Didn't your mother ever tell ya not to play with fire or you'd get burnt?" he spits at me. We're only a foot away from each other now, and his breathing's labored.

Good!

Still raging, I step right up to him, the sexual tension pulsating between us making me ache in all the right places.

I press my soft chest up against his firm one and blurt out, "I already have got burnt you fuckin' bastard."

Recognition flashes across his face, for a brief second, then it's gone. I hear him growl, and before I know what's happening, he swipes his hand out to clamp the back of my neck and presses his lips brutally against mine, stealing my breath from me.

I fuckin love that I push his buttons, so I don't fight the kiss. This kiss isn't passionate or gentle, it's something darker than I have ever had.

Tinhead stabs his tongue in my mouth, controlling the kiss. I'm just the onlooker of this kiss, my lips feel as though they are bruising, but there's something deep down inside me that enjoys the ferociousness. Its brutal, searing and branding—a kiss of the devil, pouring his darkness into me.

All at once, the immense pressure disappears from my lips, making me moan.

"Ahh," I whimper as my fingers brush my lips feather lightly, rewarding me with a stinging sensation.

Tinhead takes one massive stride back to the door, locking it, and then he's back on me like a vulture feeding on its prize. The gleam in his eyes is still black as the night, but I can already tell he's opening himself up slightly.

Something tells me this isn't just going to be a quick fuck, but cataclysmic sex I don't even get a chance to be ready for. Instead of worrying, I jump further into the black hole with him. There is no going back now.

"Fuck, Jade, you can't push me like this," he growls, fisting my hair.

Normally there is some pleasure in the pain, but it's different this time. Even the baby hairs at the base of my skull pull like a motherfucker, causing a stinging, biting sensation to shoot from my scalp.

Tugging slightly, he leads me to the sink, pushing my ass hard against the edge of the basins so it's digging and biting into my flesh. In one fluid movement, he lets go of my hair and whips my top from me as I present myself to him in my red satin bra and jeans.

"Jade…fuck it."

Thinking he's going to back out, I snatch at his wrist, and he instantly stills his movements, staring blindly at me with fury flickering in his eyes as his eyelids twitch.

He needs this. He needs to let it out, and he's unwilling to do it himself, so I'm going to help. If I have to lose a part of my soul to the Devil, so be it.

I unclip my hair from the top of my head, letting my waves fall around my shoulders, then unclasping my bra and letting it drop.

My breasts jut out, pointing right at him, my nipples already in eager peaks. I realize this is the first time he's seen me with no bra on. He stands there gawking with a fixed stare, not flinching as my breathing becomes more labored.

I wonder what the hell is going around in his head as he drops to his haunches and wordlessly grazes his teeth around one of my already-painful nipples, sending an electric current shooting through my body. The sensitivity drives me wild, running straight to my clit.

"Ahhh fuck, Tinhead..."

As soon as my words leave my lips, his tongue wraps around my nipples, licking and sucking them so hard they brush the roof of his wet, soft, warm mouth.

Flicking my jeans button open with his other hand, he jams his hand in my soaked panties. His fingers find my hole, and he pushes them deep inside of me. The pressure is hard and punishing, but the feeling is exquisite. He collects more of my juices and shoves them deeper inside me, then a 3rd finger enters me, making my walls burn.

I know he's trying to push me away with the pain; I can see through his plan. Snatching the wrist that's between my legs out of my jeans, I shift my position on the sink, shuffling my jeans down.

His eyes flash in surprise—exactly what I thought, he hoped I was stopping him completely but not a chance.

He's trying to push me away for some reason, and he knows what we have is just sex, so this isn't just about not just wanting a girlfriend. This is more, so much more that there's a chance I can't even fathom it, but turning back now isn't an option. Determination burns deep in my blood—my Momma says that I was stubborn even before I was born, deciding when I wanted to come into the world rather than waiting for my due date.

Pushing my jeans to my ankles, Tinhead spreads my knees further apart before opening my pussy lips out like a flower in bloom. His nostrils flare, then as casually as if he was licking a spoon, he scoops my juices up on one of his fingers and shoves it in his sinfully sexy mouth, instantly clenching his eyes shut and savoring my flavor.

"Fuckin' sweetest pussy I've ever tasted," he growls at me his blacker-than-onyx eyes burning back at me like wildfire. My own eyes break contact with his and stare down at his cock bulging through his jeans. He clocks where my eyes fall and grabs his jean clad cock. As I flick my eyes back up to him, I see no sparkle this time. Instead, the emptiness is there for me to see as clear as day. "Turn the fuck around Jade. Or so help me God," he growls between ragged breaths.

I know not to push this button; it's not red for danger, but big and black for self-destruct. I flip over, knowing he wants me facing the mirror in front of me. My naked breasts are now getting cold from being pressed against the porcelain white sink.

I fight the moan that is stuck in the back of my throat, pulling my hair to one side so I can look back at Tinhead as he pops open the button on his jeans. I instinctively wiggle my butt as the ache between my legs refuses to let up; I'm in desperate need of fucking.

SLAP! SLAP!

Tinhead strikes his palm across my ass, but even like this it wasn't a proper hit. If I provoked him even more, I know I could get it harder.

"Don't test me, Jade."

He tugs his jeans down his lean, tanned thighs, and in the fluorescent light of the bathroom, I see silvery white scars against his kneecaps on one side and a bigger scar on his right thigh.

Then my attention reverts back to Tinhead, and I see him fisting himself. The way his knuckles whiten suggest that his hold is ferocious and almost painful, but I'm mesmerized.

"Turn. Around. Jade," he bites in a sharp tone.

I obediently turn back around, hearing the tear of a condom. Pure anticipation shoots up my spine, leaving me breathless.

I peer into the toilet mirror to watch him take command. I see pure dominance in his stance and the way his movements are controlled. In one swift move, the breath is knocked out of my lungs as I become impaled on his dick, making both of us grunt in pure satisfaction. The pain is raw, but the way he slams into me, withdraws himself and slams himself back in over and over is deliciously sensitive.

I push my ass back at him, the push and pull between our bodies like music. He needs my body to seek solace from his hidden pain, and I welcome it, letting him drag me into his abyss.

Peering back up into the mirror, I stare at him underneath the veil of my brassy locks without letting him know I can see him. The rhythm takes over both of our bodies, building to a grand crescendo. The ache as he slams into me is phenomenal; I'm having an out-of-body experience and there is nothing else to it.

I continue watching him take and take from my body as he violently jerks inside me, building us both up to the pinnacle. He reaches down, growling into my ear,

"Fuck, Jade. You drive me wild! D'ya know that?"

He rolls and pinching my nipple in between his thumb and forefinger, never relenting even though the feeling is just short of agonizing.

I let him use me as he wants; he needs this, he needs to let whatever this is out and find himself again. My clit aches and spine tingles, I'm on the precipice of my climax and about to go over.

Sensing this, Tinhead picks up his pace in harsh, short strokes, tormenting my walls with the raw fucking he's giving me.

"Cum," he pants breathlessly into my ear. Just like that, he's pushed me over the cliff, and my body shatters into tiny pieces around him at the bottom. Looking back at the figure fucking me in the mirror I clock his face and see exactly what he doesn't want anyone else to see; pain and vulnerability. The tormented look makes my heart clench in pure fear; I've never seen anything like it, not even from Jenna or Bear after they went through what they did. It's a look of pure, harrowing anguish and distress, a look of dark torment. There's definitely more than meets the eye with this jerk...

***

We come back down from the throes of our raw, dirty, unadulterated fucking, and as Tinhead removes his now semi-flaccid dick from me, my juices smear the inside of my thighs.

Without a word, he goes and drops the used condom in the trashcan, tucking himself back into his boxers as I refasten my bra and put my shirt back on.

As I pull my thong and jeans back up, I wince; I can still feel his intrusion and punishment of my pussy.

He grazes his thumb over my brow, and as I look back up into his eyes, I see that they're back to his usual hazel coloring. Any remnants of the pure desolation I saw there moments before are gone.

"Did I hurt ya, doll?" he enquires, pure concern coating his voice,

"It was nothing I can't handle; I wanted it."

"Fuck, Jade! I shouldn't have done that, but you kept pushing."

"I know, but you needed to. That's one of the reasons why I did it. Will you talk to me at least, tell me what's going on? I'm looking in on all of this, ya know."

"Fuckin' hell Jade…Are you going to let me in on what you're holding back from me if I tell ya?"

I stay silent. None of this was meant to happen, there's no way I can tell him

Tinhead's gaze hardens. "Yeah, thought not. Leave me alone, okay? Fuck this bullshit, I don't need it! I was okay before you came along, so stay the fuck out of my life!"

"What are you afraid of, Tinhead? That maybe you're human and you're a little bit broken like the rest of us?"

"HA! That's hilarious, Jade. If I was just a 'little bit broken, I would fuckin' take it any day over—" Just as I think he's about to buckle, he stops.

"Over…?"

"Nothing. I said fuckin' leave it!"

"No, I am not leaving it! Over what, Tinhead? Fuckin' tell me!"

"Over being me."

As that statement halts me in my tracks, he unlocks the toilet door and strides out before letting it slam closed and shutting me inside.

We are all a little bit broken, but I understand now that his demons are more than that. He's utterly and completely defeated; on the edge of the mountain waiting to jump off…

I'll give him space and get out of his life if that's what he truly wants. He's resting his fist on that huge black self-destruct button, and I don't know if I or anyone else can save him now.

Just because you're living doesn't mean you're alive…

Chapter 19

We haven't spoken to each other since that night a week ago; I haven't even seen him.

It's the 22nd October and Christmas is around the corner, so me and Jenna have been putting the finishing touches to our special Christmas menus.

We're sitting in our apartment with pieces of paper haphazardly strewn across every surface—mockups for Autumn/Christmas recipe cards that Jenna wants to go out by Saturday to ease some of the strain on us.

"...so, what d'ya think, JJ?" Jenna says at the end of a long spiel, looking at me expectantly.

Shit! I wasn't paying attention...

I was in a world of my own, thinking of the man who has got my head all jumbled up.

I wonder if he's still suffering, but deep down, I know he is; he always was. They say never to judge a book by its cover, and as far as Tinhead's concerned, that's so fucking true.

I force myself back into the present as I feel my sister's stare fixed on me. "Sorry Jenna, what did you say?"

"Shall we go with the special from Menu A and mains from Menu B and D, followed by dessert selections from A? The coffee specials will be the same as last year's, unless my experiments go well tomorrow. What do you think?"

I absently just nod back at her, not paying her any mind. "Right, out with it. You haven't been the same since last Saturday when we went to the club. What is it, Jade?" she asks me with concern in her voice.

"I'm okay, Jenna…it's not even me that's the problem as far as I know. I'm trying to figure it all out right now, but once I do, I *will* talk to you." I hate placating my sister like this, but what else can I do until I manage to unjumble things for myself?

"Okay, JJ. You know I would never betray your trust."

I sigh. "The thing is, Sis, if you knew everything, you would, just not intentionally though. It's not just about me, but you have nothing to worry about, okay?" I inform her. The excuse is at least half-true; if she hears Tinhead's name mentioned, she *will* tell Bear—they don't keep secrets since nearly losing each other.

Her eyes soften, and she reaches across to me and squeezes my hand tightly, then says exactly what my Momma would if she knew. "It will all work itself out in the end."

I smile and get to my feet. "Sis, leave it with me; I'll put together the final menu and laminate it in the morning, then we can try it out tomorrow. Right now, I'm going to grab some tea and jump into bed—I'm pooped."

Jenna scans me with her eyes, smiling at me. "That sounds like a great idea."

***

"Sue, oh my God! It's been an amazing week with the introduction of the new Christmas menu; everyone is loving it. I wasn't able to create a new hot drink this year, but our new barista Maggie did—a toasted marshmallow coffee base for lattes and Cappuccinos. She's mixed some of the syrup already; Jade and I were the guinea pigs, and we couldn't believe how amazing it was. Oh, Dani came in yesterday too—she was pretty pissed that we didn't cater for her peanut butter addiction on the new menu. I tried telling her that it's not exactly festive, but you would have thought it was the worst thing anyone had ever done. She's a nut herself, God love her."

Sue chuckles from the counter. "That girl, I swear! Good job little Ryker didn't end up with a peanut allergy isn't it?"

Jenna giggles and nods. "What can I get ya, anyway?

"Well sweetheart, can I try one of the marshmallow cappuccinos, please? Doc will have a black filter coffee, are you excited for the party on Saturday? Have you decided what to go as yet?"

My ears prick up; this is the first I'm hearing of any party, Jenna and Bear haven't mentioned it.

I keep up the pretense of replacing the glittery mince pies and star shaped shortbread cookie back in the glass display cabinet so I can continue listening in while Maggie busies herself serving the few customers who have dropped by after the lunch rush.

"I've decided on a cat, but Bear is scouring the internet for a cupcake outfit for me to wear. I told him I'll only wear one if he dresses up in a jam jar costume!" Jenna lets out a snort of laughter, and Sue laughs so hard she nearly doubles over, wiping a few stray tears away.

I can't help sniggering myself; my sister would look cute as hell as a cupcake, but Bear as a jam jar would be downright hilarious. Finishing restocking the cabinet, I right myself and go to catch up with Sue—I've missed seeing her lovely face.

"Heya Sue, how are you doing?"

"Oh, Jade! I didn't see you down there! Aren't you a sight for sore eyes? I'm good, sweetheart? Are you planning on coming to the party this Saturday?" she asks right front of Jenna.

I look pointedly at her, and she blushes furiously

I turn back to Sue, "Oh I didn't know anything about a party! What party is that?"

Sue picks up the coffees Jenna places on the counter in front of her. "Oh, it must have slipped your sister's mind! It's the club's costume party. You gotta come! Make sure you bring Kelly too; you girls keep me young. I'm gonna give this to Doc, I'll see ya both Saturday." She sways her curvy body over to the booth containing the club's doctor, who just so happens to be her Ol' man.

I turn back to my sister in time to see a deep pink flush creeping up to her ears,

"Why didn't you tell me? Did you not want me to go? I don't mind if you want to go alone, ya know. You're actually a part of the club, bein' Bears Ol' Lady."

She gnaws at her bottom lip, then asks, "Jade, what day is Saturday coming up?" I blink a few times, trying to think of whose birthday I might have missed, but my brain comes up blank. "I don't know, Saturday?" I shrug nonchalantly.

"JJ, it's Halloween. I didn't tell you because I know you don't celebrate and hate it," she says with a concerned look.

How I didn't realize that it was Halloween already? The bakery has been so busy that I didn't even put two and two together when arranging the menu. Out of curiosity, I stand up on tippy-toes and look across the street to the other shops and bars around us. Sure enough, I see pumpkins, fake cobwebs, and plastic glow in the dark skeletons hanging from window displays—Jenna doesn't decorate the place for my sake, so I hadn't noticed.

I have a complete lightbulb moment, and Jenna must see something in my face, because she asks, "What is it, Jade? You look like you have just won the lottery!"

She arches an eyebrow at me as I beam back at her. grabbing her upper arms with excited force,

"I think I have solved my problem, Sis! You're a genius; thank you."

***

Saturday night—Halloween

"Well, I never thought I would see the day that Jade Smith would be glad it's Halloween, let alone excited to go to a costume party; especially after swearing off them for the rest of her life!" Kelly snarks at me as she stands there, looking like the hottest, sexiest Nala from The Lion King I've ever seen. The lioness features on her face are out of this world, complete with raised pouches holding thin plastic strips that act as whiskers—they even move when she twitches her face. Golden brown tones cover the rest of her skin, then she adds fake eyelashes and eyeliner outlining her entire eyes to make them look even bigger than they are already; finishing the look with a pale pink nose and lips. I have altered the bodysuit she wears, of course, removing the middle part of the costume so her flat stomach is on show and then adding a zip in the bottom half, as well as fashioning the legs and tail into a pair of tight pants. She looks the bomb, especially now that her gorgeous deep chocolate brown hair is loose, hanging down in waves.

"I had to do it sometime, Kel'. You were right all the other times we've had this talk; things do change…and I need to make him see that too."

She meets my eye, then breaks into the biggest shit-eating grin imaginable. "That's awesome news. I'm so glad you asked me to come with you tonight. I still haven't heard from the Russian, ya know—oh well; thank you, next!" she tells me pursing her lips.

"His loss; he's not good enough for you."

"Damn straight! 'Kay, nearly done with your make up. I can't believe you're not letting me dress you up! At least let me stick eyelashes on you?"

I inwardly roll my eyes, but relent "Oh, okay, but then I have to get ready otherwise we're going to be too late. Jenna and Bear are already there; she texted me a minute ago saying it's a really great party."

"Well, you're nearly ready, babe; you just need to put on your pants, shoes, and jacket, and hey presto! You *will* go to the ball…just not dressed as Cinderella." she smirks.

When I asked Kelly to do my make up for tonight, she stood there unblinking at first, then eventually asked if I felt alright.

"Annnnd…all done!" she announces once the eyelashes are attached. "Let me go clean my hands, and I'll help you finish getting ready," she walks off into my bathroom and returns a few moments later, toweling off her hands.

Grabbing my pants, she hands them to me and I put them on, trying to ignore the butterflies swarming around in my stomach. As Kelly passes me my shoes, my hands can't seem to grab them as my palms are so slick with sweat. She tries again, and I push my feet into them after clutching them this time.

"You wanna wear your jacket, or d'ya want me to carry it?"

I swallow the cotton-wool like feeling coating my tongue before answering her. "No, I'll wear it. You know I'll try and back out when I get there, but don't let me. I have to go, okay?"

Kelly agrees with a quick nod of her head and hands me my jacket.

I feel the cool silk lining caress my arms even through my top, and knowing I'm ready makes me panic.

Fuck, fuck! What am I doing?!

Kelly instantly comes to my rescue when she senses my fear and apprehension, wrapping her arm around me and telling me exactly what I need to hear. "Do this and there will be no more pretending, *chica*. if all hell breaks loose, you know I got ya back."

Lifting my head up high, I give her a tight, small smile, trying to not ruin my makeup.

"Let's go then," she tells me, not letting me back out.

As we get to the apartment door, I realize I forgot something I need to set this whole outfit off. I run back to my room, shuffling through the boxes under my bed and trying to find the item in question.

I know it's here...

Nope, not that box, next box...

Nope, not that one...

Eventually finding it right at the bottom of the last one, I snatch it up, shove it in my pocket, and make my way to the first Halloween party I have been to for years.

***

We pull through the club gates at 11:12pm, Wrench swaying on the spot as he opens them and follows us back to the main door. Even he's dressed up, a Trump mask over his own face.

Kelly giggles at the sight of him, shaking her head.

I haven't said a word on the drive over, too focused on tonight. I probably look crazy, but I don't care. We pull up alongside Zara's Jeep, and I stare into the night sky, distracted by the twinkling stars.

Kelly breaks the silence after a while. "Jade, you okay? We have to get out now."

Snapping back to reality, I take a big breath, and without really knowing what I'm doing, I step out of the car. Kelly is right by my side; my crutch, my best friend, and the best girl ever.

"Girl, you got this! Now let's join the party."

We stride into the main room, where the cheesy Halloween music is deafening, making the whole room vibrate—or is that just my insides? It feels like I could turn to jelly in an instant.

I scan the whole room, admiring the decorations the club have put up.

There are black and red lightning bolts lining the walls, with flashes of lime green here and there. Foam headstones in each corner give the feel of a haunted graveyard while also doubling as tables for people to put their drinks on. A vast amount of cobwebs line the walls, and realistic skulls holding candles give the room just the right amount of shadowy mood lighting.

The deep, gravelly voice of Dagger echoes from behind us—he says more than a word, which means he's had a few already. "Fuckin' hell, who ordered this hot lioness?"

His eyes linger on Kelly, and the look he gives her is even making *me* feel all hot and bothered. His eyes devour her like he could eat her up.

The next minute, I see Dani striding up to me followed by my giggling sister. Dani is dressed as Princess Leia in her classic white outfit—I couldn't imagine Axe would let her wear the bikini—while my sister kicks ass dressed as a bear, complete with a hairstyle that resembles ears Kelly did; she looks so freaking cute.

"Jade! Oh my god your outfit is amazing!" I barely register Dani's compliment as my eyes scan the room for the man I need to see. Not seeing him, I look back at Jenna, who knows exactly who I was looking for. "He's just gone to get some more beer from the back. Are you okay being here?" she enquires, her face full of concern.

I nod back at her wordlessly, and she and Dani lead me and Kelly over to where Zara is giggling on Flex's lap.

Zar' is Catwoman, and thankfully she has a wicked body to pull of all that latex Flex's effort makes me smile as I spot a Batman logo stretched across his broad chest underneath his cut, and a Batman mask propped on his forehead. He doesn't seem to mind, looking longingly at Zar'.

"*Shiiiiit!* Oh my God, Jade, is that you? You look amazing. And Kelly, you look fuckin' fierce, babe! I love it! Looks like I ain't the only one, either."

Zar' flicks her head in the direction to the bar, and we glance back at it to see Dagger staring hungrily at Kelly. There's not single flicker of emotion across the rest of his face, but his eyes say it all.

Oh, Dagger, you don't know my girl. She would have you eating out of her hand...

I spin back around to face Kelly and see her reaction. Her face still reddens underneath her makeup, so to save her any awkward questions, I mention her talent.

"Can you believe Kelly did her own look as well as mine and Jenna's tonight.

Dani's eyes practically bug out of her sockets. "Wh-what? Oh my God, are you serious?" She touches Kelly's whiskers. "These are amazing! I thought you just did makeup?"

"Yeah, I do. I love special effects make up but there's not many jobs out there that get to showcase it off, so I do the more conventional makeup..."

I don't hear the rest of the conversation, as Tinhead takes up his usual spot behind the bar. My heart pounds in my chest so loudly that I can hear it pulsating in my ears. The bowl of punch in the far corner catches my eye just the smoke machine blasts out another burst of sickly-sweet scented smoke into the room.

Knowing what I have to do, I take a last glance over my shoulder to see where he's at.

It's now or never...

I tentatively reach out to touch Axe on the forearm, but don't offer any words other than "I'm sorry."

Confusion clouds his face, and I see him frowning at me, but the rest all happens so quickly.

I grab the punch bowl, stalk up behind Tinhead, and dump the entire contents over him, including the fake eyeball ice cubes.

When it's empty, I put the plastic bowl next to him on the counter, the hollow rattle echoing in the sudden hush that surrounds us.

He whirls around, eyes wild with the pure anger radiating from him. He looks at me with utter confusion, but I don't give him time to say a thing before I place my old glasses on my face and recite the words that he said to me all those years ago; the words that made me hate him.

As true realization dawns, I watch his face fall in pure shock, his jaw goes slack, and I swear his eyes bulge out of his sockets.

My spine is poker-straight, and I look him dead in the eye as I say with venom, "Look, you're definitely not 'normal' now! Swim along, you little freak!"

Without a moment's hesitation, I turn on my heel to leave—I have done exactly what I came here to do. I silently pass the other club members as I exit the clubhouse, and as soon as I get to the bitter fresh air, I take in a gulp, doubling over as I fight the anxiety in my chest to let me breathe. The air feels foreign in my lungs.

I stumble around the backyard, then come to sit in front of a huge oak tree at the far end of the yard.

It's darker over here; easier to hide under the cloak of the low-hanging branches.

Pulling out my phone I put it on mirror mode, nearly laughing at the irony—vampires aren't meant to have a reflection, and I'm dressed as one; exactly as he was all those years ago.

Eventually my heart stops racing enough that I'm able to relax a little, but I leave my phone lying on the ground to light up with missed calls and texts. I pay them no attention.

I hear the clubhouse door open and shut, followed by the crunching of the gravel as someone walks around. I can't see the dark figure, but I know it's not Kelly as she would have hollered by now. Bear would too, come to think of it.

Shuffling around on the floor, I sit on a twig and hear it break and crunch in the silence. The sound stops the person in their tracks, then the crunching of gravel gets closer and I see the figure move agilely along the grass, drawing closer to where I'm sat until *he* stops at my feet.

Fuck…

I just stare up into his eyes. Even in the darkness, I can see his expression, and in that moment I know it will forever be burned into my head.

Hurt, confusion, and disappointment mar his face, and each flicker of emotion I see feels like a stab to my heart.

Without saying a word, he shocks me by sitting next to me. We sit in silence for what feels like only a few minutes, but I know it's been longer.

He breaks the silence first, stretching his long lean legs out in front of me, his worn biker boots sharply contrasting my men's dress shoes that are so highly polished the moonlight seems to bounce off the end of the toes.

"So, this was just revenge for what happened to you all those years ago?", he enquires, no emotion in his voice to give him away.

I try to swallow the big lump in my throat as I take a quick glance up at him in the blackness of the night, thankfully only able to see a faded gray face now it's no longer lit by moonlight.

"Yes. Yes, it was." I inform him coolly, hoping to God that this part of my plan pays off too.

"Seriously? fucking hell Jade. You hate me that much that you played me like a fool?" he bellows back at me, his black stare boring into me even in the darkness.

"Yes! You have no idea what it was like after that night. I was bullied incessantly, known as 'Ariel' for the rest of my school years, and I could never escape the memory of that horrible night that you ruined for me. It was alright for you, I heard you graduated and joined the Army, so I assumed I would never have to see you again, and even when you joined the club I could avoid you, but then you came into the bakery that day asking for my 'goodies' like nothing had ever happened. I couldn't believe you didn't recognize me—and that no one else could recognize you—so I came up with a plan to make you pay. I'm glad I did; you deserved to experience the hell you created for me all because I told you about the rules of high school. I knew it would never change; even in adult life, it was always going to be the popular kids, 'normal' kids, and then the other cliques that society creates to put us in neat pigeonholes."

"Jade, I was just a fuckin' kid! Did ya ever stop to think about the other side? I never wanted to be a jock, so I was angry too that night. If your Dad was an athlete, they'd push you as his kid to do things you hated. Those trophies were reminders of me being forced into my pigeonhole...and rather than see me, you yelled at me about the fuckin' cabinet," he snaps.

My heart sinks. I hadn't ever thought about that side of things, I naively just believed they all wanted the popularity.

His noisy breathing comes in short, heavy pants as he wrestles with his emotions. "So this is what was holding you back all this time?"

"Yes, it is. I did try and show you the real me and drop hints at the gallery. but you didn't get them, I carried on with my plan, needing to get you back for what you did. I was bullied, and taunted for years because of you, and I will never ever forgive you. I *hate* you, Dylan Anderson! Don't contact me again."

Swallowing hard, I stand up, holding my wobbling chin low to my chest, my hands hanging down limply as I walk back to the car. I pull my phone out of my pants pocket and message Kelly on autopilot.

Me: - *Babe, I'm leaving, come now if you want a ride X*

Kel: - *No, don't leave! Please don't go.*

I decide not to bother replying, and half a minute later, Kelly opens the passenger door, plopping her big booty into the seat and swiveling to face me. Her sad eyes meet mine, then the tears that I've been trying to hold in begin to cascade down my whitened face, making streak lines in my powder.

"I hate him, Kelly. I hate him!" I sob into my hands, not knowing what the hell else to do. My whole body shakes with the force of my crying as Kelly wraps her arm around me, cocooning me with her love.

"You don't mean that," she coos soothingly in my ear.

I can't even reply, silenced by the burning hole where my chest feels like it's been scooped out with a melon baller.

"You don't mean that," she repeats.

Yes! I! Do! I scream back inside my head. I hate everything he made me feel!

***

Tinhead

3am...

Fuckin' hell, I can't believe she's been pretending all this time! She had me fuckin' fooled, that's for sure!

Did everyone else know? I bet they did, and they've all been laughing about it behind my back... I knew there was something holding her back from giving into the attraction between us, but fuck! I never thought in a million years…

When that punch bowl was thrown over me, the bitter intensity of the ice-cold punch made me hold my breath, the sensation of the ice cubes sliding down my back making my eyes bulge out of my head.

As my gaze fell on Jade in costume, my head spun *with déjà* vu. I was instantly taken back to school, to the dance where I wore the exact same Dracula outfit; the black trousers, white dress shirt, shiny shoes, the dramatic black cape with red silk lining and the whitened face with dark gelled back hair. Jade's eyes shine but not with mischievousness. They're hard, shiny, and cold like a wet pebble picked up off the beach.

To my shock, she recites the words I once said to a stuck-up girl in school…then the penny drops with an almighty thud, hitting the pit of my stomach. I was frozen in time, both there in high school and here too, but the young stupid boy's words hurt me, not her. I watch her storm out of the door and replay both scenes in my head. I remember doing that to her as a younger jackass, but it was empty, a cheap laugh back when I knew nothing of my calling, nothing of how it was ripped from me, and nothing of how that very girl would shake me to my core.

***

Scanning the scarcely empty main room I nurse my 6th shot of jack since I came back in, changed, and washed myself up.

"Brother, one thing's for certain, when you pick 'em they seem to come for ya with their stinger already out." Dagger slurs out as he slips into the bar stool next to me, nearly missing it.

My chest caves in on itself as I stoop over the shots, rubbing at the back of my neck.

"Dags, she hid something huge from me and used it to get revenge; she's a sick bitch," I bite back at him as I drown my sorrows in another shot. I don't feel the burn down my throat, I don't feel anything; it's all numb, Dagger slaps his palm on my back, and then tells me,

"Tin, bro, I know you don't think she's a bitch—and if you do, don't let Jenna hear ya say that. Yeah, I know what she did was kinda messed up, but from what you've said since you came back in, she's obviously gone through a lot while you went off to the Army. ids can be cruel and vicious, and the things they do can stick with other kids until they're adults."

"She's messed up, but fuck, Dags, aren't we all in some way or another?"

He chuckles at my response.

"I hear ya, brother; I'm with you on that, but she's showed you that tonight was her letting you know her insecurities, pulling down that barrier that was stopping her all along. Most women want three things; love, respect, and to share a part of your life. So, what's stopping you from giving them to her, brother? That's what ya gotta find on your own."

I stare bewildered at Dags; he's pushing 40 and still fucks and parties like a teenager, but when he does talk to ya, it's from wisdom beyond his years.

He drains the last dregs of is bud and slapping down on my back "Right man, I'm gonna crash I'm dead to the world. Catch ya in the morning." With that and without a response he turns leaving me here at the bar grabbing the next shot I place it against my lips and the words resonate in my *ears "...tonight was her letting you know her insecurities, pulling down that barrier that was stopping her all along. Most women want three things; love, respect, and to share a part of your life."*

~ Chapter 20 Jade ~

November 24th...

It's been 3 weeks and 2 days since I last saw him. The image of him pulling and tugging at his caramel hair at the betrayal cut me deeper than it should have, but I got what I wanted. Maybe it makes me a bitch, but I thought it would be the perfect revenge, so why don't I have that sweet taste of success on my tongue? All I have is bitterness. In my heart, I know why it's there...

I don't regret it, because I did it to make him see there is nothing holding me back anymore, but as much as I want to slap his stupid face, I also want to help him. They say revenge is a dish best served cold, but that's not true if you don't have a cold heart to match.

As soon as I left the club that night, the tears I had kept at bay rolled freely down my face; not only for the teenage me, but Tinhead—I'm no better than the old him and all the other kids who hurt me now. I'm wracked with guilt, but every time I go to call to apologize my thumb hovers over the button, unable to push it. Part of me wants him to feel some of the hurt I felt, though, and doesn't see why I should be making the first move to apologize after all he did.

"You. Give me that apron now, then go upstairs, take one of my sleeping pills, and get some rest."

I look around to see that Jenna stands right next to me, but I didn't even hear her come in. I look down to see that I'm still rolling the same ball of pie dough, which now seems to have been rolled to within an inch of its life. My eyes flick up to hers, my vision swimming with unshed tears even after I blink a few times to clear my vision. "Did you hear what I said JJ? Go to bed. Go, get!"

"Sis, I'm fine."

"Let's get one thing straight, missy. You are not fine, as much as you've kept telling me that since Halloween. I know you feel ashamed about what you did, and I you've tried to reach out to apologize Jade, but sometimes as much as you try to fix it, the other person might not want it to be fixed," she says sympathetically with soft, warm look at me.

"JJ, I left him a message asking him to call me back last night. Although he's not answering my calls, at least he hasn't blocked me, right?" I joke, even though the thought makes me feel sick all over again. "Maybe you're right, though, an early night might help."

Nodding at her I hand my red spotty apron dusted with flour over to my sister, then wash up and go up to the apartment before grabbing and taking the sleeping pill Jenna offered me.

I remove my clothes, dumping them on the floor not caring where they may fall, and pulling my flannel pjs on. I climb into bed, and like every night since Halloween, I try with all my might to will myself to relax, closing my eyes and trying to ignore those hazel eyes haunting my dreams and calling me back into his world.

Even in my sleep I will him to talk to me and tell me what's happening, but there's nothing, he just smirks and winks making his eyes dance.

***

The next couple of days are the same as the past 3 weeks; get up, try to eat, work until late at the bakery or on clothes, try to sleep but fail miserably, and then press repeat. It feels like I'm stuck in *Groundhog Day*, but Bill Murray isn't here to help me.

***

At 6pm, I hear Jenna lock the door to the bakery, so I snap out of my daze and busy myself with cleaning the tables, but something's not right. I get the sensation in the pit of my stomach that I'm being watched and whirl around on my heel, stopping dead in my tracks at the sight in front of me.

In my peripheral vision, I see my Sis scampering out and up the stairs to the apartment, leaving me alone with the man who has single-handedly hurt me, fucked me, and refuses to leave my dreams. I drop my cleaning cloth onto the chrome table where I stand, but our eyes stay locked onto each other's, unmoving; I daren't blink in case he disappears.

My eyes roam over the rest of his face, but it's unreadable and stoic for the most part, void of emotion until I land on those deep pink lips of his, the corner quirked in that smile I dream about—although now he has a golden blond goatee, but it's not thick enough to rival Bear's, Daggers or even Flex's.

I flick my eyes up to his. "So what's this? You're a part of the beard brigade now?" There's a sudden lightness to my tone that I haven't had for weeks, surprising me.

His response is one that only he could get away with. "What can I say? They really *grow* on you," he retorts at with that all-American smirk as his eyes dance.

"Oh my God, Tinhead! Your ego knows no bounds, does it? That is awful, you do know that?" I throw my cleaning cloth at his face as I giggle, feeling that pit in my stomach lessen.

The cloth lands square in his face, and he breaks out into a huge grin, his eyes twinkling. Once he tugs it off, he strides in front of me, mere inches separating our bodies.

As he draws close, the air between our bodies changes, the charge of electricity tugging at me to him. Tentatively, he caresses his thumb against the apple of my cheek and rubs small circles there. When he speaks, the charge picks up again, making my heart ache.

"Jade…I'm sorry. You have to believe me. I'll do anything to right things between us."

My heart lurches, and I can't help the tears gathering in my eyes. They sting as I try to blink through them, willing them not to fall.

"Hush, Jade, it's okay. You have to believe me when I say that I was just a young naive boy. When I left and signed up…Well, let's just say I saw how the real world works. I found out it's not all about the Prom King and Queen and how many girls you can fuck behind the bleachers, and that life's a bitch. I thought you were so beautiful that day in the hall; you looked adorable with glasses. Clearly fate had its fingers around us both even then—I always did have a thing for redheads."

He grins at his own joke, and I give him a slight shove on his chest. He wraps his hand into the base of my ponytail, tugging the band free so my hair falls softly against my polo shirt.

He wastes no time in threading his fingers through my hair and kissing me like a starving man finding his next meal, devouring me. Our tongues dance, and we break apart breathlessly. I lean against his chest and he does the one thing we've never done. He wraps his arms around me and holds me, hugging me tightly against his chest.

I breathe in his sweet bergamot aftershave and the scent of freshly cut grass. I close my eyes for a brief second, basking in the moment before I open my mouth and spoil it. As I extract myself from his hold, he surveys me, confusion marring his handsome face.

I regard him again searching his eyes. I was hoping I wouldn't have to say these words, but I know I need to. "Dylan...Fuck, that sounds weird...I need to apologize to you too. You were right, I did do it for revenge. It was my intention from the first date, but with time I got to know more of you, and you surprised me. When you had that panic attack..."

"Jade, don't go there. It wasn't a panic attack, and I've got it sorted," he grinds out, adopting a defensive stance.

"No, Dylan, it was a panic attack; I've seen them enough....and experienced them too. Hear me out," I plead with him, desperation flashing in my heart. I already know he isn't going to like the next part.

He gives a quick nod, indicating I can carry on, so I take a deep breath in and try to steady my racing heart.

"As I was saying, I did what I did at Halloween not for revenge, but to show you what was holding me back because I wanted to hurt you. Now you know, and I'm not holding anything back, so can you share it with me now, please?" I implore, my throat is thick with emotion, the tears are still burning in my eyes.

His flash and narrow with momentary anger, then he blinks a few times and the look is gone like he flipped a switch.

"Jade, doll, I don't know what to tell ya...I've never had a panic attack in my life."

"Don't you dare do this, Dylan. Don't you dare." I turn away, angry that he could just lie to my face, I know I did the same to him, but not about anything like this. When he had that panic attack with me, I saw pure desolation and emptiness in his eyes. His soul was icy black, and as much as I denied it then, it was a blow to the heart to watch him like that.

"What? Jade, Come on."

"No. Don't 'come on' me, talk to me. I can get you help, I promise."

"Leave it, Jade."

"No, I won't leave it! Admit it."

"Never, there's nothing to admit."

"For fuck's sake! Admit it!" I snap at him.

"Not happening. Fuckin' hell, Jade, just drop it."

"Why? You're in fuckin' denial thinking there's nothing wrong."

"I. Said. Leave. It!" he bellows, so close that spittle speckles my face. He starts yanking and pulling at his own face, and the next thing I know he smashes his fist through the window in the main door.

I stare in complete dismay at the sight of him, the man with all the jokes who's more broken than that glass pane. I just hope I'm the right person to help put them back together…

~ Chapter 21 Tinhead ~

I don't remember punching my fist through the glass. All I remember is that Jade was going on and on about needing help and admitting I have a problem like I'm a fuckin addict. Like hell I am! Why would I want to be addicted to the fact the only time I actually feel anything is when I'm balls deep inside her and when her touch burns my skin like acid?

I had the blocking out my feelings thing down, but somehow she burns through the wall. The room spins, pressure building behind my eyes, then calms back down.

Jade's eyes roam my hand in shock, and I look down. I don't register what I see at first, but a moment later I realize I have a chunk of glass sticking out of my fist between my middle and forefinger knuckles. I yank the sizable shard out of my fist cleanly—I don't even wince at the sensation of it exiting my body. A clean towel is instantly wrapped around my fist from behind the counter, and Jade strokes my arm. Black and gold burn the edges of my sight.

"It's okay. It's okay, I'll go get help. Stay here." She tries to pull away, but I clasp my free hand around hers. Her touch scorches me and makes my heart burn, my vision starting to clear as I push the edges back into place and whisper in her ear, "I'm sorry, Jade."

"Don't you dare walk out of here, Dylan. Don't push me away," she rasps out in an attempt to fight back the tears already cascading down her cheeks. She looks painfully beautiful.

I can't admit to something I know will open a whole new can of worms, so I spare her the pain and walk away.

She deserves more than my fucked up brain. I was okay before she came along, and I'll be okay again.

***

It's been a few weeks since the last time I saw Jade, but I still remember in painstaking detail how her heartbreak was written all over her face as I turned my back on her.

It's December already, and the clubhouse has started to get decorated. I give Dani and Sue a hand with it, doing everything and anything they want. Axe asks me to do more for the club too—mainly asking for more to do, and even checking with Flex that Axe hasn't missed anything. I need to keep busy.

Even when I'm rushed off my feet, I see them all staring and hear them chatting about me. They think I don't hear, but I do.

I'm surprisingly alert even though I'm hardly sleeping and if I do it's only a few hours here and there. I think last week I probably slept 28 hours; coffee and working are my saviors. I stare up at my ceiling; it's past midnight and I'm physically and mentally drained, but it doesn't matter. Reaching into my beside drawer, I pull out one of the sleeping pills Doc gave me and grab my bottle off the side to help it go down.

I'm hoping I don't have another nightmare, but even pills can't always keep the monsters at bay.

***

"Tinhead, you're with me and Flex; I want you helping us move and distribute some of these guns. We're going to pay one of our old contacts a visit, then we have an appointment with Willy at the gun store—he said he'll buy some from us, and he's going to talk to the Irish guys over in Texas who need some more. Wrench, you go with Dags and Bear over to our Georgia chapter tomorrow, okay? I want at least 30% of these guns gone by the New Year. You okay with your instructions?"

We all holler 'aye's around the table, and he nods.

"Next thing on the agenda; I want you all to help me to plan something for Christmas Day for Dani but I need all of your help. I'm not going to say anymore yet, but I'll let you know how closer to Christmas, okay?"

Another round of 'aye's goes around the room, and then Axe slams the gavel down on the beat-up church table.

***

The next morning, we get ready to mount up to go to our first contact and see if they're interested. Axe hasn't told us who it is, he said the information is on a need-to-know basis until we arrive. Clueless as to who it could be, I shove my lid onto my head strapping on pace sunglasses for the ride—the winter sun is low in the sky today. The mic in my lid comes on and I hear the Prez's tones come through it. "Roll out."

He revs his engine, so I start up my bike. She vibrates with the need to be on the road again—I haven't ridden her much recently, I pull away, following my VP and Prez out of the clubhouse compound to our first visit of the day.

Prepared for the weather, we're all wearing thick long-sleeved shirts with our cuts over the top, but the freshness of the wind bites bitterly into my uncovered face. Most people have a face covering in these temperatures, but not me; I welcome the pain like an old friend.

***

We enter the Dyersburg Police Department, and my head spins with utter confusion.

What the hell are we doing here? I thought we were going to be meeting up with Axe's old contact…

Before the club, police stations never bothered me, but now they set my teeth on edge. My hackles rise as I start scanning the reception area, spotting the cameras in the foyer; two behind the desk and two at the front door. Looking harder, I see there's one more behind reception, another above a door down a small hallway, and a final one set into an electric door.

Axe strides up to the front desk and asks the clerk for the Chief of Police, Garth Clarke, then walks back to us with a complete poker face and waits by me and Flex.

A few minutes pass, then a heavy-set guy comes through the security door behind reception, clocks Axe, and raises his eyes in surprise. Swallowing hard, he walks casually and coolly back out the main doors we've just come through. Axe follows him first, then Flex and I trail behind, walking back down the steps.

The Chief of Police walks around the back of the vast white building and stops abruptly, whirling around.

"What's this about, Axe? Is your Pop okay?"

"Yeah, he's good. I was wondering if you wanted more guns, I have a quality shipment and I know how you liked the last load."

Whoa, fuck! This Chief is crooked!

"Sounds good to me, I can't talk about this here though, son; I'll take some as long as you have my old favorites, a Glock 22 and a Sig Sauer P226. I'll call you, but tell ya Pop that I'll be around soon."

Damn! A Glock 22 would be three figures!

Without another word, he walks back into the police station.

Axe turns to me, clearly reading my mind, "Garth's an old school friend of my Pops."

I nod, and we remount our bikes. A couple of blocks away, we pull into Willy's Gun Store. It's nothing special; a simple one-story with thick bars on all the windows and doors you have to be buzzed in to enter through. When we enter, Willy shouts across to us from behind his bullet-proof shield at the counter.

"Axe, Flex, great to see you boys! What brings you over here?" he asks, deciding to come out from behind the counter,

"Like I mentioned when I called the other night, we have…"

As Axe outlines the goods in hushed tones, I stand back near the other counters, not really looking, but I see that he has some pretty high-tech stuff that I recognize. With one ear still listening to the conversation between Axe and Willy about the Sig

Sauers he's interested in, my eyes roam the opposite glass display case…Then I see it.

I have made sure not to be around them all this time—the sight of it makes the acid boil in my stomach. Gripping the edge of the case so fiercely my knuckles turn white, I can't bring myself to pull my eyes off it.

"Tin! Tin, you okay, brother."

I spin around, flinching as the sound of Flex's voice jars me out of my trance and trying not to look back at the AK 47 gleaming at me under the spotlights in the display case.

"You all right?" he asks with a slight frown.

"Uh…yeah, VP. All good, all good."

I don't really hear the rest of the conversation in the background, but watch Axe shaking Willy's hand and clapping him on the back in the deafening silence, and then we leave.

I feel like I'm stumbling, but to my relief I get my hearing bac on the bike. Riding always clears my mind, and I love that I don't have to think.

All I want is to feel free from the turmoil. All of it.

Chapter 22

Jade

Christmas Day...

Ever since I was a little girl, I have loved everything about Christmas; the presents, family, Santa, and the need to eat anything and everything in sight until your stomach aches and don't wanna move. One Christmas when we were younger, even after we had stuffed our faces with turkey and all the trimmings and apple pie, when Momma fell asleep in front of the TV, me and Jenna snuck into the kitchen and pulled the wrapped-up turkey breast and leftover apple pie out of the fridge and sat on the kitchen floor gorging ourselves even more until we both had tummy ache.

I woke up Momma from her sleep to tell her I felt sick, but when I opened my mouth to tell her, I puked violently all over Momma and the couch. Even after I had been put to bed, my stomach still ached like it was being twisted in two. I never did that ever again, but Momma brings it up every year without fail. Jenna just laughs, mouthing the exact story word for word.

I swore to my Momma and myself that I would never have that feeling in my tummy again, but that's exactly how my stomach feels right now, twisting itself in knots and chewing itself up.

I'm standing in my bathroom staring at my reflection as the shower steam still swirls around me. I feel physically sick; I've been dry heaving for most of this morning and can't bear to eat. We're going to the club today; Bear invited us and Jenna insisted I go as we've never had a Christmas apart and she doesn't want to start now. My heart says I need to go and be there for Jenna, but he's there. I don't think I can be in the same room as him without my heart aching.

When he left that night in the bakery, he looked like a lost man on a desert island. I don't know how else I can reach him now; the only thing he knows is how to use sex to make him feel something—anything. I saw the absolute desperation in his soul clawing inside as he took me against the sink the last time we fucked.

I numbly start applying my makeup, needing to apply war paint again. I'm wearing a dress Kelly chose for me last night—even when I insisted I didn't think it was a good idea, she carried on, saying *'Fuck him, Jadey! You're better than him.'*

By the time I apply the last layer of mascara, I don't recognize myself—I have smoky gold eyes, lined like a cat's to look bigger. I walk out of the bathroom in a haze of fear and nervousness, my stomach still twisting and churning. I let my hair tumble free out of my loose bun, then carefully finger comb it out to how I want it to look.

I pull the dress off the hanger and slip it over my head, tugging it gently until the fabric hugs my curves. Once I'm dressed, I close my closet, letting it shut in a whisper to check myself over in the mirror. The girl looking back at me doesn't look like me at all. The dress fits me perfectly; it's a red leopard-print dress with capped sleeves and a deep V neckline that stops in between my breasts. The fabric hugs me, skimming down my body and stopping a bit lower than mid-thigh.

I shove my feet into my favorite black round-toed pumps, and after grabbing my black coat I storm out of my bedroom like a tornado.

I'm just not going to think about him; I'm not letting him ruin my Christmas with my sister and my friends. If he wants to talk to me, then so be it.

My sister and Bear are waiting in the lounge as I come around the corner from my room, and Jenna looks stunning in her emerald green satin dress. She has her down naturally too, but she's wearing the cutest snowflake hair grip. She gives me a big grin, beaming at me. "You ready?"

"As I'll ever be, JJ," I reply.

I just hope I'm right...

***

Tinhead

Christmas fuckin' day. Fuckin' hell, where the hell has the year gone?

I had a pretty good sleep after taking 2 of the sleeping pills—I crashed around 11ish last night and I've not long woken up at 10am—yet my head still feels like I'm in a complete fog.

I jump in the shower, the heat and pressure of the water instantly cleaning off the stickiness and sweat of sleep. I usually only sweat like this with flashbacks, but if I had a dream, I don't remember it. I squeeze shower gel into my palms, lathering it, then glance at my semi-hard dick. Without another thought, I fist myself, thinking of the strawberry-blond beauty with catlike eyes calling to me even though I know she hates me. I picture her greedy pussy dripping with the need to be fucked, and absently hum.

Happy Birthday to you, Happy Birthday to you. Happy Birthday dear me, Happy Birthday to you…

All at once, I feel the familiar tingling and shoot my cum up over the shower tiles.

Fuck that was quick…

I get out of the shower, drying myself as I walk back into my room. I need to get myself dressed fast and go to help set up the bar and table, so I pull out fresh jeans and a black Harley t-shirt before shoving my legs into my boxers and my jeans, then pulling on socks and my boots. Leaving my room, I grab my cut and t-shirt, tugging my t-shirt over my head and sliding my arms into my cut. I stride into the main room, immediately mesmerized by the sight that awaits me.

Fuckin' hell, this place looks like Buddy the Elf threw up in here!

Tree lights have been hung over the bar, walls, and any available surface—including the existing light fixtures.

"Santa's balls, the place looks like the North Pole!" I say into the room.

"Hey Tin, can you come and help me carry the chairs up from the basement?" Wrench greets me from behind the bar, popping up like a jack-in-the-box.

I snigger at his outfit, he's wearing a red t-shirt on that's got a cartoon Santa on it, but instead of a normal Santa hat, he's wearing a sombrero that says *'Santa's a Mexicana'*, fuckin' fool.

I grin at him. "Lead the way, *hermano*."

***

Once we have arranged the table and chairs and cleaned them all up, Sue, Zara, and Dani come out of the kitchen and start arranging the table settings while Wrench and Brains help me bring up the crates of beer and wine that Axe bought especially for today—along with some champagne that cost him about $300 a bottle.

As I'm walking back through to the bar, I freeze in my tracks, faced with a sight that steals the breath out of my lungs.

Her eyes burn green fire as she stares back at me, handing her coat to Bear. The world fades into silence as she stands there in the sexiest dress— deep red with large leopard spots on, the fabric leaving her creamy white legs on show.

My eyes roam her body, burning in the image into my memory. She's the first to look away, glancing to the side. When she looks back, her eyes are emotionless. She stalks over to stand by her sister's side and starts wishing everyone a Merry Christmas.

Her being here makes my chest ache; I wish I could explain things, but I don't want the filth inside me to touch her. I have to have her again one last time, like an addict craving a fix.

Just one more hit. One more taste.

***

Jade

I knew it would hurt seeing him. I had just walked through the club door, and he was standing there with his Harley shirt stretched across his arms—arms that have held me as I have come apart. We just stared at each other, unmoving.

After Bear took my coat, I could hear my sister's muffled voice calling me over to the girls, so I risked a look away, Jenna's smile giving me the strength to pull away from the gravity that's tugging at me over to him.

I hate that I feel this way; I want to help, but he won't let me in—or his brothers in the club either, given that Bear's never mentioned Tin's panic attacks.

***

I've been helping the rest of the girls in the kitchen and am busy storing the desserts that Jenna made—a sweet potato pie, an apple pie, and a Christmas-themed red velvet cake with vanilla cream frosting and edible gold glitter, finished with a sprig of holly on top.

After checking the turkey, Jenna turns to me. "I'll see you back out there, babe—Zara wants to show me the new leather jacket Flex bought for Christmas."

"Yeah, sure thang, Sis. I won't be long."

Her eyes soften. "I love you JJ, everything will be alright," she tells me with a small smile before leaving me to reorganize the fridge to accommodate the desserts.

I think I have it this time, if I just move bottle there and but the pie on top of that packet of cheese the cake should fit on the bottom shelf I'm just in the middle of sliding the cake into the fridge when I hear the kitchen door open.

I'd know that scent anywhere. It sends shivers up my body, making the hairs stand on end as I feel a wave of electricity radiating from the man behind me. I don't move from my bent position.

I hate the way we left things, but I also hate this barrier he has between us…and that my panties are soaked at the thought of him taking me from behind.

"Jade…"

My heart races knowing he's so close to me, but I straighten up and close the fridge.

I can't go there with him; he's going to leave scars on my heart if he fucks me again—each time he does, I lose more of myself. Don't look at him, you'll *crumble,* I tell myself.

I steel myself, my spine straightening. I take a deep, painful breath in, and his scent surrounds me, wrapping around my heart. I pivot on the ball of my foot and walk to the door, but just as he steps out of the way and I think I'm clear, I feel his fingers wrap tightly around my wrist.

I try to extract myself from him, but it's no use—he gives me a sharp tug and I step back into the kitchen, slamming against his firm, warm body.

I can feel his heart pounding against mine, but I still can't meet his eyes—they may seem empty and bottomless, but I see the self-torture and persecution inside.

"Red, look at me. I need to know, did you fake the orgasms I pulled from your body?" he asks accusingly.

I whip my head up, meeting his eyes, and the bastard has the dirtiest grin on his gorgeous face, his eyes glittering at me with amusement as his plan worked. The bastard!

"Fuck you, Dylan! I can't believe you!" I shove out of his hold, pushing back against his muscular body. I hate the fact that the sparks are still there, sizzling on my skin as I try to pull away.

He doesn't let me, but pushes me against the counter. Just as my butt hits the edge of the work surface, he grinds his cock into the apex of my thighs.

"Ahhh...don't. We can't keep doing this, Tinhead. I may want you to fuck me, but I didn't sign up for my heart and head being fucked over too."

"I'm not fuckin' with your heart. I want you, I want to be inside you, and when I'm not inside you, I want to be with you, inside you and claiming you." he rasps against the curve of my neck, sending goosebumps shooting up and around my body and making me tremble.

"I can't..." I whisper out into the room.

The sounds of our heavy breathing fill my ears, my skin burning from the searing heat of our bodies rubbing against each other. My gaze finally holds his and I'm utterly transfixed by his eyes—they're blazing with desire.

He bends down and captures my lips, commanding my mouth. I could drown inside the kiss; I just can't say no the hint of desperation tells me he needs this as much as I do. I squirm in his tight grasp, rubbing my pussy against his denim-clad cock, thick and rock hard.

"I need you, Jade...more than you know," he gasps.

"I know you do...so fuck me already," I rasp out between heavy breaths.

The next moment, we're all hands. He shoves my dress up my thighs with urgency, pushing it up to my waist to expose my plum-colored lacy thong and ass. Underneath it, the counter is icy cold.

I'm grabbing at his jeans, trying to unbutton them as fast as possible, but my hands are shaking. He takes control, shoving his jeans and boxers down his golden thighs. His juicy thick cock juts out at me, and I instinctively lick my lips at the sight.

"My face is up here, Sugar Tits," he chuckles, making his cock bounce around freely. My pussy clenches at the vision that is this gorgeous, dominant man.

"Shut the fuck up, Captain Crunch."

In response, he tugs my thong to the side, sliding his fingers up and down my wet slit. I moan into the quietness of the kitchen before catching myself.

Fuck, what if someone hears us?

"Don't worry they're all too busy drinking before dinner to hear us. If they could, they'd hear how soaking your pussy is," Tinhead tells me, reading my mind. To prove the point, he shoves two of his fingers deep inside of me and thumbs my bud.

"Ah, fuck! Where's your condom?"

He withdraws his fingers from inside of me painfully slowly and sucks them into his mouth, which has to be one of the most erotic things I've ever seen him do. He produces a condom from his cut pocket, rolling it down over his dick to cover.

Mmmm, it's ribbed—my favorite. I don't get to stare for much longer before his lips latch onto mine seeking my tongue, needing it like a man possessed. The passionate kiss ends abruptly, leaving me completely breathless. I find myself in a mesmerized trance as our eyes bore into each other—the heat and sensation is intoxicating.

I take hold of his cock, fisting him tightly exactly how I know he likes it.

"Jade...get off the counter and turn around," he barks at me, extracting my fingers from around his cock.

I slide off the counter until my feet touch the ground, and as soon as they do, he spins me on the spot and bends me over the counter. I can smell my arousal in the spot where I was sitting.

"Spread those fuckin' sexy legs," he orders in a gruff voice. I do as he tells me, and as soon as I do, he buries his cock inside me. We groan in unison, his cock painfully hard as he thrusts. I buck back against him, making him fuck me harder, our movements raw and needy.

As he hammers away at me, I long to see his face—the pots and pans in front of me hanging on the tiles are no good. His thrusts start get jerky, his nails digging hard enough to leave crescent moon marks on my hips. His fingers come around to my front, seeking my clit. Once he finds it, he strokes and rubs it eagerly, chasing my orgasm—he must be about burst too.

I gyrate back against him and am rewarded with the delicious feeling of him ramming me full of his cock.

"Fuck yeah, babe, just like that!" he grunts loudly.

God I love when he's like this and his barriers are down...

He tugs my hair hard, and I feel the sting in my scalp, but he doesn't relent in fucking me.

"Harder..." I mumble to him.

For a moment, I think he didn't hear, but then he pounds me like a wild animal mating, making me scream out.

"Ahhhh!"

"Fuck...Jade..." he hisses, torturing me.

He fucks me harder than ever, bringing me to the edge, then stopping and starting slow again.

I whip my head up and around to tell him to hurry the fuck up and finish what he started, but the sudden move sends the pots and pans hanging up above my head crashing onto the floor.

We stop and stand there, frozen in fear.

Shit! What if someone comes out to see what that noise was!

After a tense few minutes, we realize no one heard, and Tinhead slams back into me so hard I can feel his balls slap against my ass, not missing a beat. We don't stop working each other—he fucks me and I swivel my hips around his cock, both of us desperate for our release.

He thumbs my clit again, playing me like a harp as his movements start to become more. He grunts as he takes me again and again, and I barely hold back squeals of pure pleasure. My thighs are slick with wetness, but I don't care—I love the feeling of it. The atmosphere around us is thick with our panting and scent, making me even wetter.

He pounds harder, and I meet him stroke for stroke as a shot of ecstasy blazes around my body. Tinhead convulses on top of me, roaring loudly in my ear. Hearing him cum makes me come undone explode and shatter against him, my walls clenching the life out of his cock.

The urgency dissipates, replaced with our shared gasping for breath. After a few seconds of Tinhead practically laying on my back with exhaustion, he gingerly slides out and stands behind me.

"Fuck me that's a beautiful sight," he murmurs.

"What's that?" I ask in a breathy voice, still coming down from my high.

"Your cum dripping down your legs," he growls at me as he pockets the used condom.

"Should have taken a picture it lasts longer," I jibe with a smirk on my lips.

"Ha ha!" Tinhead replies sarcastically. "You won't need it doll; tonight you're going to be in my bed getting fucked."

"Dream on, lover-boy. I wouldn't hold my breath if I was you."

"Come on Red, you know you want to."

"I don't want to talk about this. Let's just enjoy Christmas Day, okay?" I tell him. On unsteady legs, I pull my thong back into place and shuffle my dress down.

"What d'ya mean? Why don't ya wanna spend the night here?" he asks with a boyish grin and twinkle in his eye.

"Because this was the last time, Tinhead. I can't do this again."

The twinkle disappears, but his grin doesn't slip. "Fuck no. Why?"

"You know why, I told you in the bakery. You're in denial thinking there's nothing wrong with what you're going through. You need help, and until you get it, I don't think I can do this."

I hope to God that I'm strong enough to get through to him…

"Watching you is tearing me apart inside. Please, Dylan? No one else needs to know about it, but until I can't give a part of me over to you when I get nothing back."

"Jade, what are ya—" he starts.

I cut him off before he can give me a bullshit response.

"Please!" I implore him, tears stinging at the back of my eyes. "We've come a long way since we first began whatever this is, and I can see through the cracks in your mask, Dylan! I can see who you're really hiding from everyone. *I see you.* You always want to fuck from behind so I can't see into your eyes, but guess what? I did anyway; I saw everything. I see the fragments you try to hold together. With all the chaos you've seen and been through, if you're not going to talk to me, you sho—"

"D'ya ever just stop?!" he bites back at me, his front firmly in place.

"You're just mad I figured you out sooner than your brothers! What's wrong with the Prom King, you pissed I burst your fucking bubble?"

"No. I'm pissed off you think you know me when YOU FUCKIN' DON'T! You don't know what I've seen and can't unsee. You don't know smells so putrid they would make your stomach split in two. You don't know how much blood I've seen pour out of someone…like it's a goddamn waterfall! You don't know what it's like having to kill…So don't give me that bullshit that you know me! You don't know shit all, little fashion princess! Get your nosy ass outta my life!" he growls right in my face, backing me against the wall.

Unfazed, I do what I'm good at and dig my heels in. Deep.

I stab my fingernail into his chest, near his heart.

"Well, ya know what, buddy?! I ain't going anywhere. I'm here to make your life worse! When you get your head outta your ass and realize you need to talk to someone I'll be there, but until then you know where to find me!"

With that, I do one of the hardest things I've had to do since being with Tin—I turn on my heel and walk out of the door, hoping to God he realizes and I can pull him through to the other side.

It kills me watching this happy-go-lucky man blow away like ashes from in the wind and float away until he's nothing.

If he does, it will kill me inside, shatter the very soul of me…

~ Chapter 23 Tinhead ~

Since the fight this morning, I've tried to keep away from Jade, but she was here until 10pm. After she left me in the kitchen, I had to fight the urge to grab her and force her to see there's nothing wrong with me.

There is nothing wrong with me…There's nothing wrong.

But if she thinks that, then the others must do too…

I bet she's told them things about me the way I fuck her.

Jesus, now there's something wrong with me because I love doggy-style?

I spend the rest of the night propping up the bar—I lose count of how many drinks I've had, but it's not enough.

At around 2am Flex eventually drags my sorry ass to my room, dumping me on my bed face-down.

Once I'm there, the dark abyss calls to me, clawing at my mind and soul and pulling me under. I know I'm not strong enough to pull away from it.

I don't take any sleeping tablets tonight, come what may. I'll deal with the hand I'm dealt—if I have to dance with the devil, so be it. I know Hell well, I've been there, and I always get dragged back in my nightmares…

***

I watch flashes of gold, orange and red swirl around in my mind's eye. As I stare at it, my vision turns crimson then slowly black, like blood washed away in a downpour.

Blood…

So much blood…

So much fuckin' blood…

***

"GET DOWN!" I scream from the doorframe as I watch three of my comrades go down.

It happened so fuckin' fast; the bullets came at us through the windows of this rundown shack in the pits of Hell.

I used to think there was no way anyone in their right mind would risk living here, but this is the only place some have ever had.

There's a family of 5 at the end of this cesspit they call their neighborhood—the little boy, Omar, has taken a shine to me, and when we come around the corner he wants me to play catch with him.

He's got two sisters that are too young to understand who we are, and the kid himself is lucky to have reached 4 or 5. It's a good job I trained him in advanced combat care to help the wounded when there was no medic around...

My best bud Arnold "Arnie" Thompson and I are thick as thieves, always kicking a ball around or trying to keep busy by playing pranks when we were on our down time.

As I watch him go down in front of me, I try to call for help, but I know we are surrounded. The radio lines are likely tapped by the insurgents as well—to use them would be to kill us all. I glance back over at Arnie; he *has a huge piece of shrapnel in his left arm blood dripping out of him in a slow, steady trickle.*

I know it's bad—the loss of blood doesn't help, but it's the location that's so dangerous. If I try to move it, he could bleed to death. If the shrapnel is as deep as I think it is, it could be in the axillary artery that leads to the heart…

We were outnumbered out there—I know there were more than five men firing just by the sheer rounds they shot at this shack, I stare over at the bodies of two of my closest friends scattered across the floor with all their gear and packs still on.

They're unmoving, and I know without checking that Scott "Bean" McKenzie and Corey "Paddy" O'Connor are either dead or bleeding out. At least Arnie is still conscious for now.

I can't even get to them, as if I moved across this empty shell we used as shelter, they'd hear or see me move across the shot-out windows even if I stripped down to my boxers and shimmied my body across the floor. I'd be cut to ribbons before I even had the chance with the number of shards of glass scattered across the floor. If I live, I'll still have to wait it out until nightfall to check on them and see if their radios are working— another two hours at most looking at the way the sun hangs low in the sky.

I flick my eyes back over to Arnie. He's trying to put pressure on his own wound but he's not doing it hard enough. I pull out my K-Bar knife and use it to tear off some of his combat pants at the ankle to get a piece of fabric thick enough to go around his arm twice—a lot, considering that the dude's arms are as thick as most men's calves. I split the camo fabric in half, apply pressure to the five-inch puncture wound that runs diagonally across his bicep, and strap the gauze I pull out of my pack to it.

"This is gonna hurt like a bitch, Arnie," I grimace.

"Get on with it. Don't try and get all soft on me now, ya bastard."

I stare at him, then give him a quick nod and with a sharp tug pull the tourniquet tightly to stem the bleeding. Hearing the hiss come out of Arnie as I do ain't helping feel much better about things—I've seen him take gashes and dog bites without a sound.

Moving swiftly, I tie the last of the fabric into a knot. "There ya go, keep ya panties on!"

"Fuck off! It tickles that's all, he manages, his breathing getting faster.

"Take it easy, Arnie. You have to keep your heart rate steady." I check his pulse on his wrist—slow. "Save your strength, okay? You want any more water?" I ask him, resting his head back on the makeshift pillow of his pack.

"Yeah, pass the water you greedy shit!"

"Even with a chunk of shrapnel in your arm and dripping blood everywhere, you still got an attitude Arnie. Here, try not to sup it all down." I pass him one of the canteens we have between us. "Rest up bro, I'll keep watch. It's quiet for the moment, but who knows for how long?"

***

I glance my eyes from the open windows to Arnie, then and back to our friends who are still laying unmoving.

Fuck, I need to get to them.

I scan the ground, looking through the empty window frames and back again to gauge if I could risk it from the other side of the room to where they lay near the open windows.

"Don't even fucking think about it. You're no use to any of us dead, Anderson. I'm already gonna get medically discharged for this; think of the pension and the hot nurses." Arnie tries to joke, but I hear the jumpiness in his voice; the thought of any of us getting out of the army that way guts us.

From his position in the corner of the room, he watches over our comrades.

I'm hoping to hell we get out of this together, but I know the odds aren't great—we're like sitting ducks.

"I was only judging the distance to see if I could. I know I need to wait until sundown, which by my estimation should only be another 30 minutes or so."

The only sound from outside is the wind starting to pick up and mixing with the grit on the dusty road, stones being picked up by the gusts and hurled at shot up and burnt out cars that are haphazardly scattered up and down this neighborhood. I look over to my right at the torn and faded dirty cream wallpaper peeling away from the wall like an old scab peeling away from new skin. I realize this room was once their living space and bedrooms. The chipped paint with fresh bullet holes above mine and Arnie's heads is a grubby pale blue shade, the far end of this section of the room a shade of baby pink…

If you ever needed a reality check on how we live back at home, this shack—no, this whole fucking country—is it.

Most families where we are stationed have only the clothes on their backs and their children to call their own, but to them that's all they need. We went to a nearby neighborhood this morning, and they were all hungry but ecstatic as we handed out food and clothing parcels for each family, their faces lighting up with such gratefulness. They find happiness in the simplest of things—not in having the best phone or gadget money can buy, but in each other; friends and family; that's all they need.

Just then, I come back from zoning out, glancing back down at Arnie before grabbing his wrist and checking his pulse for the umpteenth time. It's still slow, but steady; I just need to keep him alive long enough to get help.

"Quit holding my hand ya big woman, I'm still here...just."

Rolling my eyes, I check over his wound to make sure it's still stemmed and hand him my canister again, rummaging through my kit to grab my night goggles ready to use them. As we sit around and wait for the sun to set, I find myself glancing through the open window. The shells of buildings across the way have no movement in them and are too eerily quiet. It's engrained into us not to trust silence and it always expect the unexpected—our Corporal drilled that into us until we said it in our motherfucking sleep.

***

At nightfall, I start to shift around and pass Arnie more water. After I've had some too, I ask him in hushed tones, "You good if I go and make the move to check on Bean and Paddy?"

I slide my goggles over my face in preparation, pulling on the straps at the sides.

"Yeah, go and check on them I'll slide over close to ya if you need me, so kick some of the glass out the way, okay?

I gesture to the pool of blood. "Bud, there ain't any way you're going to be able to help me. You best not be using ketchup packets you stole from Smithy to make that look worse, or I'll kill ya myself for putting me through all this."

"Shut up, dick! You're just hating that ya gotta nurse my sorry ass better. Go check on them; I'll still be here ya ugly fuck!"

"I look better than you're looking right about now." Even though I was joking, his smile falls at the last part, and I instantly feel like a dick. "Arn…"

"Don't. I know what ya meant, twat."

I stare outside for a moment, then start sweeping the glass out of the way of where I'm going to be crawling, then I lay flat against the worn-out carpet and start crawling using my fists and feet to move stealthily across the dirty, dusty floor. I only move a few inches at first, listening out for an any movement outside. There's nothing, but as I move again, I hear shuffling from behind me. I lay flat against the floor as I twist my head around to glance at Arnie shuffling on his back, trying to follow my path.

"You're a stubborn motherfucker! Why didn't you wait there?" I whisper.

"Shut up. I'm trying to help you, dick; I need to see them too…"

His voice breaks off, but I know exactly what he means; we both need closure. I just give him a curt nod and turn back again, peering out of the open window across the street and finally getting a clearer picture of how things are outside the building directly across from us. My heart skips a beat as my eyes land on the far corner window and I see through a lone figure with what looks like an AK-47 in his grasp through the lime-green sight of the night vision goggles. I look to the right, where two more men with guns strapped to their sides stand behind net curtains.

Fuck!

"Can you see any?"

I hesitantly tell Arnie the truth "Yeah. Three at least. Stay down."

"Fuck!"

I shuffle across the rest of the floor, deciding I'll check the other buildings in a minute. I finally reach our friends and stay laying on my stomach but lean up on my elbows. Staring back at me is Bean, my now confirmed dead friend that I've only known this tour Bean. His face is drenched with blood from the shot to his eye, chunks of gray matter splattered across the floor behind him. I've never been squeamish, but it's chilling and disturbing to seeing your friend's brain matter strewn across the dusty carpet when only this morning you were chatting about how big the new Officer's tits were.

I know this sight will be imprinted on my mind forever…

~ Chapter 24 ~

Jade

New Year's Day 2:41am

2:41am will be a time forever engrained into my brain…

ZZZZ…ZZZZ…ZZZZ…
Turning over to my side, I look over with one eye open at my nightstand clock.
What the hell?
I feel for my buzzing phone on the nightstand and knock it clean off, then peer down at the screen and see Sue's name flash up.
What the hell is she ringing me at this time for? If she gives me another earful about not coming to the club for the New Year's Eve party I swear I'll scream. Only Kelly and Jenna know why I can't go over there again.
My phone rings out, but immediately starts vibrating again, I struggle to reach down and get it, but finally grab it after a couple of tries. Bringing my phone up to my, ear I answer with a yawn. "Hey Sue."
"Jade? Is that you?" Doc responds, shocking me.
Oh fuck!
"Oh my God, has something happened to Sue?" I start to panic, feeling guilty for taking so long to pick up.
"What? She's fine, darlin', but I need you to come to the club."

"What? Now, ya mean?" I ask curiously.

What's going on?

"Yeah darlin', as soon as you can. Come alone, he answers. His measured tone slips halfway through, and I hear his voice grow thick with emotion…fear?

"Doc, what's going on? You're scaring me."

Somewhere deep down in the pit of my stomach, I know what he is going to say, but it doesn't stop the bile rising to my mouth as the words come through the speaker.

"It's Tin. He's got a gun."

***

Tinhead

December 31st - New Year's Eve

They're all out to get me.

They think I don't know that they're trying to push me out of the club. Well I do, and I ain't going—they'd have to kill me and prize my dead fists off my cut.

Is Doc staring at me? He and Sue look up at me with curious looks across their faces.

What the hell? I haven't done anything to them. I've been a loyal soldier; always have.

The past few days since Christmas have been worse, I haven't slept since the night I relived my nightmare in hell. There's no point trying to fight them anymore; they've been getting more and more vivid since I met Jade. My muscles ache constantly and I'm always on edge, watching and waiting for something else to go wrong or be added to my list of fuck ups.

I use coffee to keep awake enough to concentrate, but even the shitload of caffeine pumping through my blood it doesn't help. Only a bit of alcohol helps to numb the pain now—all right, a *lot* of alcohol. I don't even wanna ride on my bike to calm myself anymore, and I hate that I feel even emptier than I did a year ago. The noise of this place does help a little, but my brothers and the women are too much.

I feel like I'm trapped again…like I'm back in that run-down shell in Afghan…

Her words play out on repeat, swirling in my head like a hurricane…

I can see through the cracks in your mask, Dylan! I can see who you're really hiding from everyone. I see you…

Fuckin' bitch, she knows nothing about me or anything I've gone through. This is all normal; every soldier gets this when they come back…

Yet it's been years, why has all this history come back to haunt me? I remember seeing Jade's pain etched on her face as clearly as if she'd carved it there with a rusty razor blade, I saw how tears welled in her eyes; she tried to hide it, but she gave up on me too.

There's nothing wrong with me, it's all in her head, what does she know? She hates me, so the tears were clearly from despising me.

What do you expect? You deserve it, you bastard! You killed him.

No!

YES! You left him for dead after all you went through. That's how you pay back a friend?

I didn't mean to! D'ya not think I wish I could take back what happened every day? Do you not think I hate that I got out and he died?

You killed him! And you know they're conspiring against you. They don't want you patched in anymore; they want you out. Who the fuck wants a soldier who's fucked in the head?

I'm not fucked in the head! There's nothing wrong with me.

You keep telling yourself that pal, if you say it enough times you might start believing it. But trust me, everyone is better without you.

***

The club falls silent as everyone heads to bed; eerily quiet.

Tonight's the night. Axe is at home with Dani and Ryker, Flex and Zara are at their apartment, Bear and Jenna are at the bakery, and the only ones left here are all asleep—I'm thankful my room is right at the back of the club. I don't note the time; what does that matter now?

I fall onto my bed, and I can't seem to pin a thought down. All I know is that this is it for me. This is how I should have gone out back then. Put down. Ended. Exterminated. All I can envision is me dead; me holding this gun underneath my chin and firing it.

I get off my bed, go over to my closet, and open it fully, standing up on my tip toes to reach at the back of the shelf and get what I stored up there.

Bingo.

Pulling the box, I heave it down and put it on my bed. I haven't opened this box since I came home from Afghanistan after being medically discharge, but I don't feel anything as I peel off the lid and am hit with the musty smell of dust.

I rifle through the box, reaching under my camo, badges and beret to find what I came for, tugging it to the surface. As I do, something white catches my eye and floats down.

Pain hits like a stab to the gut as I see it's a picture of me and Arnie camoed up, arms around each other's shoulders with matching big smiles. Grabbing the picture in my fist I sit back on my bed, unlocking the case I pulled from the larger box.

Here it is, my Glock 22 in all its glory…

As seamlessly as riding a bike, I start reassembling and checking it. I pull the slide back onto the frame, pull back on the it, and work it back and forth the spread the lubrication on the underside around the inside of the pistol. After pulling and holding the trigger I listen for the *click*, then pull back on the slide and slowly let up on the trigger before finally checking the magazine—five rounds are more than enough—and inserting it. I place the icy cool metal barrel of the gun underneath my chin, my finger rests on the trigger, then I go to squeeze...

There is a fine line between a hero and a monster…

My heart clenches so fiercely at Doc's words that I immediately scurry out of bed and rush to change into my jeans, not giving a shit that I'm wearing my PJ top. I put my feet into my Chucks, grab my phone and run out of my room, trying my hardest not to disturb my sister and Bear.

I practically fall down the apartment stairs and rush out of the back door to my car. As I slide behind the wheel of the car, I will myself to calm down, but my whole body won't stop trembling. My hands slicken with sweat, so I hastily rub them down my jeans and I try and calm my racing heart rubbing my palm over it.

Please, God…

It wrenches with anxiety, but I steady my breathing as I speed over to the club. The streets I pass are nearly deserted; there are a few drunken stragglers either going to or from their homes or the bars, but they all blur past in the blink of an eye. They don't matter, all that matters is that I get to the man who has claimed my heart.

Jesus, a fuckin' gun!

I know they all have them and it's normal for the club life, but this is different. After we left things at Christmas, I knew things were bad, but I would never have envisioned this. Never in a million years. I'm petrified that I'm too late.

What if I pushed him into this? Oh God!

***

I soon arrive at the club to see that Doc's left the gates open for me. I speed into the compound, not caring that I park right up in front of the club door. I fly out of the car, leaving the driver's door wide open and not giving a fuck.

I storm through the clubhouse door, my eyes scanning around wildly looking for, someone, anyone, when I hear Sue crying down the hall.

Oh God, please no! Don't do this to me...

I take a painful breath in, holding it as I round the corner down towards Tinhead's bedroom. I feel my eyes bulging out of my sockets, and I'm terrified of what I'm about to find.

I see Sue standing outside an open door, doubled over and sobbing against the wall. The next moment, I can hear Doc's gravelly voice talking in soothing tones, but then my ears are deafened by the roar of a man screaming at him.

I move closer, inching to the door as Doc retreats.

"Get. The Fuck. OUT! I don't need you."

Tinhead slams the door shut in Doc's face, the sound ricocheting off the door frame. That raw pain in his voice crumbles a chunk of my heart.

I place my hand on Doc's arm and he jumps out of his skin, pinning me with his stare.

Fear swirls in his eyes, then he recognizes me and they soften slightly. "Oh, Jade darlin', I'm so glad you're here."

Hearing my name, Sue whips her head up and launches herself at me. "Oh, honey. I've never seen anyone like it! Since Christmas he has grown more distant and insular. That happy-go-lucky boy has slipped away, and I'm absolutely terrified. We'd been laying in bed when I woke Doc up to check on Tinhead because somethin' told me I had to. I'd been seeing him deteriorate for a while, but today he was even more quiet. Doc…found what he did, and rang you while I was trying to talk to Tin, b-but he wouldn't—or couldn't—listen to me. Jade, he's lost, so lost! I don't know what has brought this on, but I love him as if he's my own." She chokes the last part out as she sobs, and my heart breaks for her.

"Jade. Please try and reason with him—he's still got the gun. We found him with it under his chin, staring into space. I knew something was going on when he asked for sleeping pills. He's not been sleeping well for months, but I didn't realize how bad he actually was, I struggled when I came back from service myself, but this? It's been a good few years now, but seeing him this reminds me a few of my old buddies. He's gotten worse since you've gotten closer," he admits hesitantly.

"I knew it; I knew I was pushing him and making him worse! How the hell am I gonna be able to help if I'm making him worse?" I screech in a packed voice as fear grips ahold of my heart, squeezing.

I hear an almighty crash of wood on wood, and guttural sobs are ripped from the broken man in the next room before he bellows through the door. "I can hear you talking about me. Just leave me the fuck alone!" The last sentence is louder, like he's pressed up against the door.

I feel tears stinging the back of my eyes, but Doc shakes his head. "No no, it's a good thing…I mean, he had to reach the bottom to face it head-on. I think he needs you more than you know."

My chin and lips wobble at the thought that I'm all who can save the man who broke down my defenses. Steeling myself, I grab the door handle, already on the verge of hyperventilation. I twist the handle and push myself through the door to find that it's pitch black except for the light of the moon glittering through his window, illuminating one side of his face and leaving the other in pure darkness—the juxtaposition isn't lost on me.

I stand frozen to the spot, taking in the sight of his bedroom in complete disarray. Broken glass decorates most surfaces, and he's sitting on his bed staring down at his hands. He reminds me of a frightened little orphan boy; I just hope I can reach him.

He doesn't hear me enter the room until I shut the door behind me, bracing myself, but nothing prepares me for the look on his face.

He's not broken; that's too mild a word. He's *imploded* on himself—he's slammed that self-destruct button, and this is what is left now, having shattered into tiny shards. His cheeky smile that made me fall for him is gone, his laughing eyes are nonexistent, and the smirk that makes me a pool of goo has disappeared.

I stand still expecting him to devour me like usual, but he just gives me a stare of nothingness that goes right through me like I'm not here. It chills me to my bones.

"You shouldn't be here. Go home, Jade," he says flatly.

My heart aching for him, I see him rocking his left wrist back and forth on the bed. I inch closer, and my heart stops at what I see. I know Doc warned me, but seeing it in his hand so casually stop me in my tracks. His gun twitches in his palm as he stares straight through the wall opposite him.

"I'm not going anywhere," I tell him calmly and softly.

At first, I don't think he heard me, but when I go to open my mouth again, he snaps, "Leave. Now. Things are about to get messy."

His words send a chill down my spine, but I stand firm. "No, I'm not going anywhere. I'm staying here, I've come…for you," I gasp out.

Fuck, that was the wrong thing to say.

He jumps up off his bed, stomping his way towards me and waving his gun around.

I can't tear my eyes away in horror; I hope to God it doesn't go off.

I risk another glance at his eyes, hoping to find some trace of the man who drives me crazy, but all I see are bloodshot, tired eyes.

"Jade, I've got dirty blood from all the people I've had to kill for this fuckin' country. It's running through my veins. The potency of which has started to infiltrate my mind. I'm nothing anymore, so you better tell me why you would come for me or I'm gonna pull this trigger. Give me one fuckin' reason not to; I have a hundred more that suggest the opposite. Well? TELL ME!" he screams, hoarseness straining his throat.

He's holding his gun loosely down by his side now, flicking it rapidly every which way he wants.

My eyes barely leave his face to look at the gun before I finally break my silence, trying as much as I can to swallow the gobstopper-sized lump in my throat.

"W-W-Why d'ya want to kill yourself? Tell me so I understand!"

His wild eyes are even more erratic at this; I barely know who this man is, even though I was the one who broke him out of his Iron mask. I stripped him bare to the world, but nothing could have prepared me for the next words to come out of his mouth.

"...I killed my best friend!" he roars, stabbing the barrel of the gun against his heart. "I let him have the grenades! I *killed* him. I fuckin' did that! I have so much blood on my hands I can't see them anymore. We were surrounded by insurgents in Afghanistan, and he was badly injured, but didn't want to get medically discharged. He...wanted to leave the Army on his own terms. He grabbed our dead friends' grenades and when we radioed for help...We were sitting ducks, Jade. We would have been fine, I swear it...but fuckin' Arnie had to be stupid about it. D'ya know what he turned to me and said?"

I can't answer; him my mouth feels like it's full of sand. I'm drowning in his pain, but I can't tear my eyes away from him. His own eyes and movements are jerky like a crackhead's as they're coming off their high, and the gun is swinging through the air as I stare on in disbelief, completely powerless to help him.

"He said...he said to me that I better run, gave me a smug smile, and recited, '*All I have in this world is my balls and my word, and I don't break them for no one. Me, I want what's coming to me... The world and everything in it.*' I tried to pull it out of his hands, I swear I did, but he held fast and said that he wanted to leave the army his way, and what a better way to do it than saving my sorry ass. I tried to talk him down, but he is…*was*…as thick-headed as me. He stood at the side of the window frame, his gun locked and loaded in his hand, grenades in his pockets ready for him to pull the pins. I…I just stood there, I did…nothing— NOTHING! —to stop it! NOTHING! Why shouldn't I die for that?! I can't go on anymore, Jade. You won. You broke me! Now let me do what I should've done that day I stood at that fuckin' door frame. I should have stayed with my brothers! I should have fuckin' died that day!"

Black desolation glazes over his eyes like he's already in Hell, so deep that I don't how to pull him out. I see a steely, determined look in his eye, and watch the man who I've fallen for point the barrel of his gun to his temple. My heart stops as he presses the barrel harder into his head.

"Tell me why I shouldn't die for that?! I see his face drenched in blood everywhere…so give me a fuckin' good reason!!"

"Of course you don't have a reason, you've never looked for one! If you would just try, you would realize you *do* have reasons—you have YOUR club and people who care about you!"

"They're not a fuckin' reason, Jade! They're better off without me. I need to pay for my sins with blood. Can't you see the poison seeping out onto everyone's life, including yours?! You fuckin' hate the sight of me, so why the fuck are you even here?! You once asked why they call me Tinhead. Because…because… because of Arnie…he used himself as a human bomb to save me. Me!"

He breaks down further, the tears silently falling down his washed-out face. I can't move from the spot until I let him get all of his story out.

"I could see at least five insurgents across from us, and the next building had at least another three. As I'm telling Arnie, he tells me he's gotta do what he's gotta do. He hands me his and our other friends' last letters home and tells me to run out the opposite way to where he's planning to distract them. I argued with him about it, but eventually he tore the tourniquet stopping him from bleeding out through the arm off. I was angry with him. So fuckin' angry."

I can't tear my eyes off of him. They burn to blink, but I won't—I can't.

He trembles and gasps as the sobs take hold of his body but carries on, needing to get it all out. "So I left my best friend, running out of the run-down shack through the back window on pure adrenaline to get as far as possible. When I turned around I saw Arnie propped up against the window frame firing rounds at the other end of the road to distract them, but they knew where the shots were coming from and were on the way to the building until one of their leaders clocked me running. The next thing I feel is fire and chunks of concrete raining down on me and I couldn't hear anything except muffled ringing in my ears. I had been thrown up into the air near a car and lost consciousness. When I came around, I was covered in rubble laying spread-eagled, and my head was killing me.

"When I got my hands free, I was able to feel a large gash from here to here," he points at the base of his skull to just behind his ear with the gun in his hand. "The explosion was from the grenades. I still have the shrapnel from the human bomb that my best bud killed himself with to save me inside me. That's what's fuckin' deeply imbedded in my head. *That's* why they call me Tinhead! What fuckin' quack can help with that shit?! I gave up on Arnie! I gave up on my best friend's life. I should have fought him harder on the decision he was gonna make for my life! And what have I got to show for it?"

My heart constricts again, this time so hard it's about to crack under the weight of what he's had to witness and go through and be strong towards for so long. I hate him, but I hate this for him…

I step closer to him tentatively, but he doesn't seem to notice. I reach the end of his bed only half a foot away, holding my breath and scared I'm going to scare him away like a frightened little bird. I don't care that he thinks he killed his best friend, I know him, I see who he was, and I know he would never have done it on purpose, mask or no mask. The turmoil and despair fills his eyes, mirroring what I've already seen from his darkened soul. I don't acknowledge the last part of what he says; it doesn't matter what he's done…

"I do hate you! You got that one right, that's for sure! I hate everything you stand for; your stupid jokes, your smug face when you think you've won me over the fact that you annoy and get to me more than anyone, I hate that you think you're the God's gift to the ladies, and I *hate* that I can't stop thinking about your arrogant, thick-headed, Casanova-wannabe ass! So, DO IT! Pull that fuckin' trigger, you sick bastard! Because you know what I hate even more than all of those things?! I hate that I fuckin' LOVE you. God I wish I didn't, but I can't and don't want to take it back. I'll jump in the deep end with you—if we drown, then we drown together."

I step closer to him until I'm nose-to-nose with him, his heavy breathing tickling my face in the sweetest caress. I risk a glance up at him, breath-stealing sobs taking the oxygen out of my lungs.

"So, is that a big enough reason? Because if not you'll have to kill me too!"

Chapter 26

Tinhead

Her words and calming presence wash over me, and I cling to the hope she gives me with everything I have.

"Will you let me call the veteran helpline? Please, Dylan."

Her words that night still ring out as clear as a bell during a Sunday service. I sit in the therapy center only a few days later, still under the watch of at least Doc and Bear when Jade isn't there.

Fuck, my mind is so lost…

I can't take the pain anymore; my mind won't stop replaying everything. Telling Jade everything every single thing was the single hardest thing I've done since discharge.

"Dylan Anderson?" A man about Doc's age comes up to me in the waiting room. He's got a short military-style buzzcut and a handlebar moustache that seems to twitch as he moves his lips. Just then, I feel Jade's hand squeeze mine, so I flick my eyes over to her.

Fuck, she's so beautiful, her eyes radiating hope as she gives me another encouraging squeeze. When she said that she loved me and that I would have to kill us both, that was a sharp stab to my heart. I would have happily died, that never bothered me, but the thought of her wanting to be killed alongside me gutted me.

"You can do this. I'll be here all the way, I promise, I love you." she whispers as a single tear rolls free down her angelic face. I can't say anything, so I press my lips to hers, trying to convey exactly what she means to me. It starts gentle and soft, then as soon as my tongue touches hers, there's a spark like an electric shock trying to bring me back to life. I lay claim on her mouth; she tastes of cakes, sugar, and a hint of freshly falling rain. I try to deepen the kiss, but she places her hand against my cheek and pulls away from me, disconnecting the electricity we share.

I place my head against hers searing and memorizing every fleck in her ocean eyes. She loves me, but I don't think I have the capacity to love her back yet. I will do anything to claw myself back and love her; I can't carry on like this, and she needs more than a husk of a man.

Wordlessly I extract myself from her hold, get up, and follow the man with my duffle bag hitched over my shoulder, leaving her sitting in the reception area. I don't look back even though I can feel her eyes burning into me—I can't. If I look back, I won't be able to turn around and keep my promise to her and to myself.

***

Jade

Watching him get up and go through the door without a single word almost ripped my heart out, but I am so proud of him for being able to do this, and he knows it too. Since he told me every single detail of what happened to him, I haven't been able to bear to think about it. I confided in Jenna and Kelly and made them swear not to breathe a word. They've all been amazing; listening and hearing everything, not judging, and letting me cry and scream because he's having to go through it all again and I can't do a damn thing about it. If I could, I would share some of the burden.

***

I sit back in the family area to see him only a couple of weeks later; they encourage family and friends coming to visit but I wasn't sure coming was the best thing for him at first.

After speaking to Doc and asking for his expertise and knowledge, he encouraged me to come, explaining that it may help his healing to see a familiar face and keep in touch with his world outside of the therapy centre. Even so, I was still hesitant; I just don't want to cause him anymore pain than he's already in.

When he reaches me, he doesn't say a word but sits down quietly next to me. I reach across for him, and as soon as I do, he clutches my hand, interlinking our fingers. I know he won't speak to me, but just seeing him makes my heart lighter; knowing he's getting the help he needs keeps me strong for him.

I make small talk, telling him about my day and what's going on in the bakery and the club to see how he reacts—he doesn't. I cautiously lay my head on his shoulder on instinct, and instantly I feel him exhale a gush of air and rest his chin on the crown of my head, sniffing my hair deeply then sighing. Just that simple act brings a smile to my face right as our hour has nearly ended. He knows it too, as he kisses my head, making me feel so precious and cherished.

Turning in the seat to face him, I meet eyes that hold so much of him, shining back at me. A small smirk tugs the corner of his lip, reminding me he's in there. I gently press my lips against his. At first he hesitates, but he soon relaxes and kisses me back. It's not as passionate or fierce as they used to be; it's a sweet kiss that you would get from a boy in middle school.

As we pull away, I recite the same words I said to him two weeks ago. "You can do this. I'll be here all the way, I promise. I love you."

***

February 1st

I haven't been back to the therapy center yet. After I left, I spoke to Dylan's doctor, Dr Thomas, about him not talking, and wanted to check whether he was speaking in his sessions. He confirmed he was, and he is progressing.

He told me to be patient, maybe leave my next visit a month, and try a telephone call to each other on his terms. I waited days—weeks, even—, and today my phone rang. It read as a private number, but I knew it was him and ran upstairs as fast as my legs would carry me. I ran straight into my room, and was too nervous to even sit down when I answer it.

"Hello?" I greet.

There's nothing at first, then then I hear shuffling around and a distant TV show. He sighs, bringing tears to my eyes.

God I miss him, it hurts so much not being able to see or hear him. If I talk, maybe that might encourage him. I remember Dr Thomas saying on the phone that touching on positive memories might help him.

"How are you? Guess what I saw today? I saw a little boy walking past the bakery eating a hot dog, it did make me giggle," I say remembering the golden-haired boy who must have been 6 at most swinging his arm around as he was munching on his hot dog with the other. he reminded me of what Dylan would have looked like when he was an innocent child.

"Donny's Dongs." The words come through like a whisper in the wind, so quiet I thought I misheard at first. There's a slight lilt to his voice.

"Oh God." Squeezing my eyes shut, I let the tears stream freely down my face, my heart aching for him even more. I follow up with questions about the gallery and the rally, and he doesn't speak again but I don't care, I'll take the win. Our call ends soon after; I don't want to scare him off but I'm so proud of him.

"Talk soon. Remember, you can do this. I'll be here all the way, I promise. I love you."

***

February 28th

I haven't heard from Dylan since February 1st, but I see him next month; although the wait is killing me inside. Jenna's keeping me busy, Kelly is inviting me here, there, and everywhere, and all the girls have been amazing. Bear and Doc have been so supportive to me, too, and when I explained to Axe that I can't go back to the club until Tinhead's home because it doesn't feel right without him there, he and Dani got it completely. I was worried about how he and the other club members would react to how things have transpired with his mental health and being diagnosed with delayed onset PTSD, but I had to eat my words when I saw tears shimmering in all of the men's eyes as I told them, and since then they have been his grounding.

At first, he would only see me, but Axe called me yesterday and said, "He looks good; he's still trying to pull off that peach fuzz he calls a beard. The CBT therapy seems to be helping, and the meds he's on are too. He did say he's not quite ready to come back, but I told him it's gonna take time, although we need to start trickling things in soon as his doc says they do encourage getting back to normal life as soon as possible too."

I'm standing in front of the coffee machine in the bakery when I hear my phone going off in the back. I pay it no mind until Jenna comes running out with it, flour sprinkled across her apron, cupcake mixture smeared across her cheek and her eyes dancing.

I leave the espresso cup I was filling where it is and within two strides, I grab the phone off her—I don't need to check the caller ID.

"Hello?" I gasp down the phone.

"Red? What is it, are you okay?"

I have to choke back tears at hearing him say my stupid nickname, but take a breath to regain my composure.

"Yeah, I was out front and my phone was in the bakery kitchen, so I ran. How are you?"

My stomach fills with butterflies in eagerness to hear his voice again. It takes him more than a few seconds to respond, but even when he finally does, the fluttering doesn't stop.

"I'm definitely getting there babe…Jade?"

"Yeah?"

"Fuck, I'm so sorry for putting you through all this and you seeing me like that," he chokes out. The tone of his voice makes me ache to comfort him—to wrap my arms around him like I did in January.

"Forget it, you jerk," I giggle, trying to break the sudden tension between us.

"Never, babe. Never. I owe you so much…I miss you and that sassy mouth," he whispers, making my heart clench for a completely different reasons. Hearing a tiny side of that man makes me so hopeful. "Come and see me?" it comes out as more of a question that a suggestion—like I can say no to him after how hard he's been working.

"Yes. Of course, I'll be there. How much notice do the center need?"

"They only need a couple of days, but can we say in two weeks, babe? I want to know I'm more me than I am now," he pleads.

It stings that he wants to wait longer, but I will wait for as long as it takes for him to be ready.

"I'll be there," I smile as the butterflies' swarm.

***

March 14th

I feel like it's our first date, and I'm sick to my stomach. I'm wearing the same outfit I wore on our second non-date, my black off-the-shoulder shirt, torn blue jeans, dusky pink pointed heels, and the cute cream sweater.

I sit in the family area, nervously bouncing my leg—the butterflies have turned to a swarm of bees now. I scan the, having not really paid much attention to it until now.

The walls are a calming cream color with and licks of pastel shades, and the odd patch of wall has a beautiful painting on it. The one to my right is of a gorgeous sunset. The buildings and trees are silhouetted in black, and the only color you see is from the sun setting; magenta, deep purple, and burnt orange swirling around the sky.

"Do you like it? It reminds me of our first date."

My heart seizes in my mouth, and I cautiously turn around, scared that if I turn too quick, I'll scare him away. When I lock eyes with him, everything else falls away, leaving just us. Seeing the sparkle back in his eyes, hope blooms in my heart more than in any of our phone calls.

I clear my throat to answer him "I love it, it's gorgeous. I can see what you mean."

"Only one thing's missing from the picture," Dylan says flatly, walking over to me so his knees are near my face. He bends down and whispers so softly that his breath tickles my face, "It's missing Donny's Dong."

Laughter ripples out of me, and I snort, making him snigger at me with a smile that turns me inside out.

God, how blind I was! I love him so much. He's so strong, more than strong enough to get through this, even though what happened to him and Arnie would have messed up the strongest of men.

***

I have been here for over an hour, and watching him, touching him, and kissing him has been amazing. He's been telling me about his therapy in depth; CBT and something called EMDR that targets underlying negative beliefs, memories, and feelings that contribute to the symptoms of PTSD and replacing them with more positive, appropriate ones.

"Dr Thomas that said in my case, the biggest belief is the one that I have to keep reliving what happened. He thinks he can access this and rewire the belief that I'm always in danger—which is no longer the case— and replace it with the one that I'm safe. We've tried it out, and it's dramatically reducing my anxiety, increasing my awareness of my triggers, panic attacks, and flashbacks. He also said that I use sex and joking around as avoidance mechanism to deal with it, so your comment about me being a sex addict was nearly exactly right. All the meds and counselling are draining me, but I definitely feel more like me. I have something else to tell you—they're planning outpatient therapy," Dylan tells me with the biggest grin.

"What does that mean?" I ask, trying not to get my hopes up as I search his eyes but hoping that I haven't misinterpreted.

"It means I can come home soon!" he beams at me.

I jump into his lap, grabbing his face, and give him the biggest kiss ever. I consume his mouth, my lips claiming his as our tongues fuse, exploring each other until we eventually pull apart; both completely breathless.

I'm so freaking excited but nervous at the same time, although Dylan reassures me that they're going to keep in contact with him and Doc.

"My man is coming home!" I squeal.

He gives me that all-American smirk and winks at me. "I take it you're happy about that?"

Chapter 27

Jade

April 10th – Two weeks home.

Axe comes through to the main room where we're all drinking and enjoying ourselves—I don't leave Jenna and Bear's side; in truth, I'm still kind of uncomfortable being here. I still get nervousness and anxiety about what happened at that early hour of New Year's Day.

I glance over at Tinhead, admiring him as he moves around the bar getting drinks,

Fuck, he's so sexy! I'm gonna grab that butt later...

When he came home on his first day of outpatient care, I picked him up...and ended up bawling my eyes out all the way home, as unbeknownst to us, the Devils had ridden out to the center while he was being discharged to give him an entourage back to the club—it was so special.

Dylan didn't think a party would help him too much, so we're all just gathered for a quiet get-together around the bar today.

When we came back in two weeks ago, Axe asked if he wanted a different club name, but Dylan just laughed.

"No way! I don't hate my name, I've learnt to embrace it. The shrapnel is as much a part of me as Arnie. The only change of name I'll accept is Big Dick!"

I remember shaking my head at him, and all the men chuckling around him. They've become even closer since he got back, embracing him not just as a member, but true family.

As my attention snaps back to the present, Axe hollers "All right! Can I have your attention? As you know, this is a party of sorts. Tinhead and Wrench, come up here!"

I flick my eyes between Dylan and Axe, but Axe's face is stoic, not giving anything away. Dylan puts down the glass he was cleaning and cautiously goes over to stand alongside Axe with Wrench. Flex and Zara walk into the room with the same facial expressions as Axe—unwavering, betraying no emotion.

I watch as Bear untangles himself from my sister, then he, Doc, Flex, Brains, and Dagger circle Tinhead and Wrench, closing in around them as they inch closer and closer.

I don't know what's going on, but I'm instantly on alert.

"Jenna? What is this?" I demand.

"Shhh, its your man's big day," she whispers back to me.

"Tinhead and Wrench, you've been prospecting for us for over a year and half, and it's time for me to decide whether you to stay or go."

Axe's face never betrays a flicker of emotion, and I watch with bated breath as the five of them move a step closer to the prospects right until they're directly behind them both. All of a sudden, they all punch, kick or knee them both.

"Shit, brother!" I hear Tinhead shout out.

"Argh, fuck!" Wrench grunts.

Bear takes Tinhead and Flex grabs Wrench, locking in a death grip on their biceps. Bear shoves Tin on the bar stool right in front of Zar', who's getting her tattoo gun ready to mark them both.

I don't tear my eyes away from Tinhead the whole time he's getting officially marked up with the Devils colors. Once it's done, he's officially the newest member of the Devils Reapers MC, the insignia still wet and shiny on his bicep.

I go over and stand right next to my man, his eyes never wavering from mine as they glitter with extreme pride.

Once Zara puts Vaseline on and film over the top he stands up, and without saying a word threads his hand through my loose hair, tugging my head up to his and latching his lips onto mine.

I have to tell him something so I gently push at his chest to free myself, and he gives me a confused look.

"I got to admit, while I was watching what they were doing, I was scared of how you were going to react, but I am so proud of how you dealt with it. You've done so well; I know you have a long way to go but I'm here every step of the way. I love you so much, Dylan."

Without a word, he rethreads his hand in my hair and pushes his tongue back into my mouth to get better acquainted.

God, I've missed him. He slips into my heart deeper with every incarnation, and this time I couldn't stop him if I tried.

I can't help myself grinding against the bulge in his pants, and as I pull away from him I lick his lips, nipping his bottom lip just as he growls and his eyes flare with lust.

Just then, Axe comes marching out of the office swinging the colors for their cuts. He strips the cuts off of both Tin and Wrench's backs, and then he lines his hunting knife up against the *'Prospect'* patches, tearing them off.

***

Tinhead

Calm and silence fills my room. It doesn't scare me anymore, but some days I seek the noise, needing to hear it—especially in bed with Jade.

Fuck, I will always need her noises; I love hearing her scream my name out as I take her over and over. I glance down at the top of the strawberry-blonde waves cascading down her bare back to where she's snuggled up after I ate her out and showed every inch of her body how much she means to me.

I see her eyes just about to close, and a rush of warmth fills me. She's precious; I can't believe I was so fuckin' close to leaving her, but I'm not finished with her.

I flex my hard dick against her stomach, tapping her soft, warm skin.

"Oh no you don't, you've wrung me out," she yawns out with her eyes still firmly closed.

"Good job you don't have to do anything then Red. Me and T-Dawg are going to do all the work."

As I extract myself from her body she wordlessly rolls onto her front and arches her back, getting ready for me to take her from behind.

Her creamy skin calls to me, and I glide my hand over the silky flesh that runs from her shoulders down the planes of her back like velvet. I cup her ass, squeezing tightly and digging my nails into her plump flesh. This sight is normal for us, but not tonight.

"Turn around, Jade," I murmur in a gruff voice.

Her gaze flicks up to mine, and she searches my eyes with caution.

After I silently nod at her, she flips over on her back swiftly not wasting any time.

That's my girl...

I fist my cock, seeing that her stunning turquoise are fixated on my movements.

I start pumping faster and her legs spread wide for me as I see a coy grin flash across her face—who is she trying to kid? Her wetness seeps out of her, her breath hitching, although she doesn't take her eyes off me as I lean over her body, letting go of my rigid cock. She brushes her palm over my forearm in encouragement, so I slide my tip over her little bean as it shimmers with her juices, then glide it up and down her slit making her arch her body off the bed.

"Ahh! Dylan..." she hisses through her teeth.

Taking that as my cue, I slam right into her, claiming her body as well, although she already claimed my heart all those years ago as the most breathtaking mermaid ever...

***

"Jade?" I whisper into the dead of the night. It's 2am, but for once, nightmares aren't what's keeping me awake...

I play with a curl of her hair, twizzling it around my finger. She's snuggled up in front of me, wiggling that sexy ass against my semi-hard dick and waking him up.

"Hmmm? What is it, can it not wait until morning?" she mumbles into her pillow.

"Nah, it can't wait babe. I just wanted to tell you something that's been bothering me."

She's suddenly wide awake, sitting up. "What is it? Are you ok?

"Yeah...I've got something I need to tell you. I don't think you're gonna like it."

Her face is full of worry and her eyes are huge and staring. I bite back a smile, knowing she's gonna kick my ass in about five seconds.

"Tell me, Dylan, I can take it..." she whispers, swallowing to clear the emotion already building up in her voice.

"If you're sure...You're gonna hate me because, Jade Smith, I am claiming your sassy ass. I fuckin' love you and your smart mouth. Be my Ol' Lady?" I grin at her.

She rains thumps down on my shoulder and smacks my fresh Devils ink, making it sting, then her face breaks out into the most dazzling, captivating smile.

"Damn straight, Captain Jerk! You're right, I do hate you for doing that, but I wouldn't be anywhere else than by your side...and your *T-Dawg*. I love you so much, " she giggles as happy tears trickle down her cheek.

She's the most amazing woman ever; she tore the mask off, saw all through the bravado and kept going even after she saw all the ugliness and carnage behind the façade. Above all, she never gave up on me.

I'll forever be grateful for her, she's my strength.

THE END

~ Dagger ~

Coming Soon…

A little taster…

Never, he would never forgive me if he didn't get a mention; he and Tinhead were fighting over who was going to go first… but I'm hoping he realizes I have saved the best till last…

Don't tell him that, though—he'll never let me live it down…

Enjoy this little snippet…

Dagger

She's too fuckin' tempting. She doesn't know what she wants and she's too young for me—I'm gonna be 40 next month and she's barely out of diapers—but I can't resist her.

I've been around the block a few times, and I never wanted to have an Ol' Lady either. I like my life the way it is; free pussy any time, any day, anyhow. If I could, I would die a happy man with a pussy on my face, fucking one with my dick, and another on my fingers. There's not just one woman out there for me—I'm like an eagle; free, lone, and that's how it's always been.

My mouth waters at the creature standing there in those tight-as-hell jeans in the middle of May, showing off that big heart-shaped ass.

FUCK. ME!

I can't lie, I want to see her bouncing on my dick as I slam into her petite little body, breaking her in. She has caramel skin with long dark mahogany hair framing her face, enhancing those fuckable lips. The sight of her has had me readjusting my dick all day, but on the surface, I'm minding my own business, chatting away to some of my brothers from other chapters after we've finished our rally across three states to raise money for the charity that helped out Bear and Jenna.

I feel her eyes on me. I can't explain the feelin', but it's like the tingling that comes over me when I'm about to shoot my load into some tight snatch. Looking over, I see her deep cocoa eyes devouring me as she licks her lips, seemingly unaware she's doing it.

Fuck me, doesn't that make me want to do shit to her...

When she came onto me at the Halloween party, she was dressed a lioness from the Lion King, and we were both drunk and chatting around the bar. As soon as she whispered into my ear that she wanted a good fucking, it took all my will power not to drag her back to my room and show her how a real man fucks, but I had to let her down easy. She was far too young for me—there's about 15 years between us—so I shut that shit down and planned to go and do what I do best; go and fuck some club pussy.

She saw me stumbling down the hall with Brandy that night and tried to hide it, but I saw the baffled reaction come across her face for a moment before she carried on drinking and chatting with the other girls like nothing was happening.

All I knew was that I wanted my dick wet and Brandy's an easy fuck. She knows what I like in the bedroom, too, there's no talking, but plenty of good long hard fuckin'.

Kelly's far too young for the likes of me. She's forbidden fruit...which only makes her that much more tempting...

I think I'm well and truly fucked!

***

Kelly

He's pure filth. Pure, dirty-talking, filth.

When he speaks, his voice is like pure unadulterated sex; rough, gravelly and smooth all at the same time, like fine whiskey.

I want his mouth, his body, his sexy-as-fuck beard that I'm dying to ride and leave my mark over...

I'm standing around the rest of the girls at the rally he organized for the charity that helped Bear and Jenna but paying no real attention to the conversation; just nodding and laughing at the right times. The girls are chatting away about the cakes we've served and catching up on gossip between the chapters, but I can't tear my eyes off the man on the opposite side of the road leaning against his aged Harley, that copper hair and matching beard shining in the sun that making it look like it has specks of gold.

My gaze roams him from his gorgeous red hair down that muscular body to those long legs stretched out in front of him…and the package between them.

God, I bet he knows what to do with his dick…

The hairs on my arms are standing on end as my gaze flicks back to his handsome face, taking in the shades covering his gorgeous eyes. Underneath them, I know he's looking at me. I can feel those intense brown-ringed green eyes hungrily roaming my body, making me sizzle.

He thinks I don't notice; he thinks I'm not gonna pursue him like I did at Halloween, but he hasn't met Kelly Isabella Davis.

"Kel' you've got it bad. I thought you said you tried it and he didn't take the bait?" Jade—my best *chica* from another Momma—whispers to the side of me.

I never move my gaze from him, not daring to because I know the current that's passing between us is gonna break if I do "Yeah, I did say that babe, but when did you ever know me to give up? He was the one who wouldn't stop checking me out at Halloween. He didn't take the bait that time, but I'll just get a bigger line for him to come take a nibble on, so I know I'll be able to reel him in," I say with a smirk. "We both know that what I want, I get!"

"What's the plan then?" she asks in a whisper.

I smile at Dagger. "Patience, just patience."

Dagger will be coming soon…

Thank you so much for reading Tinhead.

I hope you enjoyed his and Jade's story as much as me. It has to be one of the hardest storylines to write, many times being left in tears whilst writing. But as like with my other Devils books I always incorporate real life stories as well as the romance side of things.

I do hope you loved Tinhead as much as me.

I would really appreciate you leaving a review on Amazon or Goodreads. Even if it is a one liner.

Thank you again,
Love and hugs
Ruby xx

* ~ *

Read more about the Devils men...

<u>Devils Reapers MC Series</u>

<u>Axe: Book 1 is available now!</u>

Flex: Book 2 is available now!

Bear: Book 3 is available now!

Come and follow me on

Facebook:
https://www.facebook.com/rubycarterauthor/

Twitter: https://twitter.com/rubycarterauth1

Instagram:
https://www.instagram.com/rubycarterauthor/?hl=en

Printed in Poland
by Amazon Fulfillment
Poland Sp. z o.o., Wrocław

61182794R00174